A Matter

of Justice

A MATTER
OF JUSTICE

Keith Tittle

For Warren Easley,
Who writes the N.W.
as well as any author
I've ever read.

Keith

Resolute Press

PGS 44 and 60 in your honor :)

A Matter of Justice, © 2017

This is a work of fiction. Any similarity to actual events, or to persons living or dead, is purely coincidental.

COVER DESIGNED BY JOHN WEBB

Chapter 1

Vonetta Myers stepped down from the northbound commuter train onto the Max light-rail platform. Her floppy-brimmed floral hat was a vile riot of pastel petals, cornflower blue and pink and yellow, against a lime green background. She pulled it down firmly over her coarse, dark hair as protection against the unseasonably hot afternoon sun, and checked her watch.

While the train slid slowly away from the platform, Vonetta slung the faded denim bag she carried over her slender shoulder and made her way across Interstate Avenue.

She was something of a slave to routines. Coffee and a bagel every weekday morning at Arbor Lodge. Taco Tuesday with her coworkers. On Mondays and Thursdays, after work, she stopped at the New Seasons Market just across from the Max platform to pick up the groceries she and her children would need for the next few days. But today was Wednesday, so she continued past the grocery store, heading east toward the freeway overpass.

She didn't even glance in the direction of the neon-green muscle car in the market's parking lot, or at the man behind the wheel, wearing dark glasses and relaxing in the shadows.

A six-minute walk to the park … eight, at the outside. The driver made no effort to look at his watch as Myers passed by the car. He would know when to follow her. Timing had always been an innate thing with him.

With the windows rolled up, the heat inside the Dodge was stifling. He turned the key in the ignition — the metal cool even through the thin latex of his gloves — and the powerful engine rumbled to life under the hood. Then he reached over and flicked the air conditioning up two notches. As the air began to circulate, he settled back in the seat, eyes closed, and waited patiently for the minutes to tick by.

At 4:45, he backed out of the tight parking spot and eased out of the New Seasons lot. The throaty growl of the Dodge Coronet's 440 engine quickly attracted the attention of everyone in the parking lot.

The car turned to follow Myers' course, east onto Rosa Parks Way and over the freeway, already gridlocked with northbound traffic.

When the light at Albina turned red as he reached the intersection, Vonetta Myers was no more than half a block ahead of him, just passing the red brick building of the Peninsula Park swimming pool. The hem of her sundress — a crème-colored affair that contrasted nicely against her coffee-dark black skin — flicked back and forth across her thin legs as she moved.

When the traffic light turned green, the driver took his foot off the brake and the car moved slowly through the intersection, apparently too slowly for the driver behind him. The SUV's horn blared once — a brief, annoying blast — before the old Ford Bronco pulled into the inside lane and flashed past.

Myers looked up at the sound of the horn, her eyes following the battered Bronco as it sped past her down the street. Preoccupied, she didn't even seem to notice the throaty rumble of the Dodge's engine as it slowed to a near-stop behind her.

The driver picked the Belgian FN 57 pistol up from the seat beside him. As shots went, this one offered a low degree of difficulty, he realized as he rolled the passenger window down. Twenty feet, no obstructions … He squeezed the trigger, twice. Both rounds hit their target center-mass between Myers' shoulder blades. The young woman staggered … one, then two awkward steps forward before she collapsed onto the sidewalk.

As Myers fell, he snapped off three more quick shots for effect, the bullets all digging harmlessly into the pool house's outer wall.

Satisfied, he rolled the window back up and stepped on the gas. The Dodge's powerful engine roared to life. The Coronet leapt forward, trailing smoke from the overlarge tires for half a block down Rosa Parks Way.

The loud crack of the FN 57 would have attracted the attention of everyone nearby, but there was virtually no chance that any witnesses would be able to identify the driver. Not at this distance. Not through the heavily tinted glass. *But they'll remember the car,* he thought with a smile.

They will most certainly remember the car.

Chapter 2

If Alex Burwell angled his chair a little, he could just make out the peak of Mt. Hood in the distance, to the east of the Justice Building. The late-morning sun reflected like burnished gold on what snow still rested on the mountain's cap.

Four years with that outside your window, and you wait until today ... your last day ... to appreciate the view.

"Mr. Burwell?" The voice at the doorway startled Alex out of his thoughts. He looked up, a little embarrassed at being caught daydreaming, and saw the worried expression on his assistant's pretty, round face.

"Sorry, Steph, I was lost in thought." He smiled at her. "What can I do for you?"

"District Attorney Orbison is here to see you. Is this a good time?"

That brought a chuckle from Alex. "I have nothing but time today. Besides, we can't very well keep the boss waiting, can we?"

"No, sir, I suppose not." Still, her blue eyes watched him with concern.

Has she always been this protective? he wondered, *or is this a recent development?*

"It's all right, Steph. I'm fine. You can show her in."

Cynthia Orbison walked into his office like a model straight off the cover of Women of Power, with her tailored suit and oh-so-businesslike hair style. But Alex knew that there was a hell of a lot more to Orbison than her appearance. Second in her class at Harvard law, three years as a prosecutor in Los Angeles, and five more as Deputy District Attorney with a near-perfect conviction record. Her ability in the courtroom had already been well-established by the time she moved to Portland.

Frankly, Alex had been skeptical when Cynthia had shown up in the department. No one could be that good. But she was as advertised, and more.

What he'd found even more surprising, though, was that all her ability hadn't come attached to an overbearing ego. Even after winning the job as the Multnomah County District Attorney, she'd remained approachable and supportive of the team around her.

In her eyes, job titles meant nothing. What counted was the way you did your work; demonstrate a commitment to, and passion for "the ethical pursuit of justice," as she put it, and Cynthia Orbison had your back. Alex had quickly grown to admire and respect his boss.

"For god sake, Alex," she said with a smile as he stood to greet her. "Sit down. This is a friendly visit. I just came by to see how you were doing."

He shrugged as he settled back into his chair. "To tell the truth, it's been harder than I expected. Then again, I was never very fond of goodbyes."

"It's just a leave of absence," Cynthia assured him as she took a seat across from him. "You'll be back behind that desk in a few months."

"You don't really believe that, do you?"

She hesitated for a moment. "I have to believe that, Alex," she said at last. "The alternative is unacceptable."

He smiled. "Some verdicts are beyond our control. At least, that's what my boss always tells me."

Cynthia laughed at that. "Using my own words against me ... typical lawyer trick. You know, it's not too late to change your mind. I don't want to lose your expertise. Why don't you stay, if only on a part-time basis?"

"Thanks, boss, but I think I have to pass. Even the commute into town wears me out these days. Besides, we both know I haven't been on my game for a while."

"It's just the meds."

"Does that really matter? I almost cost us the Norberg case."

"We still got the conviction."

"Only because you had someone else reviewing my work." He raised his hand as Orbison started to object.

"Don't apologize, Cynthia. I would have done the same thing. The work we do is too important to jeopardize because of sentiment."

That brought a smile. "I'm going to miss you, Alex. I really am. So, what's the latest from the doctor?"

He shrugged. "I have an appointment with my oncologist on Monday. Hopefully, she'll have some good news for me this time."

"She will," Cynthia said with a certainty neither of them probably felt. Then she brightened a little. "Speaking of good news, I have a little going away present for you. It looks like we're finally going to nail Manny Cespedes."

Alex looked up in surprise. Cespedes — or *Lagarto* … Lizard, as he was known on the street — ran things in Portland for the Duarte drug cartel out of Mexico. "Someone finally roll on him for the Laurelhurst shootings?" Alex asked.

Orbison shook her head. "Not yet. This is a new one, a drive-by that happened Wednesday afternoon near Peninsula Park, in Northeast Portland."

"How solid is the case?"

"Three witnesses identified his car at the scene, confirmed by traffic cam two blocks from the shooting. A tip led us to the vehicle, parked three miles away at Lloyd Center Mall."

"His car? Please tell me that we have something a hell of a lot better than that."

His boss smiled. "What would you say to the murder weapon, tucked under the front seat?"

"Too good to be true," he told her, skeptically.

"Maybe, but as you always say; 'everybody fucks up sometime.' Ballistics was a perfect match."

"Prints on the weapon?"

Orbison nodded.

"I'll be damned. Who did he go after this time? Another dealer?"

Cynthia shook her head.

"We haven't figured out who the actual target was. Homicide thinks the victim, a social worker named Vonetta Myers, was just in the wrong place and got caught in the crossfire." The DA must have seen the expression that crossed Alex's face. "I know ... takes senseless to a whole new level. We're going to put Manny into a deep hole for this one."

Alex didn't say anything, which obviously surprised her. "Alex? Are you okay?"

"Sorry. I feel like I'm fading a little. Must be the medications." He managed a thin smile. "That's great news, boss."

"I'll keep you posted as the case develops. In the meantime, how about a celebratory lunch? My treat."

That brought another smile from him. "I never turn down a free meal. There are a couple of things I want to wrap up first, though. Can you give me twenty minutes?"

When the door had closed behind her, Alex typed his network password into the computer and navigated to a folder on his desktop named, simply, *Polyakov*. The spreadsheet file inside contained a list of names, addresses, and other demographic information from the Adam Polyakov trial. The entry he expected to find — but prayed he wouldn't — sat on row thirteen: *Myers, Vonetta Anne ... Oregon Department of Social and Health Services.*

That made three dead on this list in six months. Alex leaned back and closed his eyes in frustration. He couldn't see any way that Cespedes, or the Duarte cartel, might be tied in to the Polyakov trial. That meant this shooting had to be a setup. Not that the son of a bitch didn't deserve it.

For a moment, Alex considered just letting Cespedes go down for the murder. It wasn't like Manny's hands weren't bloody as hell, anyway.

Alex looked at the spreadsheet in front of him once more. Twenty-one rows of names and information, twenty-one people ... twenty-one lives. *If I let Cespedes take the fall for this, how many more of them are going to die before someone else figures out what the hell is going on?*

With a sigh, he leaned forward and buzzed his assistant. Sometimes, Alex realized, no matter how many options it looks like you have, there's really no option at all.

At the other end of the line, Stephanie answered. "Yes, Mr. Burwell?"

"Could you connect me with Jefferson Dawes at Ferrum Security?"

A few moments later, Alex's phone buzzed. "I'm sorry, Mr. Burwell," Stephanie said. "Mr. Dawes is out of town. I have his assistant on the line. Would you like me to leave a message?"

"No, that's okay, Steph. I can do it."

"I'll put you through, then ... Mr. Fine? I have Deputy District Attorney Burwell on the line."

Alex smiled. Stephanie always made sure that everyone knew his title.

"Mr. Burwell, how may I help you?" From the tone of his voice, Mr. Fine didn't seem particularly impressed by job titles. *Good for him,* Alex thought, *but I wouldn't want him to get too complacent.*

"Well, Mr. Fine, you could put me in touch with your boss." Even Alex hated the artificially-hard edge in his voice, but it usually got results. Usually, but not always.

"I'm sorry, Mr. Burwell. Mr. Dawes is attending a conference in Atlanta. Mr. Henderson is filling in during his absence. Shall I connect you?"

"No, thank you. This is more of a ... personal matter." Alex let a little warmth flow back into his tone. "When will Jeff return?"

"I'm afraid he's not due back in the office until Tuesday."

"You must have a number where I can reach him."

"I'm sorry, I don't." Translation: *I do have a number, but you aren't getting it from me.* "I would be happy to get a message to Mr. Dawes, however, if it's really urgent," Fine added, helpfully.

"It is," Alex assured him. "Ask Jeff to call me as soon as possible. It's ..."

He paused. It's what? A matter of life and death? *How often do we say things like that when it's anything but? And when it really is ...*

"Just tell him that it's critically important that I speak with him," Alex said, quietly.

He set the receiver back in its cradle and turned to look once more at the mountain beyond his window. Mr. Fine would pass the message along, he knew, but would Jeff respond? The Jefferson Dawes he knew and worked with — and once called a friend — *that* Jeff Dawes would call. But those days were long past. Reluctantly, Alex pulled out his mobile and hit speed dial. His wife, Kendall, picked up on the third ring.

"Hey, you," she answered, cheerfully. "How goes the last day?"

"As well as could be expected," he told her. "Listen, Babe, something's come up, and I need to talk to Jeff as soon as possible. You still have his cell number, right?" The hesitation on the other end of the line was almost palpable. "I know what you're going to say," Alex added, softly, "but I have to try."

Chapter 3

ATLANTA, GEORGIA

"Any security or investigation firm wanting to do business today has to invest heavily on the technology side." The meticulously groomed, clean-shaven sales rep from iMatt Systems flashed a well-practiced look of earnestness as he glanced from one face at the bar to the next, looking for validation. For the most part, all he garnered in return were a few bored nods from the assemblage of conference-goers.

Standing nearby at the bar, Jefferson Dawes nursed his bourbon and watched the pitch unfold with quiet amusement. The woman seated to his right, however, made no effort to hide her irritation.

"Why do they always have to interrupt Happy Hour with a goddamned sales pitch?" Megan Donovan wondered aloud. "And while we're at it, why are tech guys all so goddamned young these days? This one doesn't look old enough to even be in a bar."

"As long as his company is popping for drinks, I seriously doubt that the hotel is going to card him, are they?" Jeff pointed out. And given the top shelf stuff being poured, the tab was going to run a few hundred dollars, at least. Then again, with the high-tech solutions iMatt Systems peddled, it wouldn't take more than one decent sale to recoup their expenses.

"Well, just looking at him makes me feel like an antique," she said with an exaggerated sigh.

Jeff rolled his eyes at the comment. "For the record, Meg, you are decades away from achieving antique status," he assured her, honestly. The slender brunette could easily pass for ten years younger than her actual age of fifty, younger still when she put any effort into it at all. Her dark hair framed a face that was more beautiful than pretty, with high cheek bones and dark green, intelligent eyes.

The owner and CEO of Donovan Security shot him a half-hearted *Aren't you sweet?* look and ordered another Grey Goose martini on the iMatt tab.

The bartender nodded and turned to Jeff. "Another bourbon for you?" he asked.

Jeff shook his head, but Meg overruled him. "If you're going to come to these conferences, you're going to have to learn to loosen up," she said with a grin. "Especially when someone else is buying. Another Four Roses for my friend … on the kid's tab."

She nodded in the sales rep's direction, just to make sure the bartender understood. Then she swiveled around in her seat to face Jeff again. "So, when are you going to leave Niko Ferrum and join my team?"

He laughed. "You opening an office in Portland that I should know about?"

"The way Ferrum Security Group is taking over the West Coast? Fat chance."

"Then there's your answer."

She shook her head. "Why someone with your skill set would want to waste away in the hinterlands is beyond me."

"Portlanders prefer 'God's Country' to 'the hinterlands.' Has a much more positive ring to it," Jeff pointed out. "Besides, you couldn't afford what it would cost to lure me away from the Pacific Northwest."

Meg smiled. "Shall I throw out some numbers, just in case?"

"Weren't you the one who was just complaining about interrupting Happy Hour with a sales pitch?"

That brought a laugh. "It's different when I'm the one doing the interrupting."

As Jeff's second bourbon slid into place on the bar in front of him, he felt the phone tucked away in his suit coat begin to vibrate. He pulled it out and was about to answer when he spotted the all-too familiar number that came up on Caller ID.

Alex Burwell. The last person he wanted to hear from, now or ever. Still, his finger hovered indecisively over the disconnect icon. Before curiosity could win out over irritation, the call dropped.

"Oh, you should really see your face right now," Meg said.

"What's wrong with it?" he asked with a forced smile.

"Your expression is the most interesting mix of pensive and pissed off I've ever seen. Avoiding someone, are we?"

He ignored the question, lifted his bourbon, and drained half the contents in the short glass with one healthy — or unhealthy — swallow.

Meg watched him set the tumbler down on the bar with amusement. "You know, when I told you to loosen up, I didn't mean all at once."

Jeff managed a half-hearted smile. "I guess you're going to have to be more clear in your instructions if I ever come to work for you." The phone resting on the bar next to his cocktail napkin rumbled loudly once more to let him know that he had a new voicemail. He dropped it back into his pocket without comment.

"Interesting." Meg ran the tip of a well-manicured finger along the rim of her martini glass and studied him for a moment. "I wonder who could flap the generally unflappable Jefferson Dawes with a simple phone call? I might think you were seeing some lucky girl on the side if I didn't know you better," she added, with a decidedly Cheshire Cat-like grin.

He chuckled. "Do you?" he asked.

She looked confused for a moment. "Do I … what?"

"Know me better."

"About you and another woman?" She laughed. "If I thought for a moment that you could be tempted, we might be having a very different conversation right now."

Before Jeff could respond, he felt a heavy hand on his shoulder. He turned to see Charlie Cornwall, owner of CTG Security Specialties, who had sidled up next to them. Cornwall was tall, well over six feet, with a ruddy complexion and a physique that might once have been considered athletic before middle-age and excess had crept in.

"Well, this sounds a hell of a lot more interesting than a lame-ass sales pitch." Charlie chuckled. "Unless this *is* a sales pitch," he added, a smug look on his fleshy face. His icy-blue eyes darted from Jeff to Meg.

From the big man's vantage point, he was clearly more focused on the cleavage displayed beneath Meg's blouse than the withering glare she shot his way.

"Jesus, Charlie, could you be more of an ass?" she growled, her voice low. The question was purely rhetorical; Meg, Jeff, and half the attendees in the bar knew that Cornwall had long ago laid that matter to rest beneath a string of sexual harassment settlements and acrimonious divorces.

Jeff shook his head. "If you two are going to get into another of your famous pissing contests, I think I'll be going," he told them as he pushed his now-empty glass toward the bartender. "I have a wife upstairs who has been waiting patiently for three days for me to finish my business with you silly sons of bitches."

"Hey!"

He grinned over at Meg. "Sorry … sons and *daughters*."

She laughed. "That's better. Give Annie my love."

"Hell, give her mine too, if you think you're up to it," Cornwall offered with a smile that made Jeff want to throw a punch … *just one,* he thought, *right between those little piggy eyes*.

Instead, he swung around on the stool and stood, forcing Cornwall to step back. "See, this is why I don't like to bring Annie to these things. It's not safe to expose her to a bunch of reprobates like you."

With that he said his goodbyes, accepted a business card from the kid who'd bought his drinks, and slipped out of the hotel bar. On his way to the elevators he dropped the business card in the nearest wastebasket.

ANNIE LOOKED UP as Jeff opened the door to their room. From the look on her face, he realized he had probably overestimated the "waiting patiently" part of his comment down in the bar.

"I thought you'd forgotten me up here." She smiled when she said it, but he caught the edge in her tone.

Jeff tossed his suit jacket onto the bed and loosened his tie. "I put my phone on vibrate before the last session started. Bad form for the moderator's cell to go off during the panel."

"The panel ended over an hour ago."

"Socializing and sales pitches are part of the job at these things," he reminded her. "We talked about this when you said you wanted to come."

"Sorry." This time her tone seemed sincere, maybe even a bit contrite. "I've just been going a little stir-crazy up here. Ready for dinner?"

Jeff looked at his wife. She sat at the small vanity, dressed for the kind of restaurant that would inflict maximum damage on his expense account. The diamond necklace he'd given her for Christmas sparkled against her dark, chestnut-colored hair and the little black dress that accentuated her curves nicely. Seated as she was, the bottom of the dress rode up to mid-thigh, showing off a pair of legs that looked far too spectacular for the mother of a law student.

Annie noticed him studying her and flashed a self-conscious smile.

"The way you're looking tonight," Jeff said, "I'm not sure I want to share you with the rest of Atlanta."

The shy smile turned into a full grin. "Oh no. You are not flattering your way out of a night on the town. You owe me."

"God, you're a hard woman." he chuckled as his wife stuck her tongue out, playfully. "Let me just listen to my voicemail, and then I'm all yours."

Annie gave an exaggerated sigh as she faced the mirror to finish with her makeup.

There were two new messages. The time stamp on the first fell right in the middle of his panel that afternoon. He started the message, his attention divided equally between the voice mail and his wife's primping. It was from Markus.

"I'm sorry to bother you at the conference," his assistant was saying, "but you had a call this afternoon from Deputy District Attorney Alex Burwell. He said it was regarding an urgent personal matter, and asked that you call as soon as possible."

Jeff didn't bother to write down the return number Markus recited; he would have known Alex's office number by heart even if it hadn't popped up earlier on his caller ID.

He skipped reluctantly to the next message, the one that had managed to distract him so much down in the bar.

Alex's all-too familiar voice sounded strained, tired.

"Jeff, this is Alex … Look, I know it's been a long time — probably not long enough for you, I'm sure — but we really need to talk. There's something going on here that I … look, I can't go into it all right now. Just call me when you get this, please. It's urgent."

Urgent. Well, Alex always did have a flair for the dramatic. But this was Jeff's first real vacation with his wife in almost a year and a half. He was not going to interrupt Annie Time for some goddamned case that was none of his business, anyway. He'd put all that behind him when he left the DA's office.

Yeah, like that's the reason I'm not calling him back.

Jeff knew that ignoring Alex wouldn't make him go away, so he fired a quick email off to Markus, asking him to call the DA's office on Monday and assure Mr. Burwell that he'd be in touch just as soon as he got back to town. Anything office-related would still go to Joe Henderson, who could escalate if he felt it was critical. Then Jeff powered down his phone. The action didn't go unnoticed by Annie.

"You're turning your phone off? That's not like you."

"I'm on vacation," he pointed out with a smile he didn't really feel.

"What if Mikaela needs to get in touch with us?"

He laughed at that. Their daughter was twenty-one now, and every damned bit as independent as her mother. "If she needs something she'll call you before she calls me … and then only if the boyfriend isn't available."

"The boyfriend … He does have a name, you know," Annie said, a little of her former frostiness seeping through. "And, in case you hadn't noticed, Jim O'Connell has become something more than just a boyfriend. Which reminds me … we're supposed to be meeting his parents for dinner, the week after next. Mikaela wanted to get us together this Thursday, but I told her you'd probably be pretty busy at the office after the conference."

"Cleverly stripping me of my excuses in the process," Jeff pointed out with a half-hearted chuckle. "Well, I guess this day had to come sometime. I'm assuming you've run a complete background check on the boy?"

"Ages ago," she admitted. "What good does it do to have a husband in the security business if I can't abuse his position from time to time? Jim's father is the head of the History department at Portland State, and his grandfather is a prominent Portland attorney." Annie smiled. "Oh, and Jim's *great*-grandfather was Senator Edward Wirth."

"Oh, good. A man with a pedigree," Jeff said, sourly.

"Don't be an anti-elitist."

He shrugged unapologetically. "I promise I'll keep my proletarian views to myself when we meet," he assured her, peeling off his shirt and grabbing a fresh one from the closet. His mind was already elsewhere. *What could be so damned important that would make Alex even consider coming to me for help?*

Chapter 4

Jeff and Annie spent the weekend in Charleston, at a restored antebellum mansion within walking distance of the Battery. He hoped the thought and effort he'd put into their vacation might count as payment — or partial-payment, at least — for all the late evenings and weekends he'd worked over the last three years to get the Portland office of Ferrum Security Group up and running.

Certainly, Niko Ferrum seemed satisfied with his effort; Jeff's success in the Rose City had already led to new offices in Seattle and Spokane, with negotiations underway for another in Vancouver, British Columbia. More importantly, Jeff had just learned that he was going to be named Regional Director, managing all the company's western offices from San Diego to Vancouver. Ferrum could then focus his attention on the branches in Chicago, Dallas, and along the East Coast.

The expanded role in the company felt like a double-edged sword, however. Annie looked forward to the increased income, especially with Mikaela starting pre-law in the fall, but his new title and expanded territory also meant just that much more travel, that many more lost nights and weekends.

That had been why Jeff had pulled out all the stops for this mini-vacation … to atone for past sins, and hopefully build credit for the future ones he'd be bound to incur in his new position as Regional Director. For her part, Annie seemed resigned to the inevitable … or perhaps she'd just grown accustomed to his being away so much. Either way, the prospect didn't appear to bother her as much as Jeff thought it would …

Or should …

THEY ARRIVED BACK at Atlanta's Hartsfield-Jackson Airport Monday afternoon with a little over two hours before their flight home to Portland was scheduled to board.

Jeff guided the black Buick Lacrosse into the Thrifty lot while Annie gave the inside of the car a quick once-over to make sure they weren't leaving anything behind. As the rental car rep performed a perfunctory walk-around inspection of the sedan, Jeff finally caved in to his inner manager and powered up his phone.

Only a few texts were waiting. Most were updates on minor issues at the office. There was a reminder about a charity event that he and Annie had promised to attend on Saturday. And there was one new voice mail from Alex.

Resigned to the inevitable, Jeff played the message back. Alex's voice sounded even more tense and strained than before.

"I know we've had our issues … I promise that I wouldn't be reaching out to you if it wasn't so goddamned important, but I've found something — something big — related to the Adam Polyakov trial."

It took Jeff a moment, but then he remembered the name. Polyakov had been the defendant in a high-profile murder trial in Portland about two years earlier … accused of sexually assaulting and killing his ex-girlfriend. As he recalled, the case had been a slam dunk for Alex. Why dig into an old conviction? And since Jeff had already left the DA's office for the job at Ferrum before the murder had even occurred, what the hell kind of insight could he lend to the case?

Even if he was willing to help … which he sure as hell wasn't.

As usual, Alex had anticipated his objections. "All I need is another pair of eyes to look at this," he'd added. "An hour or so of your time, only an hour or so to go over what I've found. Just call me as soon as you get back in town."

Alex left a call back number — his home number this time, Jeff noticed, not the office — and the message ended.

"Problems at work?" Annie asked.

"No," he said as he pocketed his phone. "For some reason, the DA's office wants me to look at a file. Something about an old case."

"One of yours?"

"No. The Adam Polyakov murder trial."

She looked surprised. "Wait … the guy who chained that Russian heiress to his bed? I remember that case. Pretty damned juicy, especially for Portland."

There was no doubt about that. Adam Polyakov had been the head of security for Connections, a large regional electronics chain. The victim was his boss, Larissa Kozlov, daughter of the millionaire businessman who founded the company. A cleaning woman had found the heiress's naked body chained to a bed in Polyakov's spare room. She'd been sexually assaulted, and suffocated with a pillow.

That sort of detail was always good for a few extra ratings points with the media, regardless of who the victim was. But it makes for national news when the victim is one of the richest women in the country.

Portland had been in the national spotlight for a month or so. Every news network had covered the trial —Nancy Grace had even done a week's worth of shows in the Rose City — but they had all lost interest quickly enough when Adam Polyakov decided to roll over without a fight. No one cares about an open-and-shut case, no matter how juicy the details.

"That trial was at least a year after you moved to Ferrum," Annie pointed out. "So, why are they contacting you?"

Jeff shrugged. "Frankly, I have no idea. I guess I'll find out when I get back."

THEIR PLANE TOUCHED down in Portland a little after four that afternoon. The tarmac at PDX shimmered in the unseasonably hot June sun. Temperatures in the city had hovered in the high eighties to low nineties while they'd been on the East coast, even slipping into triple digits over the weekend.

God, I hope Mikaela remembered to go over and turn the air conditioning on, Jeff thought. Like most true Pacific Northwesterners, neither Jeff nor Annie was very comfortable when the thermometer passed eighty or so, and they were miserable when temps hit the nineties. Get into triple digits and locals started seriously contemplating moving to Alaska.

As the plane taxied to their gate, Jeff put in a call to Markus to check on their ride home.

"There should be a town car waiting for you just outside of baggage claim," his assistant assured him.

"On top of things, as always. Did you get in touch with Mr. Burwell?" Jeff sensed Annie stiffen up in the seat beside him. *Well, shit …*

"I called his office," Markus told him, "but he's apparently on extended leave."

That explained why Alex had left his home number. "I wouldn't worry about it then. You can fill me in on everything else in the morning. Oh, and set up some time for me with Henderson tomorrow, if possible."

"Mr. Henderson is on your calendar from nine to ten, if that works for you."

Jeff chuckled. "Sometimes I forget who's really running the office, Markus. Nine will be fine. I'll see you in the morning."

Annie watched him as he ended the call. "So … Alex Burwell?" she asked quietly. "Is he the one who called about that case?"

Jeff nodded.

"I must have missed that before," she said, turning to watch the tarmac roll past her window.

Thus ends the weekend, Jeff realized with irritation. *And I have no one to blame but myself … and Alex Fucking Burwell.*

Chapter 5

Business at the Portland office of Ferrum Security Group had nearly doubled over the last seven months. In return, Niko Ferrum had reinvested a significant amount of money into new offices. The branch now occupied two large suites on the top floor of the Matteson Building, in the heart of the city's trendy Pearl District, as well as the entire floor below. The new, well-appointed digs were meant to reflect the company's growing prosperity in the region.

Unfortunately, Annie had decided that Jeff's wardrobe should reflect that prosperity, as well. Today, it was a charcoal-gray Brooks Brothers suit with black Elswick Oxford loafers. The shoes alone probably cost more than Jeff's first car had, although, to be fair, the Chevy had been an ongoing work in progress. *But at least the car ran,* he reminded himself, *which is more than I can do in these things.*

Jeff had the elevator to himself, as he usually did at seven in the morning. Coming in early had been a habit he'd developed back when he was at the DA's office. The pre-workaday quiet helped him focus himself for the tasks ahead.

He pushed open the glass doors leading to Ferrum Security Group's executive suites. His assistant, Markus, sat behind a large oak desk, slender fingers tap-dancing their way across the keyboard in front of him. No surprise, there; Jeff couldn't remember the last time he'd managed to get to the office before Markus.

The young man looked up from his work, peering at Jeff over the trendy eyeglasses perched low on his long, thin nose. He bobbed his head at Jeff by way of greeting. Markus bobbed his head a lot … in greeting, in thought, in conversation. Annie always said that he reminded her of one of those birds — the ones with glass bodies and pink feathers jutting flamboyantly from their heads — perpetually bobbing their beaks into a glass of water.

Jeff smiled and nodded back, per their long-established protocol. Head bob, quick nod … no words spoken until eight o'clock, or Jeff's second cup of coffee, whichever came first.

Today, however, Markus obviously had something on his mind. "Did you see the news this morning?" he asked as soon as Jeff cleared the doorway.

Jeff noticed his assistant's anxious expression. "What's going on?" he asked.

"Deputy District Attorney Burwell made the early edition today. And not in a good way. Apparently, they found his body in a car on some private road outside of town."

Jeff stared back in disbelief.

"I put this morning's paper on your desk," Markus added. He was obviously unsure of what else to say. Jeff thanked him and headed for his office.

The Oregonian didn't have much in the way of details. Around ten the night before, Alex's wife, Kendall, had called the police to report that her husband hadn't come home from a doctor's appointment that afternoon. No one seemed to know where Alex was, and there'd been no answer on his mobile phone. Normally, the police waited at least twenty-four hours before acting on a missing person report. But a Deputy DA gone missing? That tends to garner special attention.

The initial search turned up nothing; no credible sightings, no phone activity — incoming or outgoing — and no transactions on any of his bank cards. The police hadn't released any other information before the story had gone to print.

Frustrated at the lack of details, Jeff turned the television on and tuned in to the only station that reliably carried local news in the morning. They were midway through a story on the heat wave — which the weatherman predicted would continue throughout the week — but the crawl at the bottom of the screen caught Jeff's attention right away.

… reported missing late Monday evening. The Clackamas County Sheriff's Department located Alexander Burwell's 2013 BMW sedan parked along a private …

The report faded into a Dodge commercial.

While shiny black trucks hauled unlikely cargos over absurdly rough terrain, Jeff booted up his computer.

By the time he'd keyed in his password, one of the co-anchors had come back onscreen, wearing her 'serious news' face. Jeff notched the volume on the TV up.

"We've been following a breaking story out of Clackamas County, where the body of Multnomah County Deputy District Attorney Alexander Burwell was discovered in his car earlier this morning, along a remote private road near Estacada. News 14's Andrea Torrence is standing by at the scene."

The image switched over to the live feed of an attractive young woman holding a microphone. In the distance behind her, flashing lights danced along a wooded lane. The camera was too far removed to show any amount of real detail.

"The property owner reported the 2013 BMW, registered to Alexander Burwell, to the Clackamas County Sheriff's Department around five this morning," the woman reported, her expression a study in seriousness.

Jeff pictured the classes newscasters must have to take to get jobs on television: Serious 101, Introduction to Upbeat, Advanced Empathy … This one must have gone for her Masters in Somber, he decided.

"Sheriff's deputies have positively identified the body as Deputy District Attorney Alexander Burwell, a long-time Multnomah County employee. According to the Sheriff's Department, Mr. Burwell was reported missing by his wife around ten-thirty last night."

The camera footage switched to an aerial view of a dark-blue luxury sedan parked haphazardly along the shoulder of a narrow, paved lane. A half-dozen deputies could be seen moving around the vehicle and the trees that bordered the road, like ants around sugar.

"A spokesman for the Clackamas Sheriff's department indicated that there were no signs of foul play at this time," the reporter continued, off-camera. "It isn't clear how long the vehicle has been parked here. Officials at the scene won't confirm whether any items of interest were found in, or around the vehicle. Following the initial investigation, the car will be towed to Salem for further processing by Oregon State forensics specialists."

The shot transitioned to a photo of Alex. He looked about the same as he had the last time Jeff had seen him: smiling, confident … impossible to reconcile with the all-too-familiar mental image of a body, slumped over behind the steering wheel.

"Alexander Burwell had served the Multnomah County DA's office since 1997. District Attorney Cynthia Orbison voiced her sadness at the news of his death, adding only that Mr. Burwell had recently taken a leave of absence from his position, citing health issues. We'll continue to follow this developing story throughout the day. For News 14, this is Andrea Torrence reporting."

Jeff hit mute on the remote and stared at the screen. He only became aware that he wasn't alone when his assistant set a fresh cup of coffee in front of him.

"Any word on what happened?" Markus asked, glancing over at the television.

"No official announcement, yet." But for the Sheriff's Department to already report no signs of foul play, so early in the investigation … especially in a case this high-profile? *Jesus, Alex. How the hell could you do that to Kendall and Sarah?*

Chapter 6

Jeff had just wrapped his regular Wednesday afternoon phone conference with Niko Ferrum when the cell phone on his desk started buzzing. He checked the caller ID and frowned when he saw Kendall Burwell's name. He picked up, reluctantly.

"I wasn't entirely sure you'd answer," Kendall admitted. "We haven't talked in a very long time."

"Of course I was going to answer." The near-lie tasted sour in his mouth. "How are you holding up?"

"I think I'm still numb at this point," she told him. "Thank God Alex's parents volunteered to handle all of the funeral arrangements. I'm not sure I could have made it through all of that."

"I'm glad they could be there," he said simply.

"Well, they're on the plane back to Ohio, and Sarah left for Seattle last night. I guess now I get to find out how I'm really managing."

He could hear the weight of sadness in her voice. "How is Sarah doing?" he asked.

"Better than I would have expected," Kendall confessed. "She was definitely Alex's little girl. Especially over the last couple of years. But I think she's going to be all right. Honestly, she amazes me sometimes."

Jeff smiled. "She's always been stronger than you and Alex gave her credit for."

The other end of the line went quiet for a moment. "You had something to do with that, you know," Kendall said, at last.

His smile faded. "Not that much."

Thankfully, Kendall was apparently content to leave the matter at that. "The real reason I called," she continued, "is that I found an envelope with your name on it on Alex's desk. I'm sending it by courier to your office, but I thought I'd better give you a head's up before it arrives."

"Thanks, but you could probably have saved yourself the trouble," Jeff said. "I'm pretty sure it's just related to an old case he wanted a second opinion on. Not much point of my looking at it, now."

"Well, whatever you decide to do with it is fine. One less thing for me to deal with, frankly. I was going to come downtown to give it to you, but … well, I'm not sure that I'm quite up to that, yet."

"I get it. Listen, Kendall, if there's anything I can do to help …" he offered.

"I'll let you know. It's good talking with you, Jeff. Stay in touch?"

"I will," he promised, hoping she couldn't hear the reluctance in his voice.

AROUND THREE, MARKUS stepped into the office, a small manila envelope in his hand. "A courier dropped this off, but I'm not sure who it's from."

"It's all right. I was expecting it," Jeff said as he got up and took the envelope, ignoring his assistant's inquisitive look.

He opened the envelope to find a flash-drive and a letter, folded neatly into thirds. He recognized Alex's almost obsessively neat handwriting at once. A message from a dead man … from an old friend.

> *Jeff,*
> *Since you won't come to me, I figured that I would just have to come to you.*
> *Before I go into any of the details, you should know that I have been diagnosed with a form of brain cancer. My prognosis is not optimistic, and the surgical option I've discussed with my oncologist carries risks that, frankly, seem more frightening than the cancer itself.*
> *Please understand, I'm not looking for sympathy; I've made my peace with whatever the future holds. I'm only letting you know because, between the cancer and the drugs they're giving me, I've begun to question my instincts. That's why I've come to you.*
> *Enclosed, you'll find a flash-drive with a list of the key people involved in the Adam Polyakov trial. Over the last few months, three of the people on this list have been killed.*

As far as I can tell, nothing obvious ties these deaths to each other except the trial. But you know I don't believe in coincidence, not in something like this.

You and I go way back. Despite everything that's happened between us, I still consider you a friend. You're also the best investigator I've ever worked with. There's no one I trust more. Look at the file. Tell me what you honestly think. Am I just being irrational and delusional, or is there really a connection to these deaths that no one else is seeing?

Jeff inserted the flash drive into his laptop and opened the file, a single Excel spreadsheet with three columns of data; *Name, Role,* and *Details*. Twenty-one names, from the prosecution and defense attorneys down to the court stenographers. Three of the names had been struck through.

The first was Erin Meadows, listed as Chief Defense Counsel. She'd died in late December, victim of a hit-and-run. Alex had added a comment in the third column: *No suspects. Car found abandoned, wiped clean.*

On the next row down, Jeff found another lined-through name. This one he recognized: *Gabriela Ruiz, Presiding Judge.* In the Details column, Alex had entered, *Died 5/30. Preliminary ruling boating accident (probable fuel line rupture).*

The third struck-through entry — several rows below — was Vonetta Myers, the jury foreman, who had died on the 24th of June. Alex had gone into more detail with his notes on this one: *Drive-by shooting. Manny Cespedes arrested, weapon under driver's seat. Traffic cam confirmed car not driver. Alibi soft but no known connection to Polyakov.*

Jeff leaned back in his chair and tried to consider the file dispassionately. The evidence was ... well, as far as he could tell there was no evidence. Almost six months had passed from Erin Meadows' death to Judge Ruiz's boating accident, making any connection between the two unlikely. Then again, there'd been only three weeks between Ruiz and Myers. And five days later ...

Five days later, you apparently decide to off yourself on some little country lane, Jeff thought.

Old and unwelcome instincts were whispering to him. He closed his eyes and sighed. *What the hell are you getting me into now, Alex?*

Chapter 7

District Attorney Cynthia Orbison's outer office was far less ostentatious than Jeff remembered her predecessor's having been. Where the former DA had prominently displayed photos of himself with Governors Kulongoski and Kitzhaber, and President George "dub-ya" Bush, Orbison had opted for enormous, beautifully-framed photos of the county and city she'd been elected to serve. Jeff couldn't help but wonder if the "check your ego at the door" message the décor sent was sincere or mere window dressing. Knowing politicians — and every good district attorney was, at their core, a politician — Jeff assumed the latter.

After just a few minutes' wait, Orbison's assistant, Kyle Washington, led him into the DA's inner office. The woman who stood as he entered looked younger than the fifty-three years he knew her to be. Orbison wore a smart, no-nonsense, charcoal-gray suit blazer and skirt that left no doubt that she was all business. Thick, course black hair surrounded an attractive face, with high, rounded cheekbones and full, naturally-red lips. Intelligent eyes the color of burnished copper watched Jeff as he approached her desk.

"Mr. Dawes, please have a seat," she offered, pleasantly.

As Jeff took one of the low-backed leather chairs across from Orbison, she settled into her own chair and studied him for a moment. "My assistant tells me that you have something of Alex's," she said at last. "A file that you think belongs to this department. May I ask how you happened to come by it?"

"His wife, Kendall, found an envelope with my name on it. She couriered it over to me this morning," Jeff explained. "Apparently, Alex had stumbled across something odd in one of his cases. He wanted a second pair of eyes to look over the information."

Orbison looked puzzled. "One of his cases? Why not run it by one of our people?"

"You'd have to ask Alex," he told her.

The DA smiled, thinly. "Alex always said you were a pain in the ass. Am I safe in assuming you looked at the file?"

"I did."

"Then please, enlighten me." It didn't sound much like a request.

"The file contained a spreadsheet with the names of everyone involved in the Adam Polyakov trial, all the way down to the steno and officers assigned to the courtroom. Three of the people on that spreadsheet have died since last December. Well … four, if you include Alex," he added, sliding the letter Alex had written across Orbison's desk.

A flicker of concern crossed the DA's face as she read Alex's familiar script. "And he thought they were connected," she said, stating the obvious.

"They'd almost have to be, wouldn't they, if his facts are correct?"

"You didn't confirm the information?" Her surprise was obvious.

Jeff had, but he didn't think she needed to know that. "That isn't my job anymore," he said, simply.

"But it *used* to be your job," Orbison pointed out. "According to both Alex and my assistant, you were the best investigator this office ever had. And if your personnel file is correct, you were also one of the youngest."

"I didn't feel all that young by the time I left," he admitted with a smile.

"Why *did* you leave, if you don't mind my asking?"

"My daughter got accepted into Pre-Law at Lewis and Clark," Jeff told her. "Tough to cover that kind of tuition on a county paycheck. So, when I got a better offer …"

"With Ferrum Security. How is Niko these days?" She must have caught the surprise in his eyes. "Niko and I bumped heads more than once while I was in Los Angeles. He's a great guy, not that I'd ever admit that to him. The fact that he picked you to run the West Coast operations is quite a compliment."

This time, Jeff managed to hide his surprise. Few people, inside the company or out, knew Niko Ferrum was planning to announce him as Regional Director. Cynthia Orbison had been doing her homework.

"What were the names of the people on Alex's list who have died?" she asked, bringing the discussion back to the file.

"Besides Alex, there was Judge Ruiz, Polyakov's attorney, Erin Meadows, and a woman named Vonetta Myers."

Orbison sat back in her chair, then swiveled slightly to look out at the city beyond her windows. "How did Myers fit into the Polyakov case?" she asked at last.

"Jury foreman."

The DA sat in silence for a moment. Finally, she turned back to face him. Jeff could see the concern in her eyes. "Ever hear of Manny Cespedes?" she asked.

He had. Cespedes had started making a name for himself with Narcotics about the time Jeff made the jump to Ferrum. "Duarte Cartel, right?"

Orbison nodded. "Last year, Manny shot three teenagers dealing for a rival organization … slaughtered them, really. Homicide and Narcotics both knew he carried out the hit, but no one could ever come up with any proof, or credible witnesses. Then, last week, we nailed the sonofabitch for a drive-by shooting in North Portland … or at least, we thought we had."

"And the victim in the drive-by was Vonetta Myers." Jeff remembered Alex's notes from the file. "How solid is your evidence against Cespedes?"

"Solid enough to hold him, for the time being. Positive ID on the car from witnesses at the scene, supported by traffic cams. Patrol unit found the vehicle just a few miles away at the Lloyd Center mall. Murder weapon under the driver's seat, complete with his prints. Oh, and a quarter kilo of meth in the trunk."

"Let me guess; Manny swears it was all planted." She nodded. "Any witnesses who can place him, and not just his car, at the scene?"

"Not yet," Orbison admitted.

"Doesn't sound like much of a slam dunk for your team, then." Jeff saw the irritation in her eyes. "Sorry, but it seems a little too much like a setup."

"Maybe you're right," she allowed. "Obviously, that's what Alex thought, didn't he? Of course, there's always the possibility that Cespedes has some connection to Adam Polyakov."

Alex hadn't thought so. Jeff didn't, either. None of the deaths — with the obvious exception of Myers' — felt like the drug dealer's style.

"So, what would your next step be?" Orbison asked. "If you were still working for this office, I mean," she added with a smile.

Jeff hesitated, the ex-cop inside screaming for a seat at the table. "Like I said before, that's not my job anymore," he said, finally.

"Let's say that it was, just for argument's sake." Orbison's smile was encouraging, and more than a little sly, he thought.

"All right," he said, "if this is related to the Polyakov trial — and I'd have to say Alex is probably right about that — then start there. Go down to the prison. Find out if Polyakov is pulling the strings from the inside, or if someone else is doing it on his behalf."

The DA shook her head. "Adam Polyakov isn't the one behind this."

"How do you know that?" he asked.

"Because he died in prison last year ... protecting a guard during a riot," she added. "Not exactly what you'd expect from a sociopath, is it?"

"Is that what he was? A sociopath?"

The DA shrugged. "That's what we went with in the trial. In all fairness, that's where the evidence pointed, and Polyakov offered no defense."

"He pled guilty?" Jeff asked.

"He refused to enter either a plea or a defense," Orbison admitted.

"Sounds like a prosecutor's wet dream."

She scowled at that. "Rolling over without a fight is bullshit and you know it. We had all the evidence in the world. DNA, motive, opportunity ... if he was guilty, why not just plead guilty?"

"They're usually holding out for a reduced sentence," Jeff pointed out.

"Except Polyakov didn't ask for a reduced sentence. He didn't ask for anything. Given the evidence against him, and who the victim was, he wouldn't have gotten anything, either. Both he and his attorney knew that going in."

Jeff had the feeling Orbison was expecting him to say something. He didn't. She studied him for a few silent moments, then: "I can see the wheels turning. Help me find out what the hell is going on here."

He smiled at that. "Why me?"

"Because, according to Alex, you're the best detective he ever worked with. And because I don't have the resources to handle something this speculative in-house right now. Besides, if Alex is … *was* … right," she said, measuring her words carefully, "and someone is setting all this up, I need an investigator who can look past the obvious. Frankly, I don't know if anyone on my team fits the bill as well as you do."

"You *are* a politician, aren't you?" Jeff shook his head. "Sorry, but I have enough on my plate at Ferrum as it is. I can't help you."

"Can't help, or won't?" she challenged.

"Whichever one you prefer."

Orbison sat back. "So, you'll willing to let Alex's killer go free?"

Jeff slowly leaned forward in his chair. "That's a horseshit play and you know it," he told her, his voice carrying only a little of the irritation he was feeling. "If Alex's death is part of some conspiracy, then you have plenty of resources 'in-house' to deal with it. Hell, you have a whole police department at your disposal. You sure as hell don't need me," he added.

"I do if I want to keep this low profile. And I need to keep this low profile," she admitted.

"Why?"

If his directness bothered her, Orbison didn't let it show. "Let's just say it's complicated," she told him. "Pressure from on high."

"Look, we could go back and forth all morning," Jeff told her as he stood. "The answer would still be the same. I just don't have the bandwidth right now."

Orbison nodded, but the determination in her eyes never seemed to waiver. "Well, anyway, thank you for bringing this to my attention, Mr. Dawes. Now, at least I can finally put a face to the stories. I look forward to seeing you again," she added, looking a little too confident for his comfort.

HE ACTUALLY MADE it all the way back to his office before Niko Ferrum called.

"Cynthia Orbison tells me you're refusing your civic duty."

"Good afternoon to you, too."

"You do realize that it's bad business to piss off the District Attorney's office, don't you?" Niko said. "I mean, Cynthia is good people ... and ethical as hell ... but that doesn't mean she won't poison the well a little with her counterparts in other cities."

"You really think she'd do that?" Jeff made no effort to hide his skepticism.

"Probably not," Niko admitted, "but why take the chance? A reputation of being uncooperative is not what we need when we're expanding into new markets. That's why I told her she could have you for a month."

"A month? Without a fucking word to me?"

"Language, son, language." Ferrum chuckled. "You sound more like a New Yorker than I do."

"You know, Niko, you're not exactly making me feel like a valued employee when you pull shit like this."

His boss laughed at that. "You'd feel plenty valued if you knew how much I negotiated for your services."

"Who's supposed to handle things while I'm running errands for the DA?"

"We both know that Markus really runs things around there," Ferrum said. He seemed to be enjoying himself entirely too much. "You're lucky I'm such a considerate employer, or I would have stolen him away months ago. Seriously, Jeff, you've put together one of the best teams in our business. Between Markus and Joe Henderson, the office will be in good hands. Besides," he added, "I didn't give Cynthia an exclusive on your services. Even I knew better than to do that."

"I really don't have a say in this, do I?" Taking Niko's silence as confirmation, Jeff sighed. "How the hell did I end up working for such a manipulative son of a bitch?"

Niko laughed again. "Beats me. I sure as hell thought you were smarter than that. Anyway, Cynthia is expecting you in her office in the morning."

"What time?"

"Nine," Niko told him, "so nine-thirty should be fine. I wouldn't want her to start taking you for granted."

Chapter 8

Orbison had arranged for a small office on the ninth floor of the Justice Building. The furnishings were Spartan, at best: a metal bookcase sat along one wall — empty and forlorn — while a well-used metal desk dominated the center of the room, along with a chair that creaked in protest like an arthritic old man when Jeff sat down. On top of the desk, a phone and oversized calendar completed the set up. The office looked like a set from a cheap 1960's detective movie.

"I see you spared no expense," Jeff said, glancing over at the DA. She leaned against the door frame, wearing the beginnings of a smirk.

"From what Alex told me, you weren't much for sitting around the office anyway, so I just had them pull a few things from the warehouse," Orbison admitted. "Your laptop and remote token should be ready sometime this morning. Oh, and any calls related to this case have to go through department phones, so we'll get a mobile for you to use."

"The joys of government work."

"Sorry," she said. "Turns out that getting you temporarily reinstated was easy enough … you have quite a sterling reputation, even now. But there is still the inevitable bureaucracy to wade through. You'll also have to retest on the firing range, and use a department-approved sidearm while you're with us."

"No sidearm," he told her, sharply.

She looked surprised at his vehemence. "Why not?"

Jeff held her gaze for a moment. "Because I'm not a cop anymore," he said after a moment.

"What if you get into trouble?"

"That's what the cavalry is for," he told her. "And you'd better hope they get there quickly, or Ferrum will charge you a premium for damages."

Orbison caught the edge in Jeff's tone. "You're not happy about any of this, are you?"

He leaned back in the old chair. "Does how I feel really matter?"

"It matters. It won't necessarily change anything, but it matters," she said, almost managing to sound genuinely apologetic.

"All right then ... I'm not happy," Jeff admitted, "about any of this. I don't like being manipulated. Not by you, or Niko Ferrum, or anyone else, whatever the cause. I like my job at Ferrum, so here I am ... for the moment. But from this point on, if you're not up front with me about everything ... everything ... I walk, and you can explain to Niko why I've taken a job with the competition."

"That's not a conversation I'd want to have," Orbison acknowledged. She studied him, clearly assessing his intent. "You have my word," she said at last. "Up front, from here on in."

"Good. Then let's start with why you brought me in on this case at all. And please spare me the whole 'you're the best' crap," he warned with a faint smile.

"Fair enough." Orbison glanced around the office. Realizing that Jeff occupied the only chair, she perched on the edge of his desk. The informality didn't seem to bother her much.

"I wasn't kidding when I said that I didn't have the resources to follow up on something this speculative," she said, "or that I needed to keep this low profile. I'm getting a tremendous amount of pressure to get a quick conviction in the Myers case, just to get Cespedes off our streets. Believe me when I say that no one is going to be happy if you come up with evidence that Manny wasn't involved."

"So why stir things up at all?"

She looked surprised, then irritated by the question. "Believe me, I want that son of a bitch to go away for the rest of his life. But not for something he didn't do. I don't work that way. Besides, if Alex was right, this isn't going to end until a lot of innocent people are dead."

Jeff nodded, finally allowing himself a genuine smile. "All right, Ms. Orbison, I can work with that ... for now."

A brief look of anger flashed in her eyes at the realization that he'd been testing her, but she kept herself in check. "So, where do you start?" she asked, levelly.

"At the beginning. How long will it take to pull all of the Polyakov case files together?"

"They'll be on your desk within the hour."

"Good. I'll also need everything you can get on the Ruiz, Meadows, and Myers investigations. And Alex's, of course."

Orbison nodded. "Already in the works."

"Good. When they get here, have all of the files couriered to my office at Ferrum."

Orbison leaned back in surprise. "That wasn't part of the arrangement I had with Niko," she pointed out.

Jeff looked around the dingy little office. "Let's just say that I'm accustomed to slightly better working conditions." He read the irritation on the DA's face and decided to back off on the attitude a little.

"Look, I know what you arranged with Niko," he said, his tone as conciliatory as he could manage. "And we'll keep this low profile, I promise. But I need more resources than you can apparently give me. I've put together an excellent team of people at Ferrum, and I intend to use a couple of them … at no additional charge to your department," he added before she could object again. "Besides, if Alex was right, the clock is ticking and I'm going to need all of the help I can get."

Chapter 9

Azmera reached the bottom of the stairs, turned, and started back up with a labored sigh. The last climb to the top always seemed the hardest. Still, this made his fourth time up and down the long flight of steps this morning, and all before the sun was up. It had taken months of walking to progress to this point. Along the way, he'd shed twenty-seven pounds. Jahzara would hardly recognize him when she returned home from her trip.

Well worth the aching muscles, he thought.

Even so, the last trip up the steep climb was proving a struggle, one he knew he'd pay for the rest of the day. One hundred thirty-one concrete steps — he'd counted them too many times — tying together Fairfax Terrace at the bottom of the hill with Cumberland Road at the top. He'd read somewhere that the stairs had been built back in the early 1920's, put in to shorten the distance children had to walk to and from school every day. These days, few people in the neighborhood seemed to even know the path existed. In fact, if not for The Reader, Azmera would have had the staircase to himself most mornings.

He slowed as he approached the mid-point landing. Struggling to catch his breath, he managed a soft grunt to the young man in glasses who sat on one of the concrete benches placed on either side of the staircase. The Reader, as Azmera had come to think of him, looked up from his paperback — another mystery or spy thriller, judging by the lurid cover — and nodded his encouragement.

The two had never exchanged so much as a single word, but Azmera always appreciated the quiet support. Especially as he faced the final, daunting climb. With a half-hearted smile at the younger man, Azmera started up the remaining steps. *Sixty-four,* he counted to himself. *Sixty-three, sixty-two …* Progress became comically slow as his breath came in short, shallow gasps. But he kept moving. It wasn't so much out of determination as out of the knowledge that, if he stopped to rest, it would be a long time before he'd have either the strength or the will power to start climbing again.

A few steps from the top, Azmera sensed movement ahead. He looked up to see a short, stocky man turn onto the staircase from Cumberland. Azmera maneuvered to the right to make room. The man in front of him grinned, but instead of stepping likewise to the side, the stranger brought his hands up in front of him and pushed out, catching Azmera full in the chest.

He cried out, tumbling out of control. Arms and legs flailed weakly in a vain attempt to break his fall. Azmera slammed back-first onto the steps behind him. The force of the impact knocked what little wind he had left from his lungs as he slid and bumped to a halt.

At some point Azmera must have blacked out. When at last he opened his eyes, The Reader was kneeling beside him. Confused and in pain, Azmera opened his mouth and gasped for air.

"Shhh," The Reader whispered, a gentle smile on his face as he reached out with both hands and cradled the injured man's head. He lifted it up several inches, forcing a low, agonized moan from Azmera's lips. Then, still smiling, he slammed Azmera's skull into the edge of the concrete step below.

Chapter 10

The two people sitting across the conference table from Jeff couldn't have looked more dissimilar. Samantha Ledbetter — she preferred 'Sam,' — could pass for a junior at some SoCal college. Blonde, tall, and athletic, she looked more like a cross between a beach volleyball player and a swimsuit model than the veteran of two tours in Afghanistan. But her employee profile told a different story; Sam held a black belt in the Marine Corps Martial Arts Program — or MCMAP — and could shoot hell out of her targets with either a Beretta or a Glock.

In contrast to her apparent youth, the other person in the room, Paul Maxwell, seemed much older than the thirty-six his personnel file said he was. Tall at just over six feet, stocky and athletic, Maxwell's close-cropped brown hair was already beginning to show a little gray at the temples. Paul had four years with the NYPD under his belt, and eight more with the FBI. The last two were on a joint human trafficking task force in Portland. Jeff figured that last assignment alone would probably explain the gray hair.

Both of them had demonstrated keen, analytical minds since coming to work at Ferrum, and the kind of obsessive work ethic that threatened to make them largely unsuited for quality personal relationships. As a rule, Jeff did his best to ensure they achieved some semblance of a work-life balance. The project he had selected for them this time would have to be the exception to that rule.

"None of what we discuss here goes beyond the three of us," Jeff told them. They nodded without comment. "For the next thirty days, the two of you are being pulled to work with me on a special project. You'll need to delegate everything you're currently working on to someone else."

Paul frowned. "The Menlo Industries go-live is only a week away," he pointed out. "This must be one hell of a project."

"It is," he assured them. "There's a detailed briefing of the assignment in the files you have in front of you. This is just going to be a high-level overview, but ask any questions you have along the way.

"At the request of the District Attorney's office, Mr. Ferrum has agreed to have the three of us assist in a possible murder investigation." Sam leaned forward, keen interest in her eyes. Paul's expression was much more difficult to read.

Jeff picked up the folder in front of him and turned to the magnetic white board hanging on the conference room wall.

"Last December," he said, pulling a photo from the folder, "an attorney named Erin Meadows was killed in an apparent hit-and-run. The car was reported as stolen just before she died. The theory is that some kid probably went for a joyride and lost control. The car was wiped clean, and there are no suspects," he added as he used a magnet to attach the picture of the lawyer to the whiteboard. Below it he wrote her name and the date of her death with a red marker.

"Two months ago," he continued, "Gabriella and Antonio Ruiz were killed when their boat exploded just outside of Newport harbor. The preliminary ruling is that the explosion was accidental, although the Coast Guard hasn't closed the investigation, yet."

The photo of the couple went up on the board, appropriately captioned.

"Then, on June twenty-fourth, a social worker named Vonetta Myers was killed in a drive-by shooting in north Portland. The suspect in the case is a high-profile drug dealer for the Duarte Cartel, Manny Cespedes. The working theory is that Ms. Myers was not the intended target."

Jeff placed pictures of both Myers and Cespedes on the board.

"How solid is the evidence in the drive-by?" Paul asked.

"They have the weapon with his fingerprints, and witnesses place Cespedes' car at the scene."

"His car, but not him?" Jeff shook his head. "So, he's going to walk," Paul predicted.

Jeff let the observation pass without comment. "There's one more addition to the board," he said. "Two weeks ago, Deputy DA

Alexander Burwell committed suicide in his car on a rural county road."

For the first time since the briefing began, Samantha spoke up. "I'm guessing there's some backstory we're missing here, something that ties all of these cases together."

Jeff nodded. "A little over two years ago, a man named Adam Polyakov was convicted of murder."

Only Sam's expression indicated that the name was familiar. Paul would have been at the FBI's office in Cincinnati when the murder was committed, so Jeff knew he probably didn't have a clue about the case.

"As for the connection," Jeff continued, "Erin Meadows was Polyakov's defense attorney, Gabriella Ruiz was the presiding judge, Vonetta Myers the jury foreman, and Alex Burwell led the prosecution."

"So, it sounds like Polyakov is playing executioner to their judge and jury," Paul said.

"Someone is," Jeff agreed, "but it definitely isn't Polyakov. He died in prison last year."

Sam looked troubled. "Why does the DA's office want us to investigate?" she asked. "This sounds like serial killer shit."

Without going into great detail, Jeff explained about the sensitivity of the Cespedes case and the pressure Orbison was under to get a conviction. "Besides, at this point there is absolutely no evidence that the deaths are anything but what they appear to be," he pointed out.

Sam leaned back in her chair. "Four deaths in less than a year can't be a coincidence. That's obvious."

"Unfortunately, 'obvious' doesn't equate to 'evidence' in our legal system," Jeff said, "And whoever is doing this knows it. That's why everything has been staged so carefully."

Paul nodded in agreement. He had a troubled look on his face.

"It would take a pretty specialized skill set to plan and execute these murders without leaving a trail," he pointed out.

"You mean a professional killer?" Sam asked. Her dark green eyes opened a little wider than usual.

Paul shrugged. "Any idea what Polyakov might have been into that would justify this level of retaliation?" he asked.

"Nothing that I know of," Jeff admitted, "but I'm going to do a little digging into his background this afternoon and see what I can find."

"What do you want us to do, then?" Sam asked.

"Review the files on these cases," Jeff told her, indicating the list of victims. "Find something — anything — that the investigators might have missed. Knowing what we now know about the connections between the victims, maybe something new will stand out."

"Anything else?" Sam asked.

He studied the whiteboard for a moment. "That five-month gap between Erin Meadows' death and the Ruiz murders bothers me," he admitted. "So go over the list of the other people involved in Polyakov's trial. Make sure that our body count is correct."

"It looks like they went after the judge, attorneys, and jury foreman first," Paul pointed out. "Maybe whoever is behind this has satisfied their need for revenge."

"I hope you're right," Jeff said, "but there are a lot of lives on the line if you're not."

Chapter 11

With the email from Rx International open, Kolya clicked on the embedded hyperlink. The screen opened almost immediately to a poorly designed web-site, advertising a variety of cut rate pharmaceuticals. In the navigation bar on the right side of the screen, he clicked on the *Today's Discounts* link and entered his password at the prompt.

The screen refreshed with another innocuous display of over-the-counter drugs, all priced a little higher than might be expected for an internet discount site. In the upper right corner of the screen he clicked on the hyperlink labeled *Your Account*, then spent a few minutes committing the details of his next job to memory.

Again, nothing too challenging, he realized with disappointment. Nothing that required the artistry he'd come to be known for. At least the Ruiz's boat had required something in the way of ingenuity and patience, and managing the District Attorney's suicide so cleanly ... *Still*, he thought, *it would be nice to have something that would test my skills once in a while.*

He closed out of the drop-site with a sigh and shut down his computer, then carried his glass of Barberra out to the deck. On the water, boaters soaked in the afternoon sun as their small craft — cruisers and sailboats — bobbed lazily along the Willamette River. He watched for a few minutes, appreciating the peaceful setting.

There were far more exciting places to live in the world, to be sure. But, for some inexplicable reason, he'd found few places as ... comfortable ... as Portland. Within a couple of hours' drive, he could be watching the waves break along the Oregon Coast, enjoying a cocktail at Timberline Lodge on the slopes of Mt. Hood, or horseback riding in the high desert.

Well, if I'm not going to be inspired by the work, he realized, *at least I can still enjoy my surroundings.*

He settled into his chair and picked up the next book on the stack — by a local author named Easley — ready to drink a little wine and lose himself in another dark mystery.

Chapter 12

Jeff studied the reporter sitting across the table from him, sipping at a Black Butte Porter. Rob LaSalle caught him looking and offered a half-hearted smile.

"Go ahead and say it." There was an air of resignation in LaSalle's tone. "I look terrible."

"Not terrible. Not great by any means," Jeff admitted with a half-grin, "but not terrible. I'm not quite sure about the Bohemian look you've got going with the beard, though."

The writer rubbed self-consciously at the stubble on his chin. "Sometimes it's hard to work up the enthusiasm for shaving these days, you know?"

"I can imagine. I was so sorry to hear about Laura's accident. How are you doing?"

LaSalle set his half-empty glass down on the table. "It's a process," he said simply.

Jeff nodded. Rob and Laura had been married for only about six years, but they'd been good together, the kind of marriage you compared your own to ... and usually found wanting. After Laura's death in December, Rob had more-or-less disappeared into himself. It had been months since Jeff had seen his friend's byline in the *Bridgetown Times*.

"Anyway," LaSalle said, "you told me over the phone that you had some questions about my feature on Adam Polyakov?"

Jeff nodded. "I do. You were pretty much the only one — including the police — who seemed to have really taken the time to look very deeply into his background."

Rob shrugged at the observation. "The 'why' is always more interesting than the 'what,' as far as I'm concerned," he said. "But why the sudden interest in that case? The last I heard, you traded in your Dick Tracy decoder ring and badge for a rung on the corporate ladder with some private security company. Ferrum, right?"

"We've been hired to look into the case."

Rob gave him a curious glance. "Really? By whom?" Jeff smiled in response. "All right then, be mysterious. But isn't it a little late to start digging into the Kozlov murder? After all, Adam Polyakov died in prison last year."

"I heard. So tell me what you thought of him … as a person, I mean."

"As a person? Honestly, everything I found about Adam I gleaned from the people who supposedly knew him best."

"Then let's start there. Paint a picture for me."

Rob sipped at the last of his beer as he thought about the request. "All right," he said after a moment. "In school, Adam demonstrated above average intelligence. Most of his teachers went a lot farther than that, actually. He was also a pretty decent athlete by all accounts. Lettered in both baseball and basketball. He even turned down baseball scholarships at Oregon State and Stanford … North Carolina, too, I think."

Rob slowly traced his finger along the rim of his now-empty pint glass as he spoke, his voice quiet as he remembered. Then he looked up at Jeff, a serious glint in his eyes. "You'd think he might have had an ego problem, with all of that going for him. But I must have talked to a dozen people who knew him back then — at school, at church — and I couldn't find one person who wanted to label Adam as a prick or … what is the male equivalent of a prima donna, anyway?"

Jeff chuckled at the question. "I've never really thought about it," he admitted. "Any idea why he turned the scholarships down?"

"Just before he graduated from high school, his dad got laid off from his job. Adam decided to stay home and get a paycheck while he took business classes at Bellevue Community College. His parents were disappointed that he'd passed up that opportunity, but the extra money coming in really helped."

"What was his home-life like?"

"Disgustingly loving and supportive," Rob said with a smile. "Everyone I spoke with agreed that the Polyakovs were an Ozzie and Harriet family … absolutely devoted to each other. I interviewed his father a couple of times … rough around the edges to be sure, but a nice guy."

"And his mother?"

"She doesn't speak English, so we only spoke through her husband. I do know they were both pretty torn up by what happened."

The waitress came by to collect their empties and ask if they wanted another round. LaSalle nodded, without asking Jeff. "What the hell," he said with a smirk as she headed back to the bar. "You're paying, right?"

"That's what expense accounts are for," Jeff assured him. He considered what his friend had told him so far. "Polyakov ... that's Russian, right?"

Rob nodded.

"And Larissa Kozlov was Russian. I'm assuming that had something to do with Adam going to work for Larissa's father."

"Actually, Adam took a job with a company called Whiteman Security, out of Seattle, and they assigned him to Andrei Kozlov's personal security detail ... which says a lot for Adam, I think."

Jeff thought that was putting it mildly. Kozlov — the founder and CEO of the Northwest's largest electronics chain, Connectivity — had a personal net worth of nearly seventy million dollars, conservatively. Jeff couldn't imagine a scenario where *he* would entrust the personal security of a man that prominent to a college student.

"Had Adam already started seeing Larissa Kozlov when he made the jump from security guard to Head of Security for Connectivity?" he asked.

"I don't know," Rob admitted. He must have seen the surprise in Jeff's expression. "The truth is, very few people inside the company knew the two of them were dating until after the murder, although they all noticed Larissa's attitude toward Adam become much less ... cordial ... toward the end."

"How long before the murder was that?"

"Maybe three or four months."

Then what was she doing naked and chained to the bed in Adam's apartment? "Gut feeling," Jeff said. "Do you think he killed Larissa Kozlov?"

Rob looked troubled by the question, and didn't answer for a few moments. Their waitress, Emily, dropped off their next round of beers while he considered what to say.

"To tell you the truth, I still don't really know," the reporter admitted, at last. "Somehow, I could never match the man I researched with the crime he was charged with. And I'm not alone in that. No one who knew him at all believed that he could have been guilty, even after he refused to put up any defense. That kind of blind, unwavering loyalty is usually well-deserved."

"Not always, though. Did you get a chance to talk to Adam personally while you were writing your piece?"

LaSalle shook his head. "I tried several times — both before and after sentencing — but he very politely declined each request. Even sent a hand-written apology the last time, thanking me for my interest. Believe me, that was a first," he added with a laugh.

"What struck me most about that was the contradiction," he continued. "I mean, he apologizes to me for not granting an interview but, as far as I know, he never once apologized to the Kozlov family, after all they had done for him. Then again, he never actually admitted to the murder."

"Or denied it either, for that matter," Jeff pointed out. "Anyway, a confession would hardly have been necessary to get a conviction."

Most homicide case files looked like a jigsaw puzzle with at least a couple of the pieces missing. Not so with the Kozlov murder. The girl's body had been found by the housekeeper in Polyakov's guest bedroom. His fingerprints — and no one else's — were all over the handcuffs used to chain Larissa to the bed. And Forensics had found just enough semen on — and in — the girl's body to make a positive DNA match to Adam.

Alex had everything he needed to convict. It was intriguing to Jeff, then, that an experienced and intelligent reporter like LaSalle could still be undecided about Polyakov's guilt.

"Did you run across anything else that felt … off … during your research?" Jeff asked.

"There were a couple of other things," Rob admitted, "but nothing compared to the evidence against him."

"I'll try to keep an open mind."

Rob studied his friend for a moment, as though he was gauging Jeff's sincerity. "All right," he said, at last, "the first thing that bothered me was the way Larissa Kozlov's body was discovered. Adam's housekeeping service found her on Thursday, the morning after she died. But they normally cleaned his apartment on Wednesdays."

"Why the change?"

"Who knows? But according to the cleaning service, that was the first, and only, time he'd ever changed the arrangement. And yet, somehow, he manages to let that slip his mind completely just when he's about to leave a body in his guest bedroom."

"Things happen in the heat of the moment," Jeff pointed out.

Rob frowned at that. "Oh, come on … according to the DA, Adam drugged his ex-girlfriend, handcuffed her to the bed, and raped her repeatedly before — and after — he killed her. That sounds a hell of a lot more premeditated than 'heat of the moment' to me.

"And then there's the mysterious 'other woman,'" he added. "Adam told the detectives and his attorney that he hadn't been seeing anyone since he'd broken up with Kozlov. He was adamant about that. In fact, that was one of the few things he actually did talk to the police about. But I spoke with a woman Adam socialized with. She was not only convinced that he was over Larissa, but that he'd moved on. Happily, too."

"Did your contact say who this new woman might be?"

Rob shook his head. "She never met her. Apparently Adam's new girlfriend only came to town from time to time."

That seemed a little thin to Jeff. "Any chance I can get the name of your source?" he asked.

Rob smiled. "Normally I'd tell you to go to hell before I share that kind of information, but this one you could get if you just go back and read the story: Crystal Samuels … she's a nurse at Good Shepherd Hospital, and played pool with Adam most Wednesdays at a place called Touché, in the Pearl District."

The bistro was just a few blocks from Ferrum's offices. "Shouldn't be too hard to track her down. Anything else?"

Rob shook his head. "Listen, if you do find something, will you let me know? This one means something to me. I'm not even sure why, but …"

Jeff understood completely. Sometimes these things got personal, even for him.

Chapter 13

Samantha Ledbetter was waiting for Jeff when he stepped off the elevator at Ferrum. She looked more than a little agitated.

"We need to talk," she said quietly. He nodded, and followed her back to his office in silence. They made straight for the private conference room where she and Paul had been briefed earlier that afternoon. When the door had closed behind them and they were alone, Sam turned to her boss, green eyes glowing with intensity.

"We have more victims." She nodded toward the white board. The photos Jeff had put up earlier had been rearranged to accommodate two additional photos, with new identifying captions written beneath in a neat, flowing hand.

"I cross-referenced the trial list against media reports online, and found two matches. The first one was from yesterday morning," she told him, pointing to the last photograph on the board. "A juror named Azmera Gatimo. He apparently fell while jogging up — or down — a very steep flight of steps in northwest Portland. He died of head trauma. Of course, there were no witnesses. And here's the second," Sam added, indicating the picture of a young-looking man she'd inserted between the Ruizes and Vonetta Myers. "Alan Russell … another juror, going to school in Grand River. Depending on who you talk to, he either committed suicide or accidently walked off a bridge."

Jeff studied the dates they'd died and compared them to the other murders. "Grand River … that's what, two hours from Newport?"

"More like an hour. Why?"

"Look at the date. Russell died the day after Judge Ruiz's boat blew up. Two hits in one trip?"

Sam nodded in agreement. "Makes sense. But does that help us?"

"If nothing else, it indicates that our killer is efficient. And that he … or she," Jeff added quickly, "plans ahead."

She considered that, her expression somber. "This is some serious shit, isn't it?"

"Serious shit indeed. Have you let Paul know about these two?"

"He's following up on Erin Meadows' hit and run. I figured I'd brief him when he got back." She hesitated for a moment, then said, "Can I ask a question?"

Jeff smiled. "Always."

"Why do you put the victims' pictures up on the board? Dates and details I get, but ..."

"The photos remind me that these were people, not just dates and details," he said, simply, as he perused the board once more. *There must be a thread to pull on,* he thought, *a piece to the puzzle that doesn't fit.*

Sam watched him in silence for a moment. "Looking for something specific?" she asked at last.

"Inconsistencies," he told her. "We already know what the murders have in common, but sometimes you can learn as much by looking for something that doesn't seem to fit."

"And have you found anything?"

"Maybe," Jeff said, stepping back to stand beside her. "A couple of things, actually. The first thing that bothers me is the judge's husband, Antonio Ruiz. He's the only victim so far who wasn't directly involved with the Polyakov trial. If the other murders were carefully arranged for when the victim was isolated, why not the judge's?"

"Maybe our killer didn't expect Antonio to be on the boat in the first place," Sam suggested, although she didn't sound particularly convinced of it.

"That's possible. I guess the next question is, how likely is it that Judge Ruiz would have taken the boat out to sea by herself?"

Sam considered that for a moment. "I'd think there would be people who knew them — either here in Portland, or down in Newport — who could tell us that."

"Probably worth looking into," he agreed.

Sam got up from the table and walked over to the board, studying the picture of Antonio Ruiz for a moment. "Then again, what if it wasn't an accident?" she asked, slowly. "What if the killer had a reason to go after Antonio Ruiz ... other than the Polyakov trial, I mean?"

Before Jeff could say anything, she added, "The Vonetta Myers shooting seems a little weird to me, too."

"Why is that?" he asked, not even trying to mask his smile.

"Because that's the only case where we have an obvious suspect, but Manny Cespedes doesn't seem to tie in to the Polyakov trial any more than Antonio Ruiz does. So … either Myers' death had nothing to do with the others on the board — which seems pretty damned unlikely — or Cespedes was as much of a target as she was."

Jeff grinned. "You missed your calling, Sam. You would have made a hell of a detective." He thought he saw a little color in her cheeks at the compliment.

"I like the money here," she assured him with a self-conscious grin.

"So, if either Antonio Ruiz or Manny Cespedes — or both — were bonus targets," Jeff said, "finding out why they were targeted could very possibly give us another angle to go after our killer."

"What's our next step, then?" Sam's growing excitement was obvious.

Jeff thought for a moment. "I want you and Paul to go down to Newport and Grand River tomorrow," he told her. "I'll have Orbison's office make the arrangements."

"Road trip?" She smiled. "Always nice to get out of town. What's the plan when we get there?"

"See what you can find out about the Ruiz and Russell investigations. Maybe even push a few buttons. I don't want the three of us to be the only ones digging into these deaths. If you need to play the 'serial killer' card to get their attention, then do it."

A flicker of concern crossed Sam' face. "How is the DA going to feel about that?"

"We're not going to find out much of anything if Orbison keeps our hands tied," Jeff reminded her. "Whoever is behind this is already racking up quite a body count. Maybe some pressure from the Coast Guard, or the Grand River PD, will force Orbison to order protective custody for the remaining jury members, or at least surveillance."

"Whatever you say, boss," Sam said. "And what are you going to be doing while we're gone?"

"Me? I'm headed the other direction. Orbison's office has set up an appointment for me with Polyakov's parents in Federal Way. I'm also going to Seattle to talk with Adam's boss, Reuben Whiteman, of Whiteman Security. I want to find out why he picked someone as young as Adam for Andrei Kozlov's personal security detail in the first place."

Sam shot a malicious grin Jeff's way. "A meeting with Reuben Whiteman? That should be interesting." Whiteman Security had owned the lion's share of the corporate security market in Washington State for the better part of a decade, and Reuben Whiteman had been livid when Niko Ferrum expanded into his little fiefdom by opening the Seattle office.

Jeff ignored his employee's apparent glee at his having to enter the lion's den.

"I've also got an interview with Andrei Kozlov," he added. "Apparently, he's more than willing to talk about his daughter's case. It'll be interesting to find out why."

"When do you leave?" she asked.

"Bright and early tomorrow morning. I thought about heading out this evening, but Annie reminded me that we're supposed to have dinner with the prospective in-laws tonight."

Sam raised her eyebrows in surprise. "Mikaela is getting engaged? When did all this happen?"

"She hasn't really announced anything to us, yet," he admitted. "But she and James have been together for over a year now. And this is the first time that she's ever asked us to meet the parents."

"Must be love." His investigator chuckled at the pained expression on Jeff's face. "How are you dealing with all of this, Papa?"

"I'm sure I'll adjust, eventually. Besides," he added, nodding toward the white board, "I've got plenty of more pressing things to worry about right here."

Chapter 14

Paul backed the Chevy Blazer into a shaded spot just across from the gated entrance to Pier 4 and rolled the windows down to compensate for the oppressive afternoon heat. Then he powered the driver's seat back a little. Resting the Meadow's hit-and-run case file more comfortably against the steering wheel, he reviewed the details of the investigation.

On December 20th, at a little past nine PM, the police received a report of a stolen car in northwest Portland. The car, a 2014 Toyota RAV4, was found the next morning, about 25 miles away in a Hillsboro parking lot. Its grill and front fender on the passenger-side were badly damaged, the headlight shattered. There was no glass on the ground around the car so, whatever happened, it had happened somewhere else.

A routine check on accident reports in the Metro area came up with one likely match, a hit-and-run vehicular homicide in the West Hills, just a few miles from where the Toyota had been reported stolen. The victim, Erin Meadows, had died at the scene. The timeline fit. The ME had put the time of death at between 9:25 and 9:40, PM, within a half-hour of the car theft. Forensics matched glass found on and near Meadows' body with the Toyota's broken headlight. That would be their first, and last, break in the case.

The rental had been wiped clean before being abandoned. No physical evidence, no latent prints ... not even a gum wrapper or cigarette butt left behind. The homicide case remained open but, with no new leads, detectives had more-or-less written it off as a joy ride that went sidewise. Meadows was simply in the wrong place, at the wrong time.

Paul might have reached the same conclusion himself if he hadn't known about the other deaths related to Adam Polyakov's trial. Now he was going back to the beginning, looking for anything that might have been overlooked before.

The Toyota had been reported stolen by Nicholas Averill, a free-lance travel writer based in London, who was in town on business.

Fortunately for Paul, Averill was still staying in Portland. He had sublet a floating home at the Lattimer Yacht Club, along the Willamette River, using that as a base while he explored the Pacific Northwest for a series of travel articles. The writer had immediately agreed to meet with Paul if it would help with the investigation.

Finished reviewing the Meadow's file, Paul decided to call Sam at the office to see how things were going on her end. She picked up on the second ring.

"You on your way back?" she asked.

Paul chuckled. "Hello to you, too. In answer to your question … no, not yet. Averill is still about five minutes out so I thought I'd touch base and find out how you were doing."

"We have two more victims," she told him. "So far."

Paul felt his stomach tighten. "Where do they fall on our timeline?"

"The first was killed the day after the Ruiz boat blew, about an hour's drive from Newport. The second died just yesterday. I'll fill you in on the details when you get back. Oh, and I hope you don't have any plans for tomorrow. Jeff wants the two of us to talk to the Coast Guard in Newport, and the Grand River PD."

"Well, I was planning on taking Lucy to the Gorge for some wine tasting. Fortunately, she's the understanding type."

"She'd pretty much have to be, wouldn't she, to put up with you?"

He laughed. "Cute. At least I *have* a girlfriend."

Paul could almost see her scowl over the phone. "I'll get around to it, eventually," Sam said.

The tightness in her voice made him regret teasing her. He liked Samantha a lot, but sometimes she was a little too driven to succeed, to prove herself to everyone in everything she took on. That had pretty much described Paul's own life in New York, and with the Bureau, until the spectacular crash-and-burn of one very important relationship had forced him to make some changes.

Of course, Lucy would be quick to remind him that he was still a work in progress … but at least there'd *been* progress.

Paul considered apologizing, but he knew that would just piss Sam off more. Besides, across the parking lot somebody had just climbed out of a sweet little silver Audi A4, looking around expectantly.

"I think my guy is here," he told his partner. "Listen, why don't you go home and get some rest. I'll call you when I'm done and we'll make arrangements for tomorrow."

"I still have a few calls to make," she argued.

"A case like this isn't a sprint, Sam," Paul advised her as he closed the Meadows file. "If you don't want to burn out quickly, you'll need to pace yourself a little."

He ended the call and stepped out of the Blazer. The young man in the parking lot looked his direction and smiled. "Mr. Maxwell?" he asked tentatively.

Paul nodded. "You must be Nicholas Averill."

The man extended his hand. "Nick," he said as they shook. His grip was firm and confident. "I'm so sorry to have kept you waiting," he added with an apologetic smile and only a hint of an English accent. "I'm afraid I still haven't quite figured out your rush hour here in Portland."

"No worries," Paul assured him. "None of us have."

The writer stood about two or three inches shorter than Paul's six-one. He looked to be in his mid-thirties, although he might easily be a few years on either side of that mark. His dark brown beard and hair were fashionably short-cropped, and he wore trendy, thick-framed tinted glasses that exaggerated his angular features. Not an imposing man by any means, he nevertheless appeared fit, even athletic, and moved with an easy gait as they walked down to the slip.

"Nice neighborhood," Paul observed as Averill unlocked the front door to the unit he was subletting. The floating homes, lining both sides of the slip, were clearly high-end. Many, like the one they were walking up to, had upper floors with balconies. They all appeared to be immaculately maintained, and more than a few had power boats that were probably worth more than Paul's SUV tied up alongside.

"I got incredibly lucky," Averill acknowledged as he stepped aside to let Paul enter. "The owner is working in New York until November, and didn't want to leave the place unattended all those months. Right place, right time. Can I offer something to drink?" he asked as Paul took a seat at one end of the modern, gray leather sectional that dominated the living room.

"Thank you, no. This shouldn't take very long anyway. I just wanted to follow up on your stolen car report from last December."

The young man settled into a matching armchair. Now that they were inside, the lenses in Averill's glasses transitioned from dark to clear. Brown eyes, flecked with gold, studied Paul with interest.

"You said you were with the District Attorney's office," Averill said. "Does this mean you've finally found out who killed that poor woman?"

"Not yet," Paul admitted. "But we do have some new information in the case, so hopefully something will break soon."

The writer looked pleased. "Good," he said. "Anything that I can do to help, I will."

"I appreciate that." Paul pulled his small spiral-bound notepad out, flipping the cover back to the questions he had prepared outside. "You rented the Toyota on the eighteenth, two days before it was stolen. Is that right?"

Averill nodded. "I picked it up that afternoon, when I flew in from Toronto."

"And you're a travel writer?"

"Free-lance. I came to Oregon to write a story on skiing. Mt. Hood, Mt. Bachelor …"

"How did that work out for you?" Paul asked with a smile. The previous winter had been one of the worst for skiing in decades. The snow pack on the mountains had barely reached ten percent of normal. Paul's girlfriend was an avid snowboarder, and the lack of opportunity had made her cranky as hell for much of the season.

Averill shook his head and laughed. "Not so well, obviously."

"What kept you here, then?"

"Fortunately, there's a great deal more to do in this part of the country than just skiing. I pitched a series of articles on 'The Great American Northwest' to a British magazine, and they jumped at it."

"Sounds like a pretty good way to make a living."

Averill smiled. "I can't imagine doing anything else, frankly. Getting paid to backpack, mountain climb, surf … there aren't too many places in the world I've wanted to see that I haven't been paid to visit. The money isn't always what I'd want it to be, of course."

"It can't be that bad. That's a pretty expensive car you're driving."

The writer laughed. "I wish that was mine. The owner of this house, Mr. Konigsberg, is letting me use it while he's away."

"Pretty sweet deal," Paul said with a grin as he looked down at his notepad again. "The night your rental was stolen, you said that you were parked in a lot near Papa Haydn's restaurant, correct?"

Averill nodded. "Just across the street, behind some shops off NW 23rd Avenue."

"Did you notice anyone nearby, anyone watching you when you parked?"

"Like I told the officer that night, I saw a couple just getting into their car — two spots down from mine — but no one else that I remember."

"Can you describe them?"

Averill did so, showing the kind of attention to detail Paul assumed came from being a writer. Given that the man and woman had appeared to be in their late sixties or early seventies, it seemed highly unlikely that they would prove to be of any interest in the case.

"Let's back up a little, then," Paul said. "How did you find out about Papa Haydn's?"

"The hotel concierge recommended it, I think."

"Do you remember if there was anyone in the lobby who might have overheard your plans?"

That seemed to catch Averill by surprise. "Wait … are you saying that someone staying at the hotel might have been involved?"

"It's unlikely," Paul admitted. "I'm just trying to be thorough."

Averill considered the question for a few moments. "I really can't say, honestly. It has been six months after all."

"How about on the drive there? Is there any possibility that someone might have been following you to the restaurant?"

The writer looked anxious. "This is beginning to sound like far more than a simple car theft," he said.

Paul smiled, reassuringly. "I'm sorry. Again, I'm just trying to be as thorough as possible."

Averill looked at him skeptically, but before he could say anything else, the mobile phone on the coffee table next to him rang. He picked it up and glanced at the caller I.D. "Excuse me a moment," he apologized. "It's one of my editors."

Paul decided to give him some privacy and stepped out onto the deck, pulling the sliding glass door closed behind him. It was a beautiful afternoon, and the river's surface was dotted with sail boats and small power boats.

While he watched, a Bayliner idled slowly through the 'no wake' zone. Two attractive young women — a blonde and a red head — sunned themselves on the bow.

Must be a tough life, Paul thought.

"The scenery isn't too bad, is it?"

He turned to see Averill watching him from the doorway, an amused look on his face.

"Like I said, nice neighborhood." Paul glanced at his watch. "I really should be going, Mr. Averill. Thank you for your time."

"No more questions?" His host looked almost disappointed.

Paul smiled. "No, it was a long shot anyway, and I think you've probably given us everything you can. If you do think of anything else, however, give me a call." He pulled a business card from his wallet, one of the ones Cynthia Orbison had let Jeff print up for Samantha and him when she had — with great reluctance, apparently — agreed to let them work on the case. It had the District Attorney's office direct line on it, as well as Paul's personal mobile number.

Averill glanced at the card briefly, then set it beside a paperback on the small glass table by his deck chair.

Paul saw that it was the latest mystery by Warren C. Easley. Lucy had the same novel on her nightstand.

"How do you like the book?" he asked.

Averill looked puzzled for a moment, then he saw where Paul was looking. "It's a great read. Then again, I'm something of a sucker for mysteries, especially stories set in the locations that I, myself, am writing about. Are you a fan of mysteries?"

"Not so much," Paul admitted as they walked through the house to the front door. "But my girlfriend, Lucy, is practically an addict. I lean more toward non-fiction, myself."

"Understandable, I suppose. After all, you probably get enough excitement in your job as an investigator."

Paul chuckled. "Not as much as you'd think. Mostly it's the boring, behind-the-scenes grunt work …"

"Like interviewing me?" the writer asked, a sly gleam in his eyes. "I think I should be offended."

"Present company excepted," Paul assured him.

Averill smiled. "Well, I'm sure that if you ever do find whoever ran that poor woman down, things will get exciting in a hurry."

AFTER THE DOOR closed behind Maxwell, Averill walked over to the bar and thumbed through the stack of mail he'd picked up earlier at the clubhouse. Finding nothing of interest, he poured himself three fingers of 1942 tequila and booted up his laptop.

He logged into the Rx International website and navigated to the bogus cut-rate pharmaceuticals webpage. After clicking on the *Need Help?* button and entering his password at the prompt, Averill spent a few moments typing up a summary of his visit with the DA's investigator. He included Maxwell's contact information and the name of Maxwell's girlfriend, Lucy, because … well, because you never knew what information might prove of value in the future.

Then he clicked *Send*, closed out of the site, and took a moment — per protocol — to wipe his browser history clean.

Satisfied, Averill stepped out onto the deck to watch the pleasure boats drift by in the hot July sun, and finish his book before he lost the afternoon light.

Chapter 15

Meeting the prospective in-laws … at some level, Jeff knew that he'd been dreading this event since Mikaela had morphed from little girl into a beautiful young woman seemingly overnight. Jeff's relationship with his daughter may have been a little strained over the last few years — since he'd left the DA's office to work for Ferrum, in fact — but she had remained very much her father's little girl. Until today. Until this dinner with the O'Connells.

If pressed, Jeff would have to admit that he couldn't have chosen a better man for Mikaela to fall for than James O'Connell. He was light-hearted to Mikaela's more seriousness nature, spontaneous to balance her reserve. And, as so often happens, the opposites worked together amazingly well. Mikaela seemed as happy as Jeff had ever seen her. That made accepting the prospect of his inevitable loss a little easier to bear.

The O'Connells lived in northwest Portland, in a century-old home high on a terraced hillside, near the end of Thurman Street. The location afforded a commanding view of the Willamette Valley. Their house stood out in the old, long-established neighborhood of Craftsman and classical Georgian-style homes. Quarried stone covered the outer walls on the first level, while the upper floors showed exposed wooden timber framing of a traditional English Tudor. Rather than calling attention to the home's design, the architect had managed to convey the impression that the house had risen almost organically up out of the hillside.

"This place dates back to the turn of the last century," James's father, Patrick, explained as he handed a Makers Mark over ice to Jeff. The senior O'Connell was a trim man in his mid-sixties, the gray at his temples and the beginnings of wrinkles around his gray-green eyes the only real indicators of his age. With a quick wit and a ready laugh, Patrick had proven a hard man not to like.

He and Jeff had retired to the library after dinner, while Patrick's wife, Rachel, showed Annie around the house. Mikaela and James had already excused themselves to go meet up with some friends.

"Has it been in your family the entire time?" Jeff asked.

"Mine?" Patrick laughed. "No, I was smart enough to marry into money. Rachel's great-grandfather built all of this."

"Her great-grandfather ... was that the Senator?"

Patrick smiled. "You're thinking of her grandfather, Edward Wirth. It was Ed's father-in-law, Carl Lundgren, who commissioned this house. In fact, he designed and built most of the furniture as well."

Jeff looked around the room at the beautiful, vintage Mission-style pieces. "It's all very impressive," he admitted, "and the house isn't nearly as imposing on the inside as it looks from the street."

"That's probably because it was built by the Lundgren, rather than the Wirth, side of the family. Very down-to-earth people, the Lundgrens."

"And the Wirths?"

Patrick hesitated before answering, then smiled. "There are certain ... expectations ... that come with being a senator," he said, "or even the son of a senator, I suppose. Let's just say that I'm thankful Rachel took after her grandmother Julia, rather than the men in her family," he added with a chuckle.

"What are you two talking about?"

Patrick turned at the sound of his wife's voice. Rachel O'Connell was an attractive woman in her late forties, although she had both the figure and complexion of someone several years younger. Of course, there were always products and procedures to help slow the aging process — especially for those who could afford them — but Rachel somehow struck Jeff as one of those women time simply favored.

She wasn't tall, perhaps five-two, maybe five-three. Her hair, a light brunette color, framed a face that was more pretty than classically beautiful, with soft edges and mischievous, brown eyes that seemed to be watching her husband with genuine affection.

"I was just filling Jeff in on your family's deep, dark secrets," Patrick told her with a smile.

"Oh, lord, don't tell him about *all* of our skeletons," Rachel said with a laugh. She and Annie settled into two comfortable-looking armchairs in the middle of the room. "We don't want to scare them away before the wedding."

Jeff glanced over at his wife, who looked delighted. "So there is going to be a wedding, then?" he asked Rachel.

She smiled. "Actually, the kids haven't announced anything to us, but I keep hoping. We both adore Mikaela."

"And anyone who can put up with our son is all right in my book," Patrick added, with the faintest trace of a grin.

"That's only because he takes so much after you," Rachel pointed out. Her brown eyes were laughing, even as she struggled to keep her tone serious.

IT WAS HALF-PAST nine before Jeff could drag Annie out the door, and only then after reminding her for the third or fourth time that he had a long drive in the morning. Even so, they'd stood on the O'Connell's doorstep for ten minutes, saying their goodbyes.

The drive down Thurman and back into the city was quiet. Annie seemed lost in thought, so Jeff decided to tune in to see if he could catch the end of the Mariners' game. He found the station just in time to hear the commentator, Dave Simms, announce that the Angels were down by one in the top of the ninth, with two out. That was the good news. The bad news was that the Halos had loaded the bases, and Mariner-killer Mike Trout was coming to the plate.

"What did you think of the O'Connells?" Annie asked as the Mariners' closer threw his first pitch to Trout, *Down and in …*

Patrick checked his side mirror, then signaled a left turn. "They were very nice," he said.

Slider down and away. Great block by Zunino to hold the runners. The count goes to two and oh …

"Nice?" Annie's irritation at his lack of enthusiasm was almost palpable. "I thought they were a hell of a lot more than just nice."

"I could tell." He was trying, really trying to keep his focus on what she was saying, but in the back of his mind, he wondered how Annie always seemed to wait until the ninth inning — figuratively and literally — to spar with him.

"You could tell …" Jeff could feel her glaring at him. "And what is that supposed to mean?"

Trout lines the ball hard down the third base line … Seager dives to his right …

Annie reached over and flicked the radio off just as the third baseman got to the ball. "I'm not going to apologize for enjoying their company. God knows, I wasted enough evenings hanging out with your cop buddies over the years."

"And when was the last time I asked you to do that?" he growled. "When was the last time that I even spent time with them?"

"That's not my fault," Annie said, sullenly, but they both knew better.

A heavy silence lasted for several minutes before she spoke again. "Let's go out to dinner tomorrow," she suggested, her voice almost plaintive now. "Just the two of us. Maybe we could go to Gracies?"

He sighed. *She must be doing this on purpose,* he decided. *There's no other explanation.* "I'll be in Seattle tomorrow, remember?"

"Oh, that's right. Alex's case." The glacial tone flowed quickly back into her voice. "Why do you have to be involved in this, anyway? You don't even work for the county anymore."

"Because the DA hired Ferrum Security."

"So, send Paul Maxwell … or that Ledbetter woman."

That Ledbetter woman. Jesus … "Samantha doesn't have the experience to go it alone on something like this," he told her, as calmly as he could manage. "Anyway, I'm sending them both down to Newport in the morning."

"You have other people you could send to Seattle," she pointed out.

"We've talked about this. I'm lucky Orbison agreed to my even bringing Paul and Samantha in."

He could feel her watching him in the darkness.

"I don't think that's what's going on at all," she said at last. "I think you're actually loving this … a chance to play detective again."

He glanced over at her, his patience quickly evaporating. "What the hell are you talking about?"

Annie held his gaze, stone silent.

"I'll tell you what," he said, his voice tight as he turned his attention back to the road ahead. "Why don't you call Niko Ferrum and ask him why he gave me this fucking assignment? Because frankly, I'm no happier about it than you are."

"Really? Even though Kendall Burwell is involved?" she asked, smugly, as he guided the car up onto their driveway.

Jeff put the parking brake on and turned off the engine before looking over at his wife. They sat in stubborn silence for a few moments. When Jeff spoke, his voice seemed unnaturally quiet, even to him.

"Kendall has nothing to do with this. And I am not going down that road again with you, Annie. Ever. Do you understand?"

She hesitated for a moment, then turned away from his hard stare.

"I'm serious. The subject of Kendall Burwell is dead between us," he said. "That is, unless you really feel like opening old wounds." When Annie looked up at him anxiously he sighed, pulled the keys from the ignition, and climbed out into the cool night air.

"I'm going to bed," he told her as the car door closed behind him.

Chapter 16

Sam guided her Subaru Outback down the I-5 freeway toward Salem. Traffic was still Saturday-morning light, even though there were a lot of tractor-trailer rigs on the road. When the Port of Portland had lost their two biggest shipping contracts a few months back, the number of semis on the highways had seemingly quadrupled almost overnight. Weekday traffic in the city had become an ongoing nightmare, and weekends weren't that much better.

By the time they'd reached Wilsonville, the road south looked reasonably clear. With a bit of luck — and her lead foot — Sam figured they would make Newport a little before nine.

Paul leaned back in the passenger seat beside her, his Mets ball cap down over his eyes to block the rising sun streaming through Sam's window.

"Rough night?" she asked as she slid smoothly into the left lane and passed a double-semi doing a mere ten miles over the speed limit.

"Not rough, but tiring. I told you, Lucy is very forgiving," he said, a hint of a grin appearing under the cap. A few moments later he'd dozed off, leaving his partner to the drive.

They made a quick stop for coffee in Grand River, just over an hour out of Portland. Then they turned west toward to the coast, following Highway 20. Now fully caffeinated, Paul brought his seat back into the upright position so that he could enjoy the ride and offer up a little company. He watched the town of Grand River — and the campus of Oregon Central University — pass by to their right.

"Ever spend much time in Newport while you were going to OCU?" he asked Sam.

She nodded. "Jen and I used to drive down all the time after classes on Friday. Her parents have an enormous old house just north of town, in Nye Beach, that they hardly ever use. Of course, that was a while ago," she added, almost to herself.

He processed that in silence. Sam glanced over after a few moments. "You know, you don't have to tap dance around it," she told him. "It's been two years since she left me. I survived."

"Doesn't mean you want to talk about it," he pointed out. "Believe me, I know."

Since they were running ahead of schedule, Sam resisted the temptation to go 'Gran-Prix' on the curvy, mostly two-lane road. Even so, they still made Newport in record time. As they neared the coastal town, Sam turned left off Hwy 20, following the Historic Bayfront signs down the hill. They drove past some elaborate and expensive-looking homes before the road emptied onto Bay Boulevard. The expanse of Yaquina Bay lay sparkling before them in the morning light.

"I could get used to a view like this," Paul said, wistfully. He watched as a fishing boat made its way beneath the graceful arch of an imposing steel-and-concrete bridge at the mouth of the bay.

His partner nodded. "I've always loved Newport," Sam admitted. "I mean, it's definitely got its share of tacky tourist-traps but, at the end of the day, Newport is still a fishing town."

The bay front offered ample evidence of that. Dock 5 teemed with commercial fishing vessels edging in to their slips, or offloading the catch of the day. Signs along the road enticed visitors to buy fresh fish and Dungeness crab right off the boats, and the cool morning air carried the tang of salt and seafood. At the west end of the boulevard, restaurants and galleries coexisted with commercial processing companies.

Bay Boulevard ended just beyond the last packing plant. The Coast Guard station rose like a movie set on the hillside ahead, two storeys of classic white clapboard siding, with shingles that glowed barn-red in the sunlight. A white picket fence surrounded the property, giving the place a pleasant 1950's, small town America feel.

Sam found parking on the street. The two investigators made their way to the front entrance, where they checked in with a Seaman Donnelly. He verified their identification before guiding them back to a conference room overlooking the mouth of the bay. "Captain Bailey will be with you shortly," he assured them. "Can I get either of you some coffee or water?"

They both declined, and Seaman Donnelly closed the door behind him.

"How are you going to play this?" Sam asked when they were alone. Paul looked genuinely surprised by the question.

"Why me?"

"Because you have a hell of a lot more experience at this sort of thing than I do," she pointed out.

"We're not interrogating a terrorist or a sex-trafficker, Sam. Bailey's one of the good guys, remember? We just want to know where they're at in their investigation."

"And if she doesn't feel like sharing?"

Paul smiled. "You're over-thinking this," he assured her. "If Bailey didn't intend to cooperate, she would have just told Orbison's office to piss off. She'll give us everything she can."

Sam still looked uncomfortable. "What if I say too much and raise suspicion? We're supposed to keep this under everyone's radar."

He smiled. "Sounds like Jeff isn't worried about that, one way or the other, so why are you sweating it? Just ask your questions and answer hers. Everything will be fine."

Almost on cue, the door to the conference room opened and Captain Patricia Bailey strode into the room with an air of authority that almost had Sam stand at attention, just out of habit. She was a tall woman, probably in her mid- to late-fifties, with dark hair that was still more pepper than salt, and creases at the corners of her eyes and mouth. In her right hand, she held a thick, manila file folder.

"Ms. Ledbetter, Mr. Maxwell ... I apologize for making you wait." The captain smiled pleasantly as the door closed solidly behind her, and gestured to the chairs at the table. "Please, have a seat."

They settled in at the far end of the table. Bailey joined them, placing the file folder — still closed — in front of her.

"I understand that you're looking for information about the Ruiz investigation," she said. "Why is the Multnomah County DA's office looking into a boating incident down here in Newport?"

"We're investigating a series of crimes that may — or may not — be related," Sam told her. "At this point we're just trying to look at every possible angle."

Bailey accepted that without comment and opened the file in front of her. "The vessel was the *Justice Served*," she told them. "She was a 32-foot Carver, built in 1984, and registered to Antonio and Gabriella Ruiz, out of Seattle, Washington."

Paul looked up from the notes he'd started to jot down. "Not Portland?" he asked.

Bailey shook her head. "It's not uncommon for a vessel to be registered in a different city than the one the owner lives in, Mr. Maxwell. The Willamette and Columbia are beautiful rivers, but they don't really compare to the Puget Sound for boating. Besides," she added, "my understanding is that the Ruiz family owned a condo in Seattle. I gather they spent quite a bit of time there."

"Can you tell us what you've learned about the explosion?" Sam asked.

"There were actually two explosions, not one," she corrected. "But in answer to your question, we're still waiting for the lab report on the debris we recovered. What I can tell you is that the *Justice* had a remarkably spotless maintenance record. No known issues, no major repairs since the Ruizes purchased the boat five years ago. That is, until three weeks before she sank."

"Three weeks before?" Sam leaned forward in her seat. "What kind of problems did they start having?"

The captain flipped through a couple of pages in the file before finding what she was looking for. She pulled a piece of paper from the investigator's report and slid it over in front of Paul and Sam.

"On May 8th, Mr. Ruiz discovered a fuel leak during a day cruise out of Newport. Nothing too serious ... or at least it didn't seem too serious at the time. Ruiz took the *Justice* over to Sanderson's Boat Works, on the other side of Yaquina Bay. According to Sanderson, his crew made the necessary repairs — minor repairs, at that — which should have been the end of it. But the next time Ruiz took the boat out, about two weeks later, he encountered the same issue.

"He took the *Justice* back to Sanderson's on the 23rd of May where, again, they believed they'd made the necessary repairs. Frankly, this is the only part of the investigation that has me ..." Bailey paused as she weighed her words.

"Suspicious?" Sam offered.

Captain Bailey smiled. "That's probably a little strong. I'd say more surprised than anything. Bertram Sanderson is absolutely one of the most irascible, obnoxious men I've ever met, but he and his crew know boats inside and out. Hard to believe they could screw up a simple repair like this one. And yet, apparently, that's exactly what they did. Twice."

"So, you're still leaning toward mechanical failure as the cause?" Paul asked.

Bailey looked hesitant to answer. "At this point, yes," she admitted finally. "Maybe that will change when we get the lab results back from the FBI."

"Is it standard protocol for the Coast Guard to send evidence from a boating accident to the FBI lab?" Paul asked.

"It is when one of the victims is a federal prosecutor, apparently. And we didn't so much as send it to them as they appropriated it."

"Wait, did you say federal prosecutor?" Sam asked. The captain nodded. "Gabriella Ruiz was a district court judge."

"But *Antonio* Ruiz worked for the Justice Department. I assumed you knew that." Captain Bailey looked intrigued. "Interesting. Perhaps I should ask again ... why *is* the DA's office investigating this case?"

Sam glanced over to Paul, who simply nodded his encouragement.

"Gabriella Ruiz was the judge in a high-profile murder trial in Portland a few years ago," she told the captain. "In the last seven months, a half-dozen people from that trial have died under ... unusual circumstances."

The captain leaned forward in her chair. "And by 'unusual,' it sounds like *you* obviously mean suspicious."

"That's the problem," Paul admitted. "Taken individually, not one of the deaths is terribly suspicious. Tragic, yes, but easily explained. When viewed all together, however ..."

The captain closed the file, placing her hand flat on the manila folder. "How can the Coast Guard help?"

"By doing just what I'm sure you were going to do anyway," Paul told her. "Find out exactly what happened on that boat. And perhaps put a little pressure on the FBI to speed up their lab tests. I'm guessing that they're going to find explosive residue on some of the debris sooner or later.

"As far as the remaining people from the trial are concerned," he added, quietly, "sooner would be better."

PAUL PULLED OUT his phone while they walked back to the car, putting in a quick call to one of his old friends in the Bureau's Portland office, in hopes that they could shed some light on the Antonio Ruiz investigation. The call went straight to voice mail.

"I doubt that we'll hear back from Yance until this afternoon, at the earliest," he said after leaving his message. "He'll have to run the request by someone higher up the food chain to find out what he can share and what he can't. In the meantime, why don't we head over to Sanderson's Boat Works. Clearly that recurring fuel leak was no accident."

The shipyard was on the southeast shore of Yaquina Bay. Judging by the number of commercial and pleasure boats they could see lining the long dock and in the holding area, Sanderson's did a booming business. That certainly lined up with Captain Bailey's assessment of their abilities as boat mechanics. As they drove through the gate, Sam noted the eight-foot-tall chain link fence — topped with razor wire — that bordered the property on the three land sides.

Signs for the office led the way to a somewhat dilapidated wooden building, resting on barnacle-covered pilings over the bay. It took a solid push from Paul to open the weathered, warped door, which swung back with an angry creak. A dowdy, middle-aged secretary with bottle-blonde hair looked up from the paperwork in front of her. Her expression held a mixture of irritation and curiosity.

The desktop itself was a jumble of invoices and boating magazines, fighting for space with an ancient computer monitor that Sam could practically feel the heat radiating off.

"Help you?" The woman behind the desk directed her question to Paul, as though he was the only one in front of her. Sam caught the twinkle in her eyes. *Chalk up another conquest for the old Maxwell charm,* she thought, stifling the urge to grin.

"I'm sure you can." Paul flashed her a warm smile. Clearly, he had picked up on the receptionist's interest as well. Knowing him, Sam was certain he had no qualms about using it to his advantage. "We were hoping to speak with Mr. Sanderson. Is he in?"

"Bert's been pretty busy ... that time of year, you know? But I'll see what I can do," she assured him with a wink. "What's your name, hon?"

"I'm sorry," he said, extending his hand. "I'm Paul."

"Dorothy." Plastic bracelets jangled on her wrist as they shook.

"And this is my partner, Samantha," Paul added, nodding in Sam's direction.

Dorothy didn't so much as throw a perfunctory glance the other woman's way. "So, what did you want to see Bert about?"

"The DA's office just wanted us to ask a couple of questions about the Ruiz boat," he told her.

The receptionist stiffened noticeably, her smile suddenly a tad brittle. "Like we couldn't get what we needed from the Coast Guard's report," he added with a *you-know-how-bosses-are* sigh. "But I figured, what the hell? At least it gets me out of the city for a day, right?"

Dorothy nodded sympathetically, although her previous enthusiasm seemed to have waned a little. "Let me see if Mr. Sanderson is available," she said. As she got up, the ancient-looking desk chair gave a soft groan of relief.

BERTRAM SANDERSON HAD a shock of white hair that appeared to be trying to escape his head in any direction it could find, and the kind of baked-in tan you could only manage if you've spent most of your life outdoors. Whatever warmth he'd absorbed from the sun over his seventy-some years on earth, however, it most definitely hadn't seeped into his disposition.

"There wasn't nothing wrong with that fucking boat when she left here the first time, much less the second. I guaran-goddamned-tee it," he growled, casting a look at Sam as though daring her to be offended by his language. She merely smiled in response.

"Let me guess," Paul said. "The goddamned Feds have been around, bad-mouthing your work."

The old man sat back in his chair, surprised. If he'd expected an argument, it didn't look like Paul and Sam were going to give him one. "Well ..." he rubbed at the stubbly growth on his chin, "they didn't actually come out and say that ..."

"But they implied it, I bet. That's the problem with those guys. They spend so much time sitting on their asses behind a desk, they can't see anything but the obvious. Pisses me off," Paul said. "But we did our research. You have one hell of a reputation, Mister Sanderson. Everyone from Captain Bailey on down said there was no way in hell your guys could have missed something like that."

"Damned straight," Sanderson agreed. Sam tried not to smirk at the self-satisfied look in his eyes. "But if you know all that, then what the hell are you doing here, wasting my time?"

"You know how it is ..." Paul told him, resignation thick in his voice. "We gotta cover the bases and ask all the questions, or the boss will have our asses."

That seemed to satisfy Sanderson. "All right," he said grudgingly. "Ask away."

"We'll try to make it quick," Paul assured him with a smile. "We know none of your long-time crew could have screwed up the repairs on the *Justice*. Did you have any new people working on the job?"

"Haven't hired anyone new in close to two years," the old man assured them. "I pay top dollar to my guys to keep them where they're at."

"And you'll vouch for all of them?"

"Every goddamned one. Hell, I taught them everything they know. Not everything *I* know, of course," he added, a grin on his face, "but pretty damned close."

"So, someone had to have snuck into the yard at night and sabotaged the Ruiz's boat," Sam told Paul. It was her first contribution to the conversation since they'd been ushered into Sanderson's office.

"Not goddamned likely," the old man said with an irritated scowl. "I got razor wire running along the whole goddamned fence line, and a guard patrolling the property at night."

"There has to be a hole in the security somewhere." Sam directed her comment to Paul, rather than Sanderson. If her partner wanted to play to the old man's ego, she'd push against his pride. Ignore him. Imply that his people and his business were small time.

Her partner picked up on what she was doing immediately.

"Samantha, you don't build a rep like Sanderson has by being stupid or careless." Paul shook his head and shot the old man a look of pure exasperation. "Look, I'm sorry about this," he told Sanderson, "but I know her. When her mind gets set on something, she won't let go. She's like a goddamned Rottweiler."

"Got me a wife the same way," Sanderson said.

Paul nodded sympathetically.

"Any chance you can let us take a quick look around?" he asked. "Maybe then she'll see you guys know what the hell you're doing, and we can get back to figuring out what really happened to that boat."

"Hell, whatever it takes to get you guys off my ass. Just tell anybody who asks I said it was okay."

As they left the office, Sam looked up at Paul with a grin. "I'll be damned if you don't have people skills!" she observed, feigning surprise. "Who would have guessed?"

"Hey, there's more to me than my looks."

"Jesus, let's hope so," she laughed. "For your sake."

They spent about three-quarters of an hour walking the yard together, studying the layout and security measures. More than one of the employees stopped them to find out what they were doing there. Even when Paul told them that they had Old Man Sanderson's blessing, eyes seemed to follow them everywhere.

"I think it's safe to say that whatever happened to that boat, it didn't happen during working hours," Paul pointed out.

"No shit. These guys don't let anything get past them. And I don't see anyone climbing over the fence, night or day. Not that it couldn't be scaled by someone who knew what they were doing, but they'd be completely exposed until they dropped over the other side. That leaves the water," Sam said. "How far from the yard do you think they might have gone into the bay?"

Paul surveyed the bay front to the east and west. "We'd have to check on the weather for the times in question," he said, "and the moon's phase, but I'd guess at least a hundred yards. Maybe more. Anything closer would probably have been pretty easy to spot by Sanderson's guard."

She thought about that for a moment. "Underwater approach?"

"That would be my guess," he agreed. "Snorkel or scuba."

"Jesus, who are we dealing with here, James fucking Bond?"

Paul didn't answer, but the look on his face seemed to confirm that he'd been wondering along the same lines. It suddenly began to feel like they were venturing into deep waters, in more ways than one.

Chapter 17

Adam Polyakov's parents, Fyodor and Anya, lived in a small wood-framed house on the eastern shore of Puget Sound's Dumas Bay. Jeff guessed that the home had been built in the nineteen-thirties or forties, perhaps as a guest house or groundskeeper's quarters for one of the larger properties on either side. The driveway — marked only by a weathered mailbox rising among a tangle of blackberry vines — amounted to little more than two worn tracks cutting back through the thick growth of vine maple and shore pine.

Gravel crunched softly beneath his tires as Jeff maneuvered down the narrow lane and parked near the shake-covered cottage. He climbed out and stretched, trying to loosen the kinks after the long drive from Portland. The air around him was still, the quiet broken only by the water lapping gently against the shoreline, and the soft hum of insects riding the warm breeze.

Jeff saw a detached garage to his right. Like the house itself, the smaller building was covered in cedar shakes. The siding was weathered gray by years of rain, sun, and salt air. The large, barn-like doors stood wide open. Inside a man with broad, muscular shoulders and short-cropped hair moved around the front end of a decades-old silver Chevy Camaro. He was shirtless, his upper torso covered almost completely with crudely-executed yet complex tattoos. The mechanic glanced in Jeff's direction and nodded before disappearing behind the raised hood.

"Mr. Polyakov?" Jeff called out as he stepped into the garage. "I'm Jefferson Dawes. I believe the District Attorney's office told you I was coming."

Several beats passed before the older man peeked out from behind the hood. He studied Jeff for a moment, then disappeared once more without saying a word.

Jeff worked his way around to the front of the car. Polyakov was half-buried in the engine compartment, wrestling with what appeared to be a stubborn bolt. His thick, muscular arms and shoulders tensed beneath the mass of tattoos until, at last, the bolt gave way.

Then the Russian edged his way back out to stand, wiping his oil-begrimed hands on the soiled rag hanging from his belt.

Fyodor Polyakov was tall — at least four inches taller than Jeff's own five-eleven — and very, very powerfully built. Physically, he looked younger than his fifty-four years. The gray, sprinkled liberally throughout his short hair, and in the stubble on his chin, told a different story. So did the weariness Jeff saw in the Russian's eyes.

Polyakov dropped the oily rag onto the floor. He looked down at the engine with satisfaction. "Do you know cars, Mr. Dawes?" he asked. His Russian accent was pronounced.

"Not much," Jeff admitted. "I've always been pretty inept, mechanically. Then again, all my friends in high school who were good with engines spent so much time under other peoples' hoods, they never seemed to have time to keep their own cars running."

That brought a chuckle from the Russian. "This is my favorite. 1970 big block V8," Polyakov said, smiling as he closed the hood with a solid metallic thunk. "The last Camaro body style worth a goddamn, if you are asking me. Like a shark, prowling the sea."

Jeff could see the analogy. The nose of the car came to a subtle point between the two large, round, eye-like headlights. It did give the Camaro the look of a predator.

"Everything after 1970 was shit," the Russian said flatly as he stepped over to the utility sink along the back wall of the garage and began scrubbing his hands. "Everything, except the 1971 Z ... same body style as this. After that, nothing good."

"Do you think so?" Jeff asked. "I actually like the newer body styles. In fact, I almost bought one of the 2010 Camaros when they came out."

Fyodor Polyakov pulled a clean white towel down from a rack by the sink and dried off his hands. The creases in his knuckles, and the cuticles around his nails, still showed dark, oily stains that probably no amount of soap or scrubbing would completely erase.

"The newer ones are not horrible," the Russian conceded with an amused smile. "But this one, the '70 Camaro ... this is classic."

He grabbed a worn work shirt from a nearby hook and pulled it on, covering his massive, art-covered shoulders. "So, you have come to talk about Adam?"

Jeff nodded. "Just a few questions," he promised. "It shouldn't take long."

"May I know the reason?" The older man asked, not unkindly. "My son is dead now seven months."

"I know, and I'm sure that it can't be easy to have to discuss this, again."

Polyakov shrugged. "Adam put himself in that place with those people. No one else. At least he died with some dignity." Then the Russian managed a slight smile. "I'm thirsty. Come," he said as he walked toward the open garage doors. "We will answer each other's questions in the house."

The cottage felt even smaller on the inside than it had appeared from without. A long couch, covered in a rustic, floral print, sat beneath the window along the outer wall. Two matching, overstuffed armchairs dominated the rest of the tiny, wood-paneled living room. The large furniture made the space feel cramped but, otherwise, the room was remarkably free of clutter.

Somehow, Jeff had expected to find a few Russian objects in the décor. Instead, he felt as though he'd walked into Sear's Generic Americana furniture collection, right down to the western-style coffee table in front of the couch. Magazines like *Sail* and *National Geographic* were carefully arranged on top.

"You sit." Polyakov gestured toward the couch. "I'll bring water." With that, the big man disappeared into the kitchen, where the faint aroma of bacon and coffee lingered in the late-morning air like the ghosts of breakfast past.

Jeff walked over to the far end of the room. Low cabinets with paneled glass doors had been built in on either side of the small brick fireplace. Framed photos lined both the mantle and shelves, interspaced with numerous sports trophies. Most of the pictures were of Adam; Jeff recognized the good-looking, athletic young man from the case file. There was one of him in graduation robes, flanked by Fyodor and a much shorter, very pretty woman — Jeff guessed her to be Polyakov's wife, Anya — and three showed him in his football uniform, with a helmet tucked under one arm. Several more were of Adam in his baseball uniform, in team and individual photos. On the bookshelf below, a snapshot of Mr. and Mrs. Polyakov with their son, all smiling broadly for the camera in front of Old Faithful in Yellowstone ... *How do families like these come to so much grief so often?*

As that thought ran through Jeff's mind, Polyakov came back from the kitchen with two glasses filled with ice and water.

"Sit, sit," he urged his guest again. He handed one of the chilled glasses to Jeff, who settled in the armchair nearest the fireplace, sinking down into the overstuffed cushion. Polyakov sat at the edge of the couch. He took a long draw from his drink. Then he set the glass down on the table beside him.

"Now, what questions can I answer for you that are important enough to bring you here on such a beautiful day?"

"Well, Mr. Polyakov ..."

The Russian smiled. "Perhaps first we should meet properly, then we can talk. I am Fyodor ... not Mr. Polyakov, please. And you are Jefferson ... or Jeffery, perhaps?"

"Jeff is fine."

Fyodor shook his head. "Too informal. I think Jeffery is better," the Russian said, amusement in his eyes. "Now that we have met, you may ask your questions."

Jeff couldn't help but smile. "All right, Fyodor. I know that you have been through this more times than you can count ..." he said, then hesitated as a thought occurred to him. "I'm sorry ... will your wife be joining us?" he asked.

Fyodor's smile faded. "No. Anya took her own life the day after we learned of Adam's death. She was ... not strong enough for all that happened."

The pain was clear in Fyodor's voice, but the man's face showed only resignation.

"I am so sorry, Fyodor."

His host shrugged. "My sins have returned to me, Jeffrey. Anya and Adam have paid for them."

Jeff leaned forward in his seat. "And what are your sins, Fyodor?"

The older man's smile returned, this time tight and mirthless. "Too many to speak of, I am afraid. You saw the art I wear on my body when we were out in the garage?"

"I did. I assumed they were Russian prison tattoos."

Fyodor nodded. "From the time I came to this country until Anya's death, I kept these ..." he brushed at the front of his shirt as though he were trying to rub away what lay beneath, "these reminders ... hidden from everyone but my wife. My hope was that Adam would never find out what his father once was. But, in the end, the Devil always knows where you live, doesn't he?"

He sat back, heavily, and looked at Jeff through dark, weary eyes. "Let me save you some time, my friend; my son killed Larissa Kozlov."

"Did Adam actually admit that to you?"

"No. At first, he assured us that he was innocent. But when they confronted him with the evidence ... well, he would not even let us come to see him after that. Adam knew, I think, that he could not lie anymore. Not to me. Not about something like this."

This wasn't what Jeff had been expecting. "Why are you so sure that he killed her?" he asked. "Nothing in his past indicated violence."

"In his past, no, but blood sometimes wins out. Or do you not believe in such things?"

Jeff held Polyakov's gaze a moment before answering.

"Regardless of whether I believe it," he said at last, "you clearly do. But, no, I don't believe in genetic predisposition. If Adam killed that girl, he didn't do it because of you, or anything you might have done in your past."

Polyakov studied him for a moment. "You say 'if' as though you thought there might be another truth. Why *did* the District Attorney send you here to see me?"

Jeff knew what Orbison would have wanted him to do ... hedge, find some way to get what they were looking for without giving out too much information. It was a bad way to do business, and Jeff had no real stomach for it. He decided to tell Adam's father the truth.

"Since your son died," he said, "someone has been targeting the people involved in his conviction."

"Targeting …" Polyakov frowned. "Say what you mean, Jeffrey."

"All right. Over the last few months someone has killed the judge, the attorneys, and at least three of the jury members from his trial."

The Russian looked genuinely stunned by the news. "But they were guilty of nothing. Nothing! *Bozha moi* …" Polyakov muttered, slumping back in his seat again. A deep sadness settled across his features. "Why have I heard nothing of this before now?" he asked, quietly.

"Because we've just recently begun to put the pieces together. Each of the deaths was carefully masked to look like an accident, or a suicide."

Fyodor nodded as though this was the answer he'd expected, as if this sort of thing was all too familiar. When he sat forward once more, his olive-green eyes had a hard, steely look.

"Ask me your questions, Jeffrey," he said, his voice firm. "I will tell you anything I can."

Chapter 18

Paul tossed his mobile down onto the table in obvious frustration. The phone slid across the polished wood and wedged itself under Sam's plate, knocking the last of her fries onto the lacquered table in the process.

They were seated outside at Ocean Bleu, one of her favorite places to eat in Newport. Their table was situated well away from the other diners, at the far end of the patio area. Sam couldn't help but wonder if the frustration radiating off of her partner had anything to do with their isolation.

"I gather your old FBI friend proved less than helpful," she observed as she dipped one of her popcorn shrimp in cocktail sauce.

The look on Paul's face was the very definition of a scowl. "'The Agency cannot comment on any investigations that may — or may not — be ongoing at this time involving the death of Federal Prosecutor Antonio Ruiz,'" he intoned robotically. "We're not getting anything without a written request from District Attorney Orbison's office."

"You had to have known what their answer would probably be when you called." She lifted one of his fries from his plate and popped it into her mouth.

"Doesn't mean I have to like it," he groused. "Especially when it's coming from a guy I fucking trained. Hell, Yance wouldn't even tell me what kind of cases Antonio Ruiz worked for the Justice Department."

"Organized crime, mostly," Sam told him. She grinned at the look on Paul's face and stole another fry from his plate. "The wonders of the internet, and the Freedom of Information Act. I Googled Antonio while you were spinning your wheels on the phone. In 2011, Ruiz was lead prosecutor in the Luciano Mazziato case. Two years ago he took on the Munõz drug cartel."

"Mazziato and the Columbians? Well, that's interesting." Paul considered the new information for a moment. "So, both of the people who don't fit neatly into the Polyakov case — Antonio Ruiz and

Manny Cespedes — have ties to organized crime and drug trafficking. That can't be a coincidence."

"Do you think the rest of the murders were just decoys to keep the Justice Department from putting things together?" Sam asked.

Paul shook his head. "The killer has been trying too damned hard to make the other deaths seem completely unrelated. But Antonio Ruiz and Manny Cespedes may have been bonus targets, which would mean some connection between Adam Polyakov and organized crime."

"That doesn't fit in with anything in his file," Sam pointed out, skeptically. "Until the murder, he came across like a goddamned boy scout."

"So far, not a lot of anything fits together neatly in this case," Paul countered as he signaled their waitress for the check.

"WHY DO YOU think Jeff took the job with Ferrum?" Sam asked as she guided the Subaru back onto Highway 20, away from Newport. It was a little after one in the afternoon, and their appointment with Captain Foster of the Grand River PD had been scheduled for two-thirty.

Her question caught Paul off-guard for a moment. She'd been uncharacteristically quiet since they'd left the restaurant. "I don't know. I've never asked. Why so curious?"

"Apparently, Jeff was hot shit when he was an investigator with the DA's office," Sam told him. "There was even talk that he might jump to the State AG's staff. Then he simply walked away from everything for Ferrum, just like that."

"Who told you all of this?"

"Lady I talked to in Orbison's office when I went in to get my clearance." Sam pulled into the westbound lane to pass a battered old Chevy pickup puttering along at the speed limit. "The truth is, a whole lot of people there seemed to be glad Jeff was coming back, even if only temporarily," she added as she slid back into her own lane. "But no one seems to know why he left in the first place."

"If I had to guess, I'd say it was probably a case of HWHL," Paul told her.

Sam looked puzzled by the acronym. "What the hell is 'HWHL?'" she asked at last.

He grinned. "Happy Wife, Happy Life."

That brought a frown from his partner. "You think Annie made him leave for more money?"

"I have no idea. But even if she did, I'd understand. Being married to a cop isn't easy, and Annie hung in there for a long time. A lot of them don't," he added quietly.

Sam glanced over. "Is that what happened to you?" she asked, quietly.

Paul leaned back and closed his eyes for a moment, trying to decide if this was a road he really wanted to go down.

"I'm sorry," she said. "That's none of my business, is it?"

"No, its fine," he assured her. "The answer is, yes. There were too many times when I couldn't leave work at work, and too many shifts with Janet wondering if I was going to be coming home at all."

Sam kept her focus on the road, but Paul could tell she was processing. He decided that this was as good a time as any to share a little more hard-earned wisdom.

"I guarantee I would have jumped at a job like this years ago, knowing what I know now." He looked out at the passing landscape and added, "Maybe if I had, Janet wouldn't be living in Port Winslow now with someone else."

The uncharacteristic seriousness of Paul's speech hung in the air between them for several moments.

"I still don't think Annie had any right to screw with Jeff's career," Sam said, quietly.

"I take it you're not a fan of Mrs. Dawes."

She smiled a little. "Yeah, well … I'm pretty sure the feeling is mutual."

Paul laughed. "What do you expect? You're intelligent, smoking hot, and half her age." He glanced over at Sam, expecting some biting comeback. He was surprised to see her cheeks begin to flush.

"Whatever," she mumbled.

"Of course, Annie wouldn't feel nearly as threatened if she knew you batted for the other team," he added with a smirk.

"You are such a dick." Sam looked to be trying hard not to grin. "I see those diversity classes the company sent us to really paid off for you."

"Right? I think the only reason they keep making me go back again and again is because the HR manager has a serious thing for me."

"Yeah," Sam agreed with a laugh, "You're just his type."

Chapter 19

One of the things Brandon Foster liked most about being a captain in the Grand River Police Department was just how quiet life was in the small college town, at least in comparison to his job as a detective back in Portland. The majority of the cases the GRPD handled were minor in nature: property crimes, possession of controlled substances, under-age drinking … that sort of thing. Sure, a few domestic violence cases came their way but, statistically, no more so in rural Oregon than in the larger cities.

On the other hand, the more serious crimes like aggravated assault and murder, fell well below the national averages. People in Grand River usually died of natural causes or injuries from an accident. Or suicide, like Alan Russell had.

The case report on the engineering student's death had looked pretty straight-forward when it had hit Foster's desk back in June. The ME ruled that drowning had been the cause of death. Russell's other injuries, fractures in the parietal and occipital bones of the skull, appeared to have occurred when he'd jumped into the river. Hair and blood spatter — found on the support cap that extended out a foot or so beyond the bottom of the bridge span — aligned with that theory completely.

Then there was the suicide note, found in Russell's backpack on the bridge … the usual crap about pressure at school, feeling lost, that sort of thing. Analysis of the note confirmed Russell's handwriting, and there'd been no latent prints on the paper other than his own. The investigating detectives had it down as suicide, open and shut, and Foster had agreed.

In retrospect, one of the uniforms dispatched to the scene, Sergeant Carol Banker, had voiced some doubts. She had been at the bridge that night, and had also assisted in the search of Russell's apartment. Banker had noted a couple of "discrepancies," as she'd called them, and the lead detective, Cal Harrison, had dutifully included her observations in the report. But no one had given them any serious consideration.

Until now, at least … until two people from the Multnomah County DA's office had shown up review the case.

Brandon knew one of the DA's investigators; they'd both been assigned to a Human Trafficking task force in Portland. Paul had impressed Foster as being sharp, and very, very committed.

Maxwell's partner, Samantha Ledbetter, seemed a little young for an investigator with the DA's office, Brandon thought, but Paul clearly regarded her as an equal. That kind of respect from someone with Maxwell's experience meant something … *and she's kind of a babe, to boot. Why the hell couldn't I ever rate a partner like that?*

The two of them were going through the medical examiner's report now, paying close attention to the blow Russell had sustained to the back of his head. "So the ME decided that both the primary and secondary cranial fractures were the result of the fall?" Paul asked.

"That's right," Foster said. "And his findings dovetailed with our own investigation."

Paul nodded. "The note, the autopsy findings … everything looks pretty cut and dried."

Brandon caught the glance that passed between Maxwell and Ledbetter. "Then why are you here, Paul?" he asked, flatly.

"Russell had some involvement with a case that we're looking into," Paul told him. "We're just trying to make sure that his death isn't connected somehow."

Brandon frowned at the obvious side-step. "Don't bullshit me. You two think that Russell's case *is* connected, and that my detectives missed something." When neither of his visitors said anything, he sighed. "I'm guessing that means 'yes.'"

"It's possible," Paul admitted.

"Not everyone seemed convinced it was suicide," Maxwell pointed out, glancing down at the file she was holding. "It looks like one of your people had some concerns about the suicide theory."

Brandon nodded. "Sergeant Banker."

"Any chance that we could speak with her?" she asked.

"I think it can be arranged," Brandon told her. "Let me just see if she's on shift."

He left the two investigators to their deconstruction of his department's findings. The duty room was Saturday-afternoon-quiet, and practically deserted. Two uniforms sat at their desks, filling out reports. A third looked like he was updating Facebook. His partner — Brandon recognized her as the rookie who had joined the department a few weeks back — was grabbing a cup of what passed for coffee at the station. Brandon joined the officer as she poured the thick, black brew into a Styrofoam cup.

"Morgan, right?" he asked as he pulled a cup for himself from the stack beside the coffee maker.

The woman looked up at the sound of Brandon's voice, obviously surprised to find the captain in the duty room on a Saturday. Or maybe it was simply the sight of him in Dockers and a polo shirt, instead of his usual suit and tie. "Morganthal, sir," she said, quietly.

He offered her an apologetic smile. "Sorry, I've never been too good with names. I'm looking for Sergeant Banker. Have you seen her today?"

"Sarge's shift ended about a half hour ago, sir. She changed into civies and took off."

"Any chance you know where she might have been headed?"

The young officer nodded. "She said something about grabbing a beer before going home. I'm guessing that she's probably across the street, at Maynard's."

CAROL SAT AT the bar, enjoying a cold PBR while she contemplated how to spend the next two days. For once, her off times coincided with Eddie's, and she'd been dropping hints all week about heading to the coast for a day, or maybe even running up to Portland for dinner or a show. Knowing her fiancé, however, the best she could probably hope for would be yard work and watching the Mariners lose another series on television. If she was really lucky, he might even spring for Chinese take-out.

An exciting guy, my Eddie. With a sigh, she drained the last of her beer and signaled Davey for another one. The young bartender pulled a clean glass from the stack and began to pour.

"Sergeant Banker ..." The rich, deep voice came from behind. Carol turned to see Captain Foster — in civies, no less — standing next to a man and woman she'd never seen before. The girl was a little too pretty, the kind of slender, leggy blonde Carol made a point of keeping Eddie away from. Not that he'd ever actually do anything — his girlfriend carried a sidearm, after all — *but every woman has her insecurities, right?*

As for the guy, he had cop written all over him. He was about the captain's height, a little over six-foot-tall, and trim. Carol figured he was in his late thirties or early forties, despite the traces of salt-and-pepper in his military haircut. He looked muscular under his buttoned-down blue shirt. Not beefy, by any means, but well put-together. *And definitely attractive,* she decided. As the thought crossed her mind, Carol noticed the blonde girl watching her, an amused, knowing look in her eyes.

"I'm glad we caught you before you headed home," Captain Foster said. He nodded toward the people he'd come in with. "Sergeant Banker, this is Paul Maxwell and Samantha Ledbetter, investigators with the Multnomah County DA's office. They're here looking into the Russell case, and wanted to ask you a few questions."

Banker nodded. Maxwell she'd assumed was a cop, but the other one ... *Shit, she can't be more than, what? Twenty-three? Twenty-four? She makes investigator with the fucking DA's office, and I'm still spinning my goddamned wheels in uniform?*

She swallowed her irritation and shook hands with them both. "Anything I can do to help," she said. "But Detective Harrison told me that the case was closed. Suicide, straight up."

"True," Foster agreed with a crooked half-smile, "but Maxwell and Ledbetter are working on something else that they think might be related. They've been reviewing Harrison's notes on the case, and saw that you expressed some doubts about the suicide theory."

"Nothing concrete," she hedged. Frankly, Carol was surprised that her dissenting view had even made it as far as the Captain's office, since that prick, Harrison, had been completely dismissive of her suspicions. "More of a hunch, really."

"Still, it can't hurt to discuss it, can it?" Foster said with a reassuring smile.

"Like I said, anything I can do to help. Do you want me to come back to the station?" she asked, eyeing the fresh PBR in her hand.

"I don't think that will be necessary." Foster glanced around the bar. "Why don't we grab a table, and I'll spring for the next round."

Paul Maxwell smiled. "Sounds good to me."

The four of them found a booth in the back and settled in. Foster ordered IPAs for both himself and Maxwell. Samantha Ledbetter opted for coffee, black. "Designated driver," she explained.

"So, what do you want to know?" Carol asked, when the waiter had wandered back to the bar.

"The morning Russell's body was found," Maxwell said, "you were sent to the bridge where he allegedly jumped in, is that right?"

Carol nodded. "One of our patrolmen found the vic's shoes, socks, and backpack — along with a half-empty beer bottle — on the Van den Burg span," she told him. "I was assigned to secure the site until the detectives finished with the body."

"What did you see there?" This from the woman, Ledbetter.

Carol hesitated. The last thing she needed to do was show Detective Harrison up. She glanced over to see Captain Foster, smiling his encouragement from across the table.

"A couple of things that seemed iffy," she admitted, "for a suicide, at least."

"Like what?" the girl pressed.

Carol took a deep breath. *Oh, what the hell,* she decided, *it's not like playing it safe is getting me anywhere.*

"All right … for one thing, there's the spot where Russell went in," she said. "He's got an entire bridge to choose from, and he decides to jump from the upriver side, almost on top of one of the concrete supports. Not only is he going to get swept up against the support, but he didn't even clear the damned cap on the way down."

She paused as the waiter brought their order, only continuing when he was out of earshot.

"Then there's the thing with his belongings," she continued. "All neatly arranged, socks carefully rolled and placed inside the shoes, and set side-by-side in front of the backpack."

"And why did that stand out?" Maxwell asked.

"When the detectives finished up at the bridge, I went with them to Russell's apartment. Pizza boxes all over the place, empty beer cans under the coffee table … the kid was a goddamned slob. Hell, he made my Eddie look like a frickin' neat freak. And we're supposed to believe in the last moments of his life he's going to get anal about how he leaves his shoes and socks behind?"

"You've got good instincts." Maxwell smiled and looked over at Foster. "I'm beginning to think you had the wrong detective working this case," he said.

"I'm thinking along the same lines," he admitted. Then he turned to Carol. "If you tell Detective Harrison I said that, however, I'll have your ass."

Carol couldn't quite decide whether Foster was shining her on or not.

"It looks like I'll be reopening the Russell case," the captain continued. "Banker, how would you like to join the investigation?"

"Absolutely, Captain," she said. "I mean, I'm supposed to be off until Tuesday, but …"

Foster smiled. "I think you can at least take tomorrow off, Sergeant. Frankly, I think it may take the others a day or two to catch up to you, anyway. Besides, I have to clear it with your boss, first." He turned to Maxwell and Ledbetter. "Now, why don't you tell us how Russell fits into the case you're investigating?"

Chapter 20

Jeff listened to Paul's theory about organized crime while he watched the sun set over the Puget Sound. He'd placed a call to his associate as soon as he arrived in Anacortes, where Orbison's office had arranged a room for the night.

"So, where does that leave us?" he asked.

"Both the Grand River PD and Captain Bailey in Newport have promised to keep us posted on anything they find in their investigations," Paul assured him. "I don't think there's any doubt that we have their attention."

"How much did you tell them about our case?"

"Bailey, not much … just that we're looking into a series of murders and Judge Ruiz might — or might not — have been one of the targets. She put in a call to the Bureau's lab while we were there, asking them to expedite their review of the evidence. As soon as she knows something, we'll know something."

"And the Grand River PD?"

"Foster wanted everything we had, so I gave it to him. The good news is, he's reopening the Russell case, starting from scratch. If there's anything to be found, Foster will make damned sure they find it this time."

"Let's hope," Jeff said. In truth, he wasn't feeling overly confident. The hit on the Ruizes, and the way Alex's suicide had been so neatly arranged … Paul's organized crime theory only bolstered what they had already suspected: they were dealing with a professional.

"Yeah, I'm with you." Paul's voice carried the same level of optimism as his boss's. "How'd you make out with Adam's parents?"

"Not the interview I'd been expecting, that's for sure." Jeff told Paul about Mrs. Polyakov's suicide, and how Fyodor Polyakov had assured him that Adam had killed Larissa Kozlov.

"Did he say why?"

"Bad genes. Judging from the prison tats I saw today, I'd say Poppa Polyakov had a pretty colorful past back in Russia."

"If Fyodor Polyakov had ties to organized crime, that might be our link from Adam back to Antonio Ruiz and the Duarte Cartel" Paul pointed out.

The thought had occurred to Jeff as well. "It's certainly worth looking into. If Fyodor *is* connected, think your friends at the FBI might have a file on him?"

"I'll see if I can't guilt Yance into looking into it for us, since he's not exactly winning any points with me on the Ruiz investigation. So, mom killed herself? Do you think …" Paul let the question trail off.

"That she might be another one of our victims? I considered it, but it looks doubtful. She'd been struggling with depression since Adam's arrest. Her doctor had her on anti-depressants, but Fyodor told me that she'd stopped taking them a couple of weeks before she died."

Paul asked about the cause of death.

"She OD'd on oxycodone. An old prescription of Adam's, from a football injury. Fyodor said he didn't even know that his wife still had them."

Paul agreed that probably ruled out any connection between Anya Polyakov's death and the ones they were investigating. "By the way, did you get anything from your meeting with Whiteman Security?"

"Only that Reuben Whiteman is a pompous jackass of the highest order," Jeff told him.

Paul chuckled. "So he's no Niko Ferrum, huh?"

"Oh, believe me, Niko can be a jackass, too," Jeff assured him. "But when it comes to arrogance and condescension, Whiteman wins hands down. One interesting thing did come up, though. During my interview with Fyodor, he told me that Adam's cousin, Eveginy Polyakov, had arranged for the job with Whiteman Security. When I mentioned Eveginy to Reuben Whiteman, he got more than a little twitchy."

"Any idea why?"

"Not yet, but it might be worth looking into. Whiteman told me that Eveginy is just a business acquaintance who asked for a favor. When I pushed for more, Whiteman suddenly had an important engagement that he'd forgotten about."

"Nothing suspicious about that," Paul said with a chuckle. "Did he at least tell you how Polyakov ended up on Andrei Kozlov's personal security team in the first place?"

"Adam spoke fluent Russian; apparently, it's a requirement for that detail. In fact, it might be the most important requirement, since I got the distinct impression that Whiteman had never actually met Adam before he assigned him to watch Kozlov."

"Maybe he's just not a hands-on kind of guy like you and Niko."

"Maybe … but let's do some digging. I'm betting there's a connection we don't know about between Reuben Whiteman and Eveginy Polyakov. Maybe even Andrei Kozlov, too. Let's find out what it is before it bites us in the ass."

JEFF HAD A reservation on the first ferry to Orcas Island, leaving Anacortes at 7:30 in the morning. Even at that hour, even on a Sunday, the line of cars waiting to board was long with mainland day trippers headed over to the San Juans for a little island time.

When it was time to board, Jeff followed the crew's instructions and guided his Audi Q5 onto the upper car deck of the *MV Hyak*. In no time, the lanes beside and behind his car were packed tight.

Up on the passenger level, he purchased a cup of coffee from the onboard café, then went out on deck to enjoy the view. The morning air coming off of the Sound was brisk. Jeff zipped his light jacket up and took a position aft, where he would be more protected from the wind.

When all of the vehicles had been loaded and secured below, the ferry's engines rumbled to life beneath his feet. Working with practiced efficiency, the crew cast off and the vessel eased away from the dock. Jeff drank his coffee in contentment while he watched Anacortes fade slowly into the distance.

The scenery was breathtaking. The small islands on either side were rich with Sitka spruce and Western Red cedar, Pacific yew and Madrone trees. For the most part, the shorelines the *Hyak* sailed by appeared largely untouched by what passed for civilization.

Here and there Jeff saw small, secluded coves where rich men's toys — power boats and sleek sailboats with polished teak decks — bobbed beside private docks jutting out into the quiet water. Houses both expensive and expansive rose in testament to the kind of money required to afford that kind of solitude.

As he watched the private little enclaves pass by, Jeff found himself wondering what a man as rich as Andrei Kozlov might have carved out for himself.

You can buy a lot of privacy when your bank balance has seven or eight zeroes … but not always peace, he realized.

The passage to Orcas Island took a little less than an hour. When the announcement sounded on the overhead that the *Hyak* would be coming into the town of Orcas, Jeff left his spot on the rail and made his way back to the car deck to wait for the crew to finish docking.

His appointment with Andrei Kozlov had been scheduled for eleven, leaving Jeff almost an hour and a half with nothing to do. Breakfast sounded like a good idea. He hadn't had anything but coffee that morning. He followed the rest of the ferry traffic toward the town of Eastsound. He and Annie had stumbled across some pretty good restaurants there on their one trip to Orcas Island, the summer before Mikaela was born.

Finding a likely eatery in Waddell's Bistro — a quaint little café that overlooked the water — Jeff ordered a bay shrimp and bacon omelette, along with a tall orange juice and more coffee.

While he waited for his food, he called his wife … or tried to. Annie's phone went unanswered, as it had both times he'd tried to reach her the night before. He recognized her silence for what it almost certainly was … she was still pissed off, and this was the long-distance version of the silent treatment.

All of the steps forward we've managed over the past three years, and now it feels like we're right back where we started.

Silently damning Annie — and Alex Burwell, and Cynthia Orbison, and Niko Ferrum, too, for good measure — Jeff ended the call without leaving a message. Like it or not, he had more immediate matters to deal with.

As the waitress filled his coffee cup, he powered up his Lenovo notebook and began to review what he knew about the man he had come to meet.

Andrei Kozlov was fifty-eight. A widower, father of two daughters: Larissa had been the oldest, Stefanya seven years younger. Originally from Leningrad — now Saint Petersburg — Andrei Kozlov and his family immigrated to the United States in 1992. They'd settled in Portland, where Kozlov started a small television and stereo store on Sandy Boulevard. Within fifteen years that one store — Connectivity — grew into six, with locations from Portland to Seattle. Over the next decade, Connectivity had continued to expand throughout the Pacific Northwest.

According to the trades, they had become the number one retailer for electronics in the region, with online sales rivalling those of even the larger national chains.

Kozlov's personal fortune was estimated at between thirty-five and forty million dollars … not Bill Gates or Paul Allen territory by any stretch, but pretty respectable for someone who had grown up in the shadow of Communism.

Jeff couldn't help but wonder whether some connection to the *Bratva* — the so-called Russian mafia — might account, at least in part, for Kozlov's success.

Unlike the public's traditional perception of organized crime, the *Bratva* in the United States wasn't one grand, overarching syndicate so much as a group of fifteen or so loosely organized groups, spread out across the country. Most of their operations were on the East coast, but they had established themselves in the Northwest, as well. The *Bratva* had its hand in the usual things, like smuggling, drugs, prostitution, and extortion. Usually, they tried to camouflage those activities behind legitimate businesses such as Connectivity.

At this point, Jeff had no proof — circumstantial or otherwise — to suspect a relationship between Kozlov and the *Bratva*. He hoped Paul's friend at the Bureau could provide some insight.

Jeff began to lay out his strategy for the upcoming interview. It was an old habit, writing out a list of the questions in advance, the whats and whys that would help him start to put the puzzle together.

Face-to-face with the interviewee, the preplanned questions simply resided in the back of his mind, as a framework.

Satisfied, he powered the notebook down and ordered another cup of coffee. Out on East Sound — the body of water that nearly bisected Orcas Island — a handful of sailboats rocked gently at anchor. He tried his best to enjoy a few more moments of quiet, unable to shake the feeling that the tranquility around him was just an illusion. The real world ... at least *his* world ... rarely had much room for peaceful interludes. He wondered how long this one would last.

Chapter 21

THE OLYMPIC PENINSULA, WASHINGTON

Porter's eyes opened slowly. He tried to work through the fog that had settled around his thoughts ... tried to remember where he was, and why he was lying on the ground. He'd been looking for firewood, and then ... he squeezed his eyes together in frustration. The memory had been right there. *Right there ...*

"Relax. Just let it happen."

Porter looked up at the source of the voice. He couldn't place the bearded, sunglasses-wearing, young man smiling down at him. Calming smile ... pleasant ... reassuring. Probably a hiker, he decided, or someone camping nearby. A miracle, really, that anyone would have come across him this far up the trail.

"Did I fall?" Porter managed. The words sounded as hesitant and awkward to him as his thoughts were muddled and confused.

"No," the hiker said. "Your heart is failing. You are dying."

Somehow that made sense to Porter. The doctors had warned him, hadn't they? They'd told him he had to slow down, that he shouldn't try to do too much.

"At least, that is what it's going to look like," his new companion added, the faintest hint of an accent in his voice.

The fog around Porter's thoughts cleared a little, just enough to register the implication of the man's words. He felt a touch of panic.

"Ah, now you understand, I think." The young man smiled again, reassuringly. "It's going to be all right. No pain, I promise. No pain. Just close your eyes and let go."

Desperately Porter tried to rise, to roll over, but his muscles refused to obey. The best he could manage was to twist his upper body a little away from the man hovering ominously over him. A few inches only ... the effort was simply too much to sustain. His arms felt all but useless, and his legs ... his legs didn't feel, at all.

"You have fight. Good for you." The stranger studied him for a moment.

"This really isn't personal for me, you know," he said, gently. "You and the others were only doing what you thought right. But then again, so am I."

"Wh … why …" The words snagged in Porter's throat. He squeezed his eyes shut in anger and frustration.

"Why? *Vozmezdiye,*" his killer said, his voice so calm it was almost soothing. "Recompense. Retribution."

Retribution? Porter forced himself to open his eyes once more. He looked beyond his killer, beyond the thick canopy of Douglas fir branches above, into the almost painfully-brilliant blue sky. A Red-tailed hawk flashed into view, circling slowly above. Another hunter searching for its prey.

The young man stood slowly, idly brushing a bit of dust from the knees of his pants as he straightened. "I should be going, I'm afraid," he said, almost apologetically. "It's a long hike back. I do hope someone will be along soon. No one should die alone."

Porter closed his eyes. The sound of boots on the stony forest trail faded, leaving only the rustle of branches, the whisper of grass in the faint breeze … his own slow, labored breathing.

No one should die alone, he thought, sadly, *but we all do.*

Chapter 22

Andrei Kozlov lived in a fortified compound along the western shore of East Sound, behind a tall, electrified fence and a gate of reinforced concrete and steel.

Jeff pulled to a stop at the bunker-like gatehouse. A broad, well-muscled man in his mid- to late-thirties stepped immediately up to the open passenger side window of the Audi. His facial features — high, rounded cheekbones and slightly almond-shaped eyes — strongly suggested a Slavic family tree. From his build, and the short, sandy-blonde hair on his head, Jeff guessed ex-military. He wore a generic uniform of blue-gray, with a wide, military-style belt and heavily polished black boots. The butt of a large-caliber handgun protruded from the holster at his side.

Bending at the waist, the guard eyed Jeff critically for a moment. "Can I help you?" he asked at last. His voice carried only a trace of an accent, just enough to confirm Jeff's earlier assessment that the man came from Eastern Europe … Russia perhaps, or one of the other Slavic countries.

"Jefferson Dawes; I have an appointment with Mr. Kozlov at eleven."

The guard studied him for a moment more before nodding impassively. "Wait here," he ordered. Then he turned and strode back inside the gate house. Jeff noticed a second man watching from the shadows beyond the doorway. Taller, but fully as broad-shouldered as the first, he ducked back out of sight when Jeff looked his way.

The first guard was speaking in Russian to someone on the phone. The language always sounded to Jeff like an argument in progress, with its sharp, clipped consonants and rapid-fire delivery. When the conversation ended, the man walked slowly back to the car and crouched down to talk to Jeff once more through the car window.

"May I ask the nature of your business with Mr. Kozlov?" he asked.

"No." Jeff smiled thinly. "I either have an appointment and you're going to open the gate, or I don't, and you're not."

The gatekeeper seemed to take no offense. He nodded to the guard in the shodows, and the heavy steel barricade lifted up slowly. "Follow the drive," the first man said. "Mr. Kozlov will be waiting."

Jeff thanked him and started down the asphalt-paved road. Behind him, he saw the two men watching his car as the gate came back down. The second guard held what looked to be a cross between an automatic rifle and an AK shotgun at his side, an ugly-looking weapon designed to inflict maximum damage on whoever was at the receiving end when it went off. Jeff was more than happy to be leaving it — and them — behind him.

Of course, God knew what still lay ahead.

The drive followed serpentine turns through Pine and red-barked Madrone. The trees looked as though they would be much happier growing on the California coast than here in the far corner of Washington State. Jeff had read somewhere that the San Juans had a much more temperate climate than most of the Pacific Northwest, but it hadn't occurred to him that there could be such a dramatic difference between the islands and the nearby mainland.

A large, apparently single-level house came into view to his left. The low-slung building ran along the edge of the hillside overlooking the water. The home's profile — as well as the materials used to build it — certainly spoke of money, but not millions. Jeff guessed that there was probably more to the house than met the eye.

He had expected additional security to be waiting for him at the front door. Instead, he found only a lean, middle-aged man with graying hair out by the drive, pulling weeds from the bordering flowerbed. The gardener straightened at the Audi's approach. He removed his work gloves and smacked them against his faded jeans a couple of times to shake free the dirt and dust. Seemingly satisfied that he had gotten most of it, he wandered over as the car pulled to a stop.

"Mr. Dawes?" His Russian accent was understated, but still obvious. Jeff nodded as he climbed out and closed the car door behind him. The older man smiled and extended his hand. "Andrei Kozlov. Thank you for coming."

"Thank you for seeing me," Jeff said as they shook. "Somehow, I'd expected a more formal greeting, given the welcoming committee out front."

Kozlov's smile turned apologetic. "I'm sorry about that. My brother's idea of security is somewhat more heightened than my own. He means well, of course, so I humor him," he added with a laugh. "Please, come inside."

Leading Jeff into the house, Andrei Kozlov paused for a moment in the entryway to free himself of his dust-covered tennis shoes. As he kicked them off, Jeff couldn't help but notice with amusement the well-worn tread on the inexpensive sneakers. Whatever he'd imagined his millionaire host would be like, this wasn't it.

Kozlov straightened as a slightly stocky, muscular young woman appeared through a nearby doorway. She had to be at least six feet tall, with an almond-shaped face and short, chestnut-brown hair. Her clothes — pressed black slacks and blue polo shirt — looked as though they might be a housekeeper's uniform, Jeff thought. But her dark, almost black eyes studied him in the same critical way as the guard at the gate had, and she moved a little more like an athlete than a servant.

Kozlov smiled when he saw her. "Ah, Marie. Could you bring some ice water, please?"

Marie nodded. "Of course, sir," she said, her accent much more pronounced than her employer's. "Will there be anything else? Coffee perhaps?"

"Mr. Dawes?" Kozlov looked to his guest.

"No, thank you. I just finished breakfast. But please, go ahead."

"Never after nine for me," his host admitted. "Caffeine and I do not see eye-to-eye these days, I'm afraid. Water will be fine, Marie, thank you. We'll be outside."

He led the way through the living room and out onto an expansive deck that overlooked East Sound. Along the house's outer walls sat a full outdoor kitchen. There was an enormous built-in grill and a long, apparently fully-stocked bar. A teakwood table large enough to seat fourteen dominated the center of the outdoor space. In addition, a half-dozen Adirondack chairs — also made of teak — were arranged around a gas fire pit set into the deck.

"So, when did you arrive on the island?" Kozlov asked as they settled in at the table. A large canvas umbrella shielded them from the sun overhead.

"Just this morning. I had some business to attend to in Seattle, yesterday."

"And when do you return to Portland?" Kozlov asked, amiably.

"I have reservations on the last ferry back to Anacortes, this afternoon," Jeff told him.

"Oh, that's a shame. A very quick trip, then." Kozlov smiled up at Marie as she positioned a tray with a pitcher of ice water and two glasses on the table. She filled a glass for each of the men. "I think we have everything we need, Marie," he said as she finished. "Thank you."

Kozlov waited until the door to the house had closed behind her before he spoke again. "My assistant tells me that you have some questions regarding Adam Polyakov."

Jeff nodded. "Actually, this is about another investigation. But I think there may be some connection between our case and your daughter's death."

His Russian host looked genuinely intrigued. "In what way?"

Jeff had decided to run with Paul's theory and see where it might lead. "We think that Adam Polyakov may have had ties with organized crime," he said.

Andrei leaned back in his chair and laughed. "That may be the most absurd thing I've ever heard."

"And why is that?"

"Because I knew Adam. Organized crime would not have been in his nature," he said, simply.

"We are talking about the same Adam Polyakov, aren't we? The one who murdered your daughter?"

A strange light flickered behind Kozlov's hazel eyes. He nodded, almost imperceptibly, as he reached out for the glass of water closest to him.

"That must seem strange to you," he acknowledged, absently running a finger along the condensation forming on the glass.

"In truth, I've always had my doubts about Larissa's death. With Adam now gone, who can say what actually happened that night?"

"You say 'actually happened …' Do you have doubts?" Jeff asked.

Kozlov smiled again, sadly. "Oh, I know what the evidence points to, Mr. Dawes. I don't think that it tells the whole story. Anyway, even if Adam did what the detectives claim, the idea that he might also have been associated with organized crime …" He shook his head. "No. Absolutely out of the question."

Jeff decided to try a different approach. "Are you familiar with a man named Eveginy Polyakov?" he asked.

Kozlov considered the question for a moment. "No, I don't think I know him. I assume that he is somehow related to Adam."

Jeff nodded. "His cousin. Eveginy is the one who arranged for Adam to get the job with Whiteman Security."

He caught another flicker of something in Kozlov's expression, a flash of surprise behind those soft hazel eyes at the mention of Whiteman's company.

"And this Eveginy … he is somehow connected to organized crime?"

"We're not sure, yet," Jeff admitted, "but we're looking into it. I was wondering … how did Adam come to be on your security detail?"

"My brother, Vasily, hired Whiteman Security to provide protection for my family. Adam was simply one of many sent by the company."

"And when was that?"

Kozlov considered the question for a moment. "About five years ago, I think," he said.

"So, Adam would have been around twenty-four at the time. That seems a little young to be protecting a man of your standing."

The Russian laughed at that. "Like my brother, I think you severely overestimate my importance. In truth, I have never actually felt the need for protection of any kind. But, to your point, I must admit that Adam did look like a child compared to the others on his detail."

"I can imagine. The two I saw coming through your gate were certainly … intimidating," Jeff pointed out. "Ex-military, I'm assuming."

Kozlov nodded. "Most are, if not all. Some of them are quite nice, however," he added with a smile, "despite their fearsome appearance."

"How long did Adam work for you before you offered him the job at Connectivity?"

Kozlov thought about the question, resting the chilled glass against the side of his neck as he did so. The July afternoon had grown hot, and both men were perspiring, even in the shade.

"Perhaps a year and a half," he said at last. "No more, certainly."

"And was the decision at your daughter's request?" Jeff asked.

Kozlov shook his head at the suggestion.

"Mr. Dawes, if I made business decisions based on sentimentality, I think would be out of business very quickly. No, I hired Adam because I thought him capable of handling the job, nothing more.

"In any event," he added, "Larissa met Adam only after I offered the position to him, when she stepped into her own role with the company."

"And what role was that?"

"General Manager … and, before you ask, her appointment was also not a sentimental decision on my part." Kozlov took a long drink of his water, before continuing. "My daughter grew up with Connectivity from a very early age. She enhanced her knowledge by earning a degree in Business from the University of Southern California."

"Still, putting her in charge of a multi-million-dollar company at twenty-seven …"

"Twenty-eight," Kozlov corrected with a smile.

"Even so, I would think that must have struck some as being a bit unusual."

"Only those who had never met Larissa." Kozlov assured him. "I have no doubts that my daughter would have proven to be twice the business person I am. She had the instincts, the drive, and a certain …

toughness ... that allowed her to make the hard decisions I have always struggled with."

"It sounds like she'd been groomed for the position."

Kozlov smiled at the suggestion. "Tell me, Mr. Dawes, do you have children of your own?" he asked.

"I have a daughter" Jeff told him. "She's in her first year of law school."

"And was law school your choice, or hers?"

Jeff laughed at the thought of making his headstrong daughter do anything she didn't want to do.

Kozlov smiled, knowingly. "I can tell you know exactly what I faced with Larissa. It was always her intention to take over the family business when I stepped down. Fate simply forced our hand a little sooner than either of us had expected."

"How so?"

"Three years ago, I was diagnosed with cancer," Kozlov explained. "It's in remission now but, at the time, the prognosis looked not so promising. My treatments left me largely incapable of handling the day-to-day pressures of running the company. Larissa stepped in and handled the challenge well."

"How did your other daughter, Stefanya, feel about all of this?" Jeff wondered.

At the mention of his youngest, Kozlov smiled as sad a smile as Jeff had ever seen. "Stefanya is ... she is very much like her late mother. Too naïve, too kind-hearted, I think, to run a business like ours. There are often difficult decisions which she would be ill-suited to make. In truth, even I wrestle with them at times."

"And how did Larissa handle them?"

The Russian's eyes flickered at the question. "She was not so burdened by her conscience as I might have thought," he admitted frankly.

Jeff detected disappointment in the observation. "You daughter Stefanya is, what, twenty-four?" he asked. Kozlov nodded. "And what does she do?"

"She was studying art and psychology at the University of Washington," the older man told him, "But, since Larissa's death, I'm afraid we both retreated from the world a bit. Stefanya is with me almost always, now."

"She's here now?"

"Somewhere," Kozlov said, vaguely. "When I have guests, she generally retires to her room. I'm afraid that the ordeal with Larissa has left her especially fragile. And she was very fond of Adam as well, which made the whole affair doubly painful."

"I can imagine. So, how long before the murder did Larissa start seeing Adam romantically?" Jeff asked.

"To be frank, I'm not entirely sure," Kozlov admitted. "I didn't learn that they had been dating until after Larissa's death."

Jeff tried not to show his surprise. "Your daughter never mentioned it to you?"

The Russian shook his head. "I suspect she knew I would have been against it," he said.

"As a father, or professionally?"

Kozlov tilted his head slightly as he considered the question.

"Certainly professionally," he said. "Romantic entanglements in business are, at best, ill-advised. At worst, they are a disaster. But my concerns would have been greater as a father, I think."

He looked out at East Sound, watching a large cabin cruiser quietly making its way to deeper water. After a moment he added, "I loved my daughter, Mr. Dawes, but I do not believe Larissa would have been a good match for Adam. She could often be ... cold is too harsh a word for a father to use, I think. Difficult, perhaps."

Again, Jeff heard disappointment in Kozlov's voice. He decided to move the interview back toward motive. "The file said that Larissa tried to have Adam fired before she died."

Kozlov nodded. "I know the District Attorney's office felt that gave Adam a strong motive for killing my daughter. They were wrong, and I told them as much. I had already refused her demand to let him go."

That fact hadn't been in the file. "When was that?" Jeff asked.

"Almost a month before the murder."

"But, did Adam know his position was safe?"

Kozlov nodded. "I assured him that Larissa had absolutely no authority to terminate his contract — or those of any of the company's officers — as long as I retained my position as CEO. You should also be aware, Mr. Dawes, that Adam offered to resign from Connectivity and return to Whiteman Security rather than create any family friction. I refused to allow it."

Jeff asked why. Kozlov looked uncomfortable with the question. He leaned back in his chair and ran his fingers through his wiry gray hair.

"Because I had already come to realize," Kozlov said, finally, "that, for all of Larissa's intellect and business acumen, she generally lacked the capacity to consider anyone's needs but her own. It is not an easy thing for me to admit, even now, but my daughter was a cold, unfeeling person with almost everyone but me.

"But beyond that, Mr. Dawes, I was personally very fond of Adam," he added, with a trace of a smile. "He was a man of character … in some ways, he was the son I never had. The Adam I knew could not have done the things to Larissa that he was accused of," he told Jeff, seriously. "Regardless of what the evidence says, or the jury decided, I am still convinced of that."

Chapter 23

Fyodor Polyakov put the last of the dishes from his afternoon meal in the drain board and dried his hands. The clock on the wall showed that it was only a little past two. It felt later somehow, as though he'd spent far more of the day beneath the hood of the Camaro than he had.

But then, what else have I to do with my time? Work, eat, sleep … and then work some more. He had begun to feel stretched and worn, an old man at fifty-seven.

Beyond his front porch, on Dumas Bay, weekenders on sailboats guided them quietly through the gently rippling water. Even those piloting powered craft — sleek little speedboats and luxurious cruisers — seemed content to take the afternoon slowly, to enjoy the high summer day while it lasted. Fyodor frequently heard the sound of laughter through his open windows, or the splash of some adventurous soul brave enough — or foolish enough — to jump from the deck of their boat and test the chilly waters of the Puget Sound.

He and Anya had planned to buy a boat of their own to sail in their retirement, perhaps even to live on. A sailboat large enough to take down the coast, should they choose. Anya had dreamt of Mexico. "Sunshine and palm trees," she would say, her eyes sparkling at the thought, "and beaches with real sand."

"Coconuts filled with rum, and beaches covered with scantily-clad women," Fyodor would add, earning himself an admonishing wag of the finger from his laughing wife. She knew he had little interest in anything more than spending his days on the open water with the woman he adored.

And now I spend my days with grease-covered hands, working on an automobile I will never really drive anywhere.

He was about to return to the garage when he heard someone coming down the lane. Tires crunched on the loose gravel as the vehicle approached. An unfamiliar little silver sports car cleared the trees and rolled slowly past the kitchen window. The automobile came to a stop somewhere near the front of the house.

He opened the door to find a young man standing there, hand raised as he prepared to knock. Eyes hidden behind dark glasses, the visitor smiled at the older man, a friendly smile, surrounded by a close-cropped beard and neatly trimmed mustache.

"*Dyadya* Fyodor?" he asked.

Fyodor wasn't sure which surprised him more; hearing someone speaking Russian, or being called 'uncle' by someone he didn't know.

"I am Fyodor," he answered warily in the same language. It seemed strange to hear his native tongue coming from his own mouth after all this time. "And you are?"

The young man smiled. "Your nephew, Nicholas," he said, "although I would have been surprised if you *had* recognized me. It's been a very long time."

"Nicholas ... *Kolya*?" Fyodor blinked in confusion. The man on the doorstep grinned as he removed the clip-on shades from his glasses. Immediately, Fyodor saw the resemblance to his sister-in-law, Ludmilla, in the younger man's eyes, and in the shape of his face.

"Kolya!" He pulled his nephew into a fierce hug. The two men held tight for a few moments, patting each other's backs, caught up in the reunion. At last, Fyodor stepped back and took a long look. "I need to have a talk with your mother. She's let you grow up much too fast."

Nicholas laughed. "I'm sure she would agree. She and my father send their love, by the way. May I come in?"

"Of course, of course. Forgive me." Fyodor stepped aside, pushing the door closed after Nicholas. "Have a seat. Can I get you something?"

His nephew shook his head. "Nothing, thank you."

"So, your mother tells me that you've become a writer," Fyodor said when they were both settled. "Do we have another Ivan Bunin on our hands, or Leo Tolstoy?"

"Nothing so grand," Nicholas assured him with a laugh. "I write travel stories for European journals. There is no Nobel Prize for literature in my immediate future, but it keeps food on the table."

"You write under your own name?"

His nephew grinned. "No, Papa suggested I use a *nom de plume*, for obvious reasons."

Fyodor smiled. "The name of Krupin does have a certain reputation, doesn't it? So, nephew, what brings you to my doorstep?"

"I've been working on an assignment in Oregon, but this weekend I had to come north. I thought I should see how my favorite uncle has been doing."

"I am also your only uncle," Fyodor pointed out.

"But still my favorite, nonetheless. How have you been?"

Fyodor shrugged. "As well as can be expected. And you?"

"Busy," Nicholas said. "Very busy. And I'm afraid I owe you an apology, uncle," he added, seriously.

Fyodor cocked his head, puzzled.

"I wanted to be here for Aunt Anya's funeral," Nicholas explained, "and Adam's. I should have been here."

The older man waved off his nephew's distress. "Please don't. There is no need. And anyway, there would have been little that you could do. Now, tell me about the family … what of your sister?"

Nicholas spent the next twenty minutes sharing stories of his last visit to St. Petersburg; his parent's thirty-fifth anniversary celebration — where the vodka and wine had flowed for days — and of his sister Dina's engagement.

"To a police lieutenant?" Fyodor asked, incredulous. Nicholas nodded with a grin. "Things have indeed changed for your family," his uncle chuckled.

"My father still struggles with that, himself," Nicholas admitted with a laugh. "But Anton is a good man, and Dina is happy. Before I forget, Papa wanted me to ask … that is, he wanted me to remind you that, if you need anything, the door is always open."

Fyodor smiled. "Tell your father that I thank him, but I am fine. I have money, and my work." *Good, clean, honest work,* he added silently. *I will not fall into old habits. Anya would not have approved, even if I wanted to.*

"He expected as much," Nicholas said, "but he wanted me to ask, nonetheless."

"Your father was always a good friend. A very good friend ... but I'm through with that life. The cost is too high." The older man regarded his nephew with a smile. "I am glad that you seem to have escaped the family business as well."

Nicholas leaned back in his seat and grinned. "My writing keeps me too busy," he assured his uncle. "I am not cut out for the life of a *hooligan.*"

"Good. Good." His uncle brought the palms of his hands down onto his thighs with a loud clap and stood. "Let's drink a toast to that. I have a bottle of *Putinka* that's been waiting for a special guest."

"I shouldn't," Nicholas protested. "It's a long drive back to Portland."

"Please. One drink. This is a luxury I don't allow myself very often, and who knows when we may have another chance?"

WHILE HIS UNCLE went in search of the vodka, Nick wandered through the living room, looking at the family photos. Most were of cousin Adam with Aunt Anya. There was even a picture of the three cousins — Nicholas, Adam, and Eveginy — taken when they were children. Uncle Fyodor appeared in only a couple of the shots, no doubt because he spent more time behind the camera than in front of it.

Nick heard his uncle moving around in the kitchen. The man some had once called The Bear of Vostok hummed softly to himself while he rummaged through cupboards. Was it truly possible to sweep so much history under the rug? Nick wondered. To forget the man you once were? Somehow, he'd like to think so.

Then again, perhaps this is who Uncle Fyodor really had been all along. Nick's father liked to say that Aunt Anya had tamed The Bear, but he doubted even his formidable aunt could have affected such a dramatic change if Fyodor hadn't been willing all along.

"Found it!" he heard his uncle call out. "Now for the glasses."

Nick smiled and moved to the couch once more. As he sat, he noticed a business card atop a small stack of mail. He reached over and picked it up, uneasiness sitting like a hot stone in his belly.

Jefferson Dawes, it read, *Special Investigator Multnomah County District Attorney's Office.* Nick glanced at the mail beneath the card. The postage dates were recent. He frowned. The card must have been placed on the table within the last day or two.

Shit.

He set the card back on top of the letters and took a quick picture with his phone just as Uncle Fyodor hurried back into the room with a bottle in one hand, two glass tumblers in the other.

"I'm sorry that took so long." The older man smiled ruefully. "I couldn't remember where your aunt liked to hide the vodka."

He settled into his oversized armchair and leaned forward, carefully filling the two small glasses near to the brim. "To family," he said as he handed one of the glasses to his nephew.

"Boodyem zdarovye!" To our health. Nick touched his glass to his uncle's and drank, his mind somewhere else completely.

Chapter 24

ORCAS ISLAND, WASHINGTON

Jeff sat in the cool darkness of the bar at Waddell's Bistro, staring at his laptop screen. The restaurant and lounge around him were largely empty. The bartender called it the "Sunday afternoon doldrums," the lull between the day-trippers heading back to the mainland and the next wave of tourists checking into the various resorts. Jeff took a bite out of his corned beef sandwich while the bartender set a second pint of Stella down in front of him. He nodded his thanks before turning his attention back to the notes from the Andrei Kozlov interview.

As with Fyodor Polyakov, the interview with Larissa Kozlov's father had definitely not gone the way Jeff had anticipated. Andrei's attitude made no sense. Not only did he doubt the prosecutor's version of Larissa's murder, Jeff had the distinct impression that Andrei felt his daughter might have even shared some responsibility for her own death.

Something just felt a little … off. Andrei claimed to have brought Adam on to head Connection's security department because of his maturity and intelligence. But would those traits alone account for his hiring a junior college student still shy of thirty years old, and with so little experience? It seemed unlikely to Jeff.

There was the organized crime angle, but no proof yet that Kozlov, or any of the Polyakovs, were directly or indirectly connected to the *Bratva*. And even if they found evidence, what reason could Kozlov have for continuing to defend Adam in his daughter's murder?

Jeff's cellphone started to vibrate against the polished oak bar. He checked the name on caller I.D. "Tell me you have good news," Jeff said when he picked up.

"Doesn't anyone say 'hello' anymore?" Paul groused.

Jeff smiled. "Sorry, I'll work on my manners. Now, tell me you have good news."

"I have news," Paul confirmed. "Hopefully it turns out to be good, or at least a little helpful. My buddy at the FBI still won't give up anything related to Prosecutor Ruiz, but Yance was a fount of information when it came to Adam's cousin, Eveginy. Definitely *Bratva*, and definitely on the Feds' radar. Oh, and you were right about there being a link between the Polykovs and the Kozlovs. There's a small, but well-established *Bratva* organization operating out of the Northwest. Eveginy Polyakov is the number two man, and a bit of a bad-ass from the sounds of it. Yance described him as 'unstable, unpredictable, and violent.' A real triple threat."

"How does that tie into the Kozlovs?"

Paul laughed. "Did I forget to mention who the number one man in the organization is? Andrei Kozlov's big brother, Vasily."

Jeff let out a soft whistle. "And do the Feds think that Andrei is *Bratva*, too?" he asked.

"The theory got bounced around for a while ... they even got as far as subpoenaing Andrei's personal and corporate financials. The FBI brought in forensic accountants to go over everything with a fine-tooth comb, but they found *nada*."

Jeff considered the relevance of that news while he took a draw on his beer. "So, what are the chances Eveginy is our killer?" he asked at last.

Paul hesitated. "Hard to say," he admitted after a moment. "From what Yance told me, Eveginy would definitely be capable — and probably more than willing — to kill anyone who crossed him. But he doesn't sound to me like someone who could manage the kind of finesse our murders have been carried out with. He would have the contacts, though, and probably the finances, too, to hire someone with that skill set. Anyway, it's our best lead so far."

"Anything on Adam's father, Fyodor?" Jeff asked.

"Yeah, about him ... there's the official version, the unofficial version, and a hell of a lot of gray in between," Paul said. "To tell you the truth, none of it makes much sense to me."

"Run it by me, anyway."

"Okay. The official version is that Fyodor was a political prisoner at *Butyrka* Prison, in Moscow, when the Soviet Union collapsed in '91.

He was released that December, and emigrated to the U.S. about a month later."

"And the *unofficial* version ...?"

"Well, rumor has it that Fyodor Polyakov was called The Bear of Vostok, an enforcer for one of the more notorious crime organizations in Leningrad. Wind up on their shit list and The Bear was the last person you wanted to see ... and sometimes the last person you did see."

A mob enforcer? That certainly didn't fit Jeff's impression of Fyodor. "If that's true," he said, "I'm surprised that we even let him in the country."

"Apparently, the Feds didn't pick up on the rumors until they started looking into Eveginy. By then, Fyodor had been living quietly in the Seattle area for almost ten years. As with Andrei Kozlov, the Bureau dug pretty deep looking for anything they could use against Eveginy, but Fyodor has been a model citizen."

Jeff felt a surprising sense of relief at that. "All right. I'll be back at the office in the morning. We can go over the rest then. In the meantime, keep me posted if anything comes up."

"When are you heading home?"

"My ferry boards in a couple of hours ..." Jeff told him, his voice trailing off. In the mirror behind the bar, he'd seen two men enter the restaurant and take seats near the door. One of them looked all too familiar. The last time Jeff had seen him, he'd been holding a vicious-looking automatic shotgun at Andrei Kozlov's gate.

Paul picked up on the shift in his boss's tone. "What's wrong?"

"Company," Jeff said, as casually as possible. "One was a guard at Kozlov's gate this morning. Not sure about the other one."

"What are they doing?" The concern in Paul's voice was obvious.

In the mirror, both men were conspicuously trying not to look in Jeff's direction.

"I'm guessing that they're waiting for me. Let me see if I can get a good picture to send to you. I'll be in touch soon," Jeff added as he hung up, silencing any potential objections. He switched his phone to camera mode and touched the selfies icon.

It took a little maneuvering to get the camera to pick up the two men sitting behind him. He zoomed in as best as he could and snapped the picture. Then he messaged the photo to Paul.

In touch within the hour, he texted. *Find out who they are.* That accomplished, he slid off of his stool and headed toward the entrance.

The two men watched him approach in silence. 'Shotgun' appeared visibly irritated by Jeff's preemptive strike. His companion looked more amused than anything else. Jeff assumed he was in charge. It was to this second, older man Jeff gave his attention, ignoring the other completely.

"I'm assuming you're here for me," he said, hopefully sounding a hell of a lot more casual than he was feeling at the moment.

The man smiled a thin, confident smile and nodded. Like the other security personnel Jeff had seen at Kozlov's compound, he appeared to be ex-military. He had short, dark hair, square features, and a neck that looked as thick as Jeff's thigh. Across the table, the guard from the gatehouse — 'Shotgun' — started to rise, but his companion waved him back down.

"I have a ferry to catch, so let's get this over with," Jeff said, pointedly ignoring the junior member of the team. "Let me pay for my lunch and we'll go."

"We've got that." The leader's voice was deep, and free of any real accent. "Why don't you and I head outside while Victor takes care of what you owe?" he suggested as they both stood.

Now that they were vertical, Jeff had a better idea of what he was up against. It wasn't good. The man named Victor was tall ... close to six-three, with broad shoulders, absurdly thick biceps, and a hard body his tight blue t-shirt did little to conceal.

Surprisingly, the other man was several inches shorter, around five-nine. But Jeff guessed he weighed in at well over two-hundred well-muscled pounds. He looked as though he could snap Jeff in half without much effort, which probably accounted for the man's relaxed air. *That*, Jeff thought, *and whatever weaponry he's undoubtedly carrying.*

The stocky man led the way toward the front entrance of the restaurant. "What about your friend?" Jeff asked as he fell in behind, nodding in 'Shotgun's' direction.

"Victor will be right behind," he was assured.

By the time they reached the street, Victor had, indeed, reappeared at Jeff's side. A silver Cadillac Escalade with tinted windows was parked in front of the restaurant. Victor held the back door open while the other two climbed into the luxury SUV. Then he settled in beside Jeff, closing the door behind him.

The interior smelled strongly of leather upholstery and cologne. The vehicle had been modified, so that the middle seats faced the back of the vehicle. On the plush leather bench across from Jeff, a very large man sat, studying him. Completely bald on top, tufts of gray hair hugged the sides of his head. Wiry gray eyebrows protruded out like little antennae.

His barrel chest filled his Tommy Bahama sports shirt to its maximum. Thick, hairy legs protruded out from khaki cargo shorts. The smile on the man's florid face was familiar to Jeff. So was the intelligent look in his hazel eyes, even if his features were much broader than the man he'd just left.

"I'm assuming you must be Vasily Kozlov," Jeff said as he made himself comfortable.

"A safe assumption," his host admitted. He didn't seem too surprised that he'd been recognized. "And you are Jefferson Dawes, of the Multnomah County District Attorney's Office ... or should that be Ferrum Security?"

"At the moment, both." The subject of Ferrum Security hadn't come up with Fyodor Polyakov, or with Vasily's brother. In fact, only one other person he'd talked to that weekend knew that he worked for Niko Ferrum. Jeff filed that away for future consideration.

"I hope this won't take too long," he said as the SUV pulled away from the curb. "I have just a little over an hour before the last ferry. That is, if I'm still going to be on the last ferry."

Vasily looked amused. "I see no reason why you won't be," he assured Jeff. "I have just a few questions."

"My first mob interrogation?"

Vasily smiled. "We will try to be gentle."

"Shouldn't you have searched me for weapons, first?"

"No need. We both know you aren't armed. Your automobile was searched while you were talking to my brother, and we would have known if you had carried a weapon into the house."

Jeff cocked his head at that. "Metal detectors?"

The Russian nodded, flashing a Cheshire Cat grin. "State of the art, in the entryway. My brother has no idea," he added. "So, now we know where we stand. Shall we discuss business?"

"Whose? Yours, or mine?"

"Yours, I think."

"From what I've heard, your business would probably make for more interesting conversation," Jeff pointed out. Kozlov simply held his smile. "No? Well then, what would you like me to tell you?"

"What did you and my brother talk about?"

"I suspect you already know exactly what we talked about."

Kozlov looked annoyed by the evasion. "Humor me," he said, all traces of his smile gone.

"I'm investigating a case that I thought might be related to your niece's murder, and Adam Polyakov's trial," Jeff added, probing gently.

"What is this case of yours?"

"If you want the details, ask the DA," Jeff said flatly. The men on either side of him shifted slightly at his tone. Jeff ignored them, keeping his attention on Vasily Kozlov.

The Russian frowned. "And what did you want from Andrei?" he pressed.

Jeff realized he was in no position to push his luck too far. "I just had a few questions, to get background on the case."

"And what did you learn?"

"That your brother seems to be a very forgiving man where Adam Polyakov is concerned."

The elder Kozlov studied Jeff for a few moments. "Andrei has always been the forgiving one in the family," he admitted with a smile. "Me, not so much. But in this case we are in agreement. Perhaps not for the same reasons, but in agreement nonetheless. You see, I never met Adam, but I knew my niece all too well. What do you know of Larissa's childhood, Mr. Dawes?"

"Only the basics," Jeff told him. "Eldest of two children, born into money. Larissa's mother died giving birth to her little sister ..."

Vasily nodded. "Larissa was almost eight when her mother died. Old enough to know what she'd lost, but too young to really understand what had happened. I've never seen so much anger in a child ... anger at the doctors who — in her mind, at least — hadn't done enough to save her mother. Anger at Katya for leaving her." He shook his head sadly. "Whatever love Larissa may have been capable of before, I'm afraid most of it lies buried in the same grave as her mother. Except where her father was concerned."

"What about her sister, Stefanya?"

Kozlov chuckled at that, a dry, rasping laugh that held no real humor. "Theirs was a ... special relationship. I'm afraid that Stefanya bore the brunt of her older sister's venom."

"Larissa blamed her for their mother's death?" Vasily merely shrugged in response. "How did your brother handle that?"

"Oh, Larissa was always careful to never let Andrei see the darker edges of her personality. And Stefanya ... little Stefanya endured her abuse in silence."

"Why?" Jeff asked.

"Who can say? Guilt, perhaps? Or maybe fear. When your sister is a sociopath ..." He let his thought fade

"It's quite a leap from emotionally distant to 'sociopath,' isn't it?" The Russian shrugged once more. Jeff leaned back in his seat, considering this new perspective on the woman everyone had considered a victim. "So, like your brother, you think Larissa somehow provoked her own murder?" he asked skeptically.

"Isn't that how the prosecutor portrayed her death? And Polyakov never denied it. In truth, I don't blame him for killing the bitch."

So much for family loyalty, Jeff thought, unless Kozlov's cold attitude was simply window dressing.

The Russian leaned forward, the soft leather upholstery groaning under his bulk. "So now, you tell me," he said quietly, "how could your case be related in any way to Larissa's murder?"

"Frankly, I don't I think it is," Jeff lied. "The DA was just grasping at straws. Personally, I don't see any reason to dig any further."

Kozlov studied him, no doubt trying to read beneath the surface. Then he smiled once again. "Good. Then I think we are finished here. Misha," he called, "*vozvrashchat'sya!*"

"*Khorosho,*" the driver answered, turning left at the next intersection.

"Is that it?" Jeff asked.

The Russian looked amused. "You sound disappointed."

"No, just surprised. This seems like a good deal of trouble to go to for a couple of questions."

Vasily leaned back in his seat. "My only concern is for my brother and his daughter," he said, perhaps a little too casually. "They have been through too much already."

The SUV pulled up in front of the bistro, and Victor scrambled out to hold the door open. Before Jeff could get out, however, Vasily stopped him with a beefy hand on his shoulder.

"One more question, Mr. Dawes," he said. "I understand you have not worked for the District Attorney for some time, so why have they brought you in on this investigation?"

Jeff smiled. "Because I'm just that good," he answered lightly. As he stepped down onto the sidewalk, he heard the Russian laugh.

"ARE YOU ALRIGHT?" Paul asked as soon as he answered Jeff's call.

"What? No hello? What about all of those 'niceties' you were lamenting earlier?" Jeff wondered if his humor sounded as forced as it felt to him. "I'm fine. I just had a little chat with Vasily Kozlov."

"Vasily Kozlov? What the hell did he want?"

"If I had to guess, I'd say he wanted to find out if we were looking into his niece's death."

Jeff unlocked the Audi and got in. Reservation or no, he had to get to the ferry soon or he would, literally, miss the boat.

The Audi started up, its engine throbbing quietly. *No bombs wired to the ignition,* Jeff mused. *I guess I haven't pissed anyone off too much … yet.*

"Why would we be reopening a solved murder investigation?" Paul asked.

"That's what I was wondering. But it's a thought, isn't it? One way or another, this whole mess can be traced right back to that damned case."

"Agreed, but I don't see that getting us closer to finding our hired gun," Paul pointed out.

"Maybe you're right," Jeff acknowledged, even though his instincts had begun to tell him otherwise. "We'll talk about it in the morning."

After Paul disconnected, Jeff tried Annie's phone. No answer … again. He hung up in frustration. *Dammit, Annie! I don't fucking need this right now,* he thought as he directed the Audi toward the ferry dock. He queued up for the last boat back to Anacortes, and set the Q5's parking brake. Then he set off in search of some shade to sit in until they started loading. He'd just settled in at a small picnic table when his phone started to ring. Without bothering to look at the caller ID, he answered.

"Hey, Dad. It's me," Mikaela said at the other end. She sounded tired, or stressed. Or both.

"Hey, Kiddo! This is a surprise. What's going on?"

"Mom's here with me. I thought you'd want to know."

"Is that where she's at? I've been trying to reach her all weekend."

"Yeah, I know. She, ah … she doesn't want to talk to you right now."

Jeff's neck and shoulder muscles tightened as his anger started to build. He forced himself to take a deep breath. Losing it now wouldn't be productive, and it sure as hell wouldn't be fair to Mikaela. *But damn you, Annie, for putting our daughter in the middle of … of whatever the hell this is.*

"Dad? You still there?" Jeff could hear the concern in her voice. It killed him to have her part of this.

"Yeah, Kiddo," he said softly, "I'm still here."

There was a long, tense pause at the other end. "Mom says she's afraid you're having another affair with Kendall Burwell."

It was all he could do not to laugh. *You have got to be fucking kidding me,* he thought bitterly. Could she possibly be so angry that she'd play that card again? And with their daughter? He wanted so badly to tell Mikaela the truth, to blow this whole goddamned thing wide open once and for all. But in his mind he could see his daughter sitting there at the other end of the phone, caught in the middle of something she didn't deserve.

"There is no affair, Kiddo," he assured her instead. "There never has been, with anyone."

"Then why would she say something like that?" Mikaela's tone held a mix of relief and doubt.

Because it's easier for her to live with the truth that way.

"I don't know, honey," he lied. "But I promise that I'll do everything I can to fix whatever this is." At least that was the truth, although Jeff couldn't work up much enthusiasm for what was to come.

Too many times down this road, Annie ... too many times.

Chapter 25

I-5, SOUTHBOUND

"Were you successful?" The voice coming through the car's speakers sounded irritated.

"Of course I was," Nick said. "That's not why I called."

"Why then?" Eveginy asked. "You know the proper protocol."

Nick sighed as he guided his car south toward Portland. Such a stickler for procedure, his cousin. Such an officious ass. "I called because we have a situation you need to know about. One that couldn't wait until I got back to Portland."

"What?"

"Another investigator from the District Attorney's office. Jefferson Dawes," Nick told him. "He visited Uncle Fedya."

That got Eveginy's attention. "When was this?"

"Yesterday, maybe the day before."

"You didn't ask?"

"The opportunity didn't come up, and too much curiosity would have aroused suspicion. Uncle Fedya is far too sharp to chance it."

"The Bear would understand ..."

"He's not The Bear anymore, cousin. That life is behind him and I, for one, am happy to let him do so. I won't put that at risk. It's over, cousin."

"We tell him nothing," Eveginy agreed after a few moments, "but this is far from over, Nikki. There are still eight more."

"Not for me. They've made the connection back to Adam."

"You don't know that. This could be nothing ... you don't know," his cousin argued, his voice edging toward frustration.

"But the risk is becoming too great."

"If you won't finish this, then I will do it myself," Eveginy vowed, quietly.

Nick frowned. "You don't know how."

"What about Meadows?"

"That took no finesse, no skill … you're a hammer, when you need to be a scalpel …"

"Then help me, Nikki," his cousin begged him. "Help me finish this, for Aunt Anya."

Nick wanted to beat on the steering wheel, to vent a stream of well-deserved obscenities at his cousin. *No one could be this fucking stupid,* he thought. *No one could be this desperate for revenge.* But this was Eveginy, and Eveginy would do what he set out to do, or die in the trying. That was the reason, the only reason, Nick had agreed to any of this in the first place. He'd loved his aunt and his cousin, but hadn't Adam brought all of this down upon them? Still, Eveginy would see justice … or what passed for justice in his strange little world. Nick couldn't let him go it alone, then, or now.

"All right, we stay the course a while longer." Even he could hear the resignation in his own voice. "Just a little while longer."

Chapter 26

Jeff guided the Audi down I-205 through Oregon City. Traffic had been practically nonexistent from Olympia, south, and he'd kept the cruise control near eighty the entire way back to Portland. Fifteen more minutes and he'd be home.

What he might be coming home to was anyone's guess.

He turned right off of Willamette Drive and followed Holly Street up the hill, past houses he'd never imagined sharing a neighborhood with back when he was an investigator for the county. He still couldn't figure out how Annie had convinced him to move from their comfortable Beaverton home to the land of inflated real estate prices. He'd loved that little house. Mikaela had grown up in that house. And it had been theirs, practically free and clear.

Now it was just the two of them — Jeff and Annie — living in a house three times the size of what they actually needed, and with an obscene mortgage to match.

He took another right, this time on Grove, and pulled up in front of his garage. The house sat dark, not even a porch light to greet him. The empty driveway confirmed what he'd expected since his phone call from Mikaela; his wife wouldn't be coming home tonight.

With a sigh of irritation, Jeff punched in the alarm code. He stepped inside the house and pulled the front door closed behind him. The darkness that surrounded him seemed heavy, almost oppressive. The only sound in the house was the steady, soft *tick-tick-tick* of the vintage hall clock Annie had bought at an upscale antique store a couple of years earlier. To his wife, the overpriced time piece — like the house itself — somehow represented the new economic status working at Ferrum had secured for them.

But what the hell does all of that money really buy? Jeff wondered as he headed upstairs. Look at Andrei Kozlov and his daughter, in their posh island retreat on Orcas, living in virtual isolation. All of their money hadn't guaranteed anything. Not security. Not happiness. Not a goddamned thing.

Jeff dropped his overnight bag by the door of the master bath. Then he stripped down to his skivvies and climbed under the covers on his side of the bed.

He lay there for a few minutes, listening to the faint ticking of the hall clock downstairs. Somehow he thought he should be feeling more … *More what?* he wondered. *Sadness? Anger?* But he didn't feel anything at all, he realized. At least not tonight. He was as spent emotionally as he was physically.

Twenty minutes later the distant ticking of the clock lulled him into a restless sleep.

HE CALLED THE DA's office at eight AM to give her an update. The call went about as well as Jeff had expected. Orbison had especially loved the possibility that they might be dealing with a *Bratva* assassin.

"If Manny Cespedes' lawyer gets wind of this, we won't have any choice but to let him walk," she'd pointed out.

"He didn't kill Vonetta Myers," Jeff reminded her.

"Maybe. We don't know that for sure, yet. Anyway, there's still the meth they found in Manny's car."

"When you drop the murder charge, his attorney will argue that the drugs were planted by whoever planted the weapon."

"Tell me again why we're doing this," she asked. He could hear Orbison's frustration over the phone.

"Because it's the right thing to do. Because at least nine people's lives depend on you making the right call."

In the end, Orbison agreed to give Jeff what he'd wanted: protective surveillance for the remaining jurors. Cespedes could stay in jail until his lawyer figured out how Myers connected to the Polyakov investigation, or until the DA's office could put together a case against the juror's real killer. But sooner or later, the murderous little prick would walk. Jeff knew it, and Orbison knew it.

Chapter 27

Sam and Paul were already at the conference table when Jeff arrived for the morning debrief. Neither looked as though they had gotten much more sleep over the last two days than he had. Jeff opened with the news that Orbison had finally agreed to police surveillance for the remaining nine jurors, hoping that might lighten their mood a little.

"Not nine jurors," Sam told him, her voice quiet and strained. "Eight." She nodded in the direction of the board where they'd posted the victims' pictures. A new one had been added to the bottom of the gallery.

"Porter Richardson went camping on the Olympic Peninsula last week," she told him. "A day hiker found his body a hundred yards or so from his tent yesterday. The preliminary ruling is heart failure."

The Olympic Peninsula ... While Jeff had been in the San Juans, their killer had been operating in the same general area, probably no more than fifty miles away. It almost felt to Jeff as though he was being taunted.

"Let me guess ... Richardson had a history of heart problems." he said. Sam nodded. "All right, I'll call Orbison and see if we can get the ME to do a tox screen for anything that might have triggered cardiac arrest, or mimicked it. In the meantime, we have our own work to focus on. What's the word from Newport and Grand River?"

"I talked with Captain Bailey in Newport this morning," Paul told him. "She's expecting to hear from the FBI lab within the next two or three days on the Ruiz investigation. If there's explosive residue on any of the debris from the *Justice Served*, we'll at least be able to nail this down as a murder investigation. Not sure how that gets us any closer, however, since our killer isn't following any particular MO."

"If nothing else, it gets the FBI working the investigation from another angle," Jeff pointed out, "and we can use all of the resources we can get. How about your meeting in Grand River?"

Sam leaned forward. "Well, we made the morning news," she said with a half-smile. "They've officially reopened the Russell suicide case and labeled his death a 'possible homicide.' Foster has his team re-interviewing potential witnesses. Maybe something will shake loose."

"Let's hope so," Jeff said. "In the meantime, I think we need to keep our focus on the organized crime angle. Dig into everything you can find on the Myers shooting, and particularly Manny Cespedes. Let's figure out why — and how — they set him up for her murder.

"Paul, I also need you to reach out to your friend at the Bureau again. When I went on that ride with Vasily, he knew I work for Ferrum. Reuben Whiteman was the only person I spoke to this weekend who should have known that. As far as everyone else was concerned, I'm with the DA's office. That means there's got to be a direct connection between Whiteman Security and Vasily Kozlov. I want to know what it is."

"I'm using up my favors with Yance pretty fast," Paul joked as he jotted a note on the legal pad in front of him. "You still planning on digging in to Larissa Kozlov's murder?"

"I am," Jeff admitted, "if only because Vasily doesn't seem to want me to. There's a link between that case and this, beyond the obvious … there has to be. I want to find out exactly what that is."

He saw the skeptical expression on his investigator's face and smiled. "Just for a couple of days," he promised. "If I can't find something that helps by Wednesday, I'll drop it. Any ID on that picture I sent you yesterday?"

"Vasily's men?" Paul shook his head. "Yance hasn't gotten back to me on it."

"Well, then, I guess we just keep pulling on the threads we have." Jeff got to his feet. "If anything breaks, I'll be in my office for the rest of the morning."

Jeff followed them to the doorway of the conference room. Sam stepped out into the hallway, but Paul held back.

"You go ahead and start getting the Cespedes files together," he told her. "I'll be down in a minute. I need to talk to Jeff about something."

When the two men were alone in the room, Paul turned to his boss with a troubled look in his eyes.

"Okay, Paul, tell me what you're thinking," Jeff said.

"I could ask the same thing of you. The only reason we were brought in on this thing was because the DA didn't have enough evidence to open an official investigation," he pointed out. "Between the Coast Guard and the Grand River PD, there should be plenty for Orbison to work with. Are you sure she's still going to want us poking around?"

"She didn't say anything about taking us off the case."

"And you didn't ask, I suppose?"

Jeff hesitated. He hadn't asked, hadn't even considered it in fact. *A week ago, I wanted nothing to do with this mess, and now …* "What's your point, Paul?"

"My point is, looking into the Polyakov case again after you've been warned off by Vasily Kozlov is a huge risk. If you're going to fuck with the *Bratva*, you better make damned sure we at least have the DA's office on our side … especially if you're involving Sam."

As JEFF SETTLED in at his desk, he considered what Paul had said. He couldn't completely dismiss the risk, but as long as Paul and Sam kept directing their attention toward the trial murders — and away from the Polyakov case — Jeff was confident that he could shield them from any fallout that might come from Vasily Kozlov.

The real question was why he'd become so obsessed with reopening Adam's case. Paul had been right; the odds were slim that digging into a three-year-old murder would help them solve the string of killings they were dealing with now, no matter how they were related. Still, there was that niggling little feeling, that once-familiar whisper in the back of his mind urging him forward.

Just until Wednesday, he promised himself. *And I can always drop this if something more promising comes along.*

Rationalizations firmly in place, Jeff picked up the phone and called Rob LaSalle. He tried the offices of the *Bridgetown Weekly* first. The receptionist told him that Rob was on an extended leave of absence. He thanked her, letting her know that he'd try Rob at home.

The home number Jeff had for his friend went straight to voice mail. He had better luck with the mobile number, however. Rob answered on the third ring. His friend sounded distant when he answered … tired, or distracted, but he perked up a bit when he found out who was calling.

"Did you find out something about Adam?"

"I'm still working on it," Jeff assured him. "Right now, I was hoping for your insightful, unbiased opinion of Larissa Kozlov. You really didn't write much about her in your series, and I was wondering … why not?"

The question was met with silence on the other end.

"Rob, are you there?"

"Yeah, I'm here." His friend sounded hesitant. After a moment he said, "I didn't write much about her because I really didn't find much about the woman I could use."

"Okay. You worded that pretty carefully," Jeff pointed out. "What are you trying so hard not to say?"

"Look, Jeff, the case had been making headlines for a couple of weeks before I got involved, and the court of public opinion had pretty much made up its mind the minute news of the murder hit the street. It was one thing to show a different side to Adam, offer a little perspective. It's another thing entirely to cast stones at the poor, innocent murder victim."

"So, you *did* find something."

"No. Nothing in particular," Rob assured him, quickly. "Certainly nothing concrete. But the ones who seemed to know her best — classmates and professors at USC, and the people she worked with at Connectivity — well, the picture they painted didn't exactly resemble your typical girl next door."

Jeff leaned back in his chair. "How did they describe her?" he asked.

"Cold, manipulative, self-absorbed …" Rob paused a moment, then added, "Remember how everyone I talked to liked Adam? With Larissa, it was the polar opposite. Bottom line, the consensus was that she was a royal bitch."

"That bad?"

"Oh, some were a little more inclined to give her the benefit of the doubt than others, but no one I spoke to harbored any real affection for her, and more than a few hated her … off the record, of course."

Jeff thought about something Vasily had said when they were discussing Stefanya: *When your sister is a sociopath …*

"So, what was I going to do?" Rob asked. "Paint the victim as some horrible person? We would have been opening up the paper to a potential lawsuit, and it wouldn't exactly have played well with my readers, would it?"

"No," Jeff acknowledged, "I don't suppose it would have."

He thanked his friend for the information. Before he hung up, he also got the contact information for Crystal Samuels, Rob's source for the *other woman* angle of the feature, but not before promising to fill him in on all the details when the case was resolved.

Chapter 28

According to the police report, Larissa Kozlov's body had been discovered by Polyakov's cleaning lady the morning after the murder. The maid service operated out of a strip mall in Gresham. Jeff arranged to meet with the regional manager, Margaret Guthrie, to discuss the case. She'd agreed, but she hadn't sounded thrilled at the prospect.

"I had hoped all of this was over and done with," Mrs. Guthrie said, irritably, as she sat down behind her desk. She was an elderly woman, and tiny, five-feet tall, at a stretch. She seemed even smaller perched on her oversized office chair. Guthrie ran a hand through her reddish-gray, permed hair and looked at Jeff over the top of her glasses. "Anyway, didn't I read that the guy who killed the girl is dead now?"

"This is just a routine case review," Jeff lied.

Guthrie frowned, adding furrows to an already pinched face. "Well, I really don't know what I can tell you that I didn't tell the other detectives."

Jeff gave her what he hoped was a sympathetic smile. "I understand, and I'll try to make this as brief as possible," he promised. "According to the report, your company had been cleaning Mr. Polyakov's apartment for four months?"

She nodded. "A little more than four months, yes."

"Was this a weekly service?" She nodded again. "And was there a set schedule, or did the day you came in vary?"

"No, we came in every Wednesday … well, every Wednesday except for that week."

"Why the change, that week?"

Guthrie looked exasperated by the question. "Look, I know that I went through this with the detectives. Over and over again."

"Humor me."

She sighed for dramatic emphasis, and said, "We received an email from Mr. Polyakov a few days before, asking us to switch to Thursday for a week."

"And you spoke to Mr. Polyakov to confirm?" Jeff asked.

That question seemed to catch her off-guard. "No," she said after a moment. "Why would we? The request came from his email account, the same one he had used when he'd initially inquired about our services."

"So that Thursday, did anyone from your service notice anything out of place, or unusual?"

"You mean, besides a dead body?" she asked, sarcastically. "Frankly, I have no idea what else my girl saw. She was hysterical when she called to tell me what she'd found. By the time I got there, the police had already taken her statement and let her leave. The last I saw or heard from her was when she came by to pick up her final check."

"She quit?"

"Would you want to clean houses after seeing something like that?"

Chapter 29

Police reports and crime scene photos from the Vonetta Myers case, and Manny Cespedes' arrest, were strewn haphazardly across the long conference room table. Sam scanned the organized chaos, hoping that whatever they were looking for would somehow miraculously announce itself.

The first thing she and Paul had reviewed was the file on the drive-by. On the 24th of June, at around 4:40 in the afternoon, Vonetta Myers had been walking from the Max light rail station in the Arbor Lodge neighborhood. The stop was at North Interstate and Rosa Parks Way, just seven blocks west of her home. According to multiple eye witness accounts, as she passed Peninsula Park a distinctive-looking muscle car — also heading east along Rosa Parks — slowed to a near-stop just behind Myers. Seconds later, shots rang out ... some witnesses stated they'd heard three, others at least a half-dozen. The vehicle, later positively identified as Manny's avocado-green 1970 Dodge Coronet, then drove from the scene at high speed.

It took the people in the park a few moments to realize what had happened, and several more to discover that the woman had been hit during the shooting. A nearby patrol unit arrived within a couple of minutes, but Myers was already dead. She had sustained two gunshot wounds between the shoulder-blades. The ME later ruled that either one would have been fatal.

The Dodge had continued east on Rosa Parks Way, through the intersection at Vancouver Avenue. Traffic cams snapped a photo of the car as it ran a red light. Cameras picked it up again, now headed south, at Martin Luther King Jr. Boulevard. Somewhere between Ainsworth and Alberta, the driver had apparently left MLK and taken to side streets.

The Dodge's windows were heavily tinted, so neither the witnesses at the park nor the traffic cams managed a clear look at the occupant — or occupants — inside the vehicle. But the plates had shown up on the camera footage. The DMV confirmed that the car was registered to one Manuel Diego Cespedes.

At 5:19 PM, about forty minutes after the shooting, an anonymous call came in reporting that a Dodge Coronet matching the description of the shooter's vehicle was parked in the Lloyd Center Mall parking lot.

Uniforms confirmed the license plate number, and put the vehicle under surveillance. About an hour later, Manny Cespedes and his girlfriend, Damita Rojas, were arrested without incident as they attempted to get into the car.

A search of the Dodge turned up a hand gun under the driver's seat, a Belgian FN 57, later confirmed as the weapon used in the shooting. Detectives also found a little less than a quarter-kilo of meth, duct-taped to the top of the trunk compartment. Manny swore both the gun and the drugs were planted. The lab found that the meth packet had been wiped clean, but a pristine set of Manny's fingerprints were on the pistol's grip. Manny claimed that someone had approached him about buying the handgun a few days before, but the unidentified seller wanted too much for it so he'd passed.

"Pretty fucking smart, Manny," Paul had observed as he'd read from the report. "Handle a black-market pistol and then give it back. Brilliant."

Sam nodded. "So we have a positive ID on the Dodge Coronet and Manny's prints on the murder weapon. Tidy. How about an alibi? What does he claim he was doing when Myers was shot?"

Paul checked the file in front of him. "Watching a movie at the multiplex across the street," he said. "Theater staff confirmed that Manny and his girlfriend had gone into the auditorium about twenty minutes before the film started, and one of the cashiers was pretty sure she'd seen them leave at about the time it ended. No one could say for sure that Manny hadn't left in the middle of it, however. His girlfriend told detectives that she'd won tickets to the new Melissa McCarthy movie through a contest she didn't remember entering."

"Did she pick them up from someone?"

Paul shook his head. "She said the tickets were mailed to her. Detectives weren't able to find the envelope they'd come in, or the letter telling her that she'd won."

"Convenient. What about security footage in the parking lot?" Sam asked. "Maybe we can get a shot of whoever stole the Dodge."

Paul shook his head. "No working cameras in that part of the lot. We have footage of the car arriving a little before four. It left about twenty minutes later, then *reentered* twenty-five minutes after Myers was shot. Unfortunately, because of the tinted windows, that footage didn't help any more than the traffic cameras had. How about you? Did you come up with any reasons why someone might have wanted to set Manny up?"

Sam laughed, but there wasn't much humor in it. "It might be easier to ask who *wouldn't* want to set him up. Manny Cespedes is a fucking maniac, and seems intent on making sure everyone knows it." She flipped through the thick file in front of her. "In addition to dealing drugs for the Duarte cartel out of Columbia, his name has come up in a half-dozen murders across Portland in the last fifteen months, including two of his own crew. Detectives haven't been able to make him on any of them. Remember those three kids who were gunned down in the park on the east side?"

"The teens dealing coke ... or was it meth?"

"Meth," Sam confirmed. "The night of the shooting a homeless guy saw three men — one matching Manny's description, perfectly — enter Laurelhurst Park and start beating on the kids. Then, when the boys were so broken up they could barely move, Manny pulled a pistol and started capping them in the head, point blank. Here's what was left." She slid one of the crime scene photos across the table to Paul.

"Jesus!" he said, quietly. "That's a hell of a statement." He lifted the note stapled to the upper left corner of the picture — the one with the names of the three victims — and studied the photo for longer than Sam had been able to manage. "It's amazing the ME could even identify the bodies. They bring Manny in on this?"

She nodded. "But they couldn't hold him. The witness was deemed unreliable because he'd been drinking ... a lot ... and five of Manny's *compadres* gave him a convenient alibi for the time of the shooting."

Paul still held the photo, studying it intently. As he looked again at the paper with the three dead teens' names, the beginnings of a grim smile spread slowly across his features.

"You find something?" Sam could feel the energy in the room shifting as her partner looked over at her. "You did, didn't you? You found something."

"As a matter of fact," he said, his smile growing wider, "I think I may have just found our connection to Eveginy Polyakov."

Chapter 30

GRAND RIVER, OREGON

Carol Banker sat at her desk and looked out the window at what was left of the afternoon. The thermometer on the savings and loan building across the street flashed 93°, ungodly hot even for July in the Willamette Valley. *At least the station is air conditioned,* she thought. So far that was the only positive thing she could find about this goddamned assignment.

She'd expected Detective Harrison to be unhappy about being ordered to reopen the Russell case. She'd been right. But Carol hadn't expected to be treated like a pariah when she'd joined the investigation. Now, Harrison and Detective McCormick were off unenthusiastically re-interviewing Russell's friends and classmates, while Carol had been left behind to review the case files for "anything that catches your eye."

Be still my fucking heart.

She glanced down at the paperwork on the desk blotter, absently running her finger back and forth over the edges of the top page. She knew she'd find nothing there that they'd overlooked during the original investigation, because the original investigation had never even started. Harrison and McCormick had followed the path of least resistance. That's all the initial evidence seemed to require. Suicide, straight up.

Even now, when everything pointed to murder, Harrison couldn't seem to get out of his own fucking way. He was still investigating Russell's death as if it was an isolated case. But it wasn't isolated at all, not if those other deaths were related. He'd waste time asking Russell's friends and classmates the same questions as before, because that was procedure, and God knew they couldn't deviate from procedure. In the meantime, somewhere the clock might be ticking down for another juror.

And just what are you doing, besides feeling sorry for yourself? Carol reminded herself.

She got up and walked over to the wall where the big state map hung, hoping a visual would help her see things differently.

Russell went over the bridge one day after Judge Ruiz and her husband were blown up on their boat over in Newport. But all of the other deaths Ledbetter and Maxwell were investigating had occurred in or around Portland. Whoever was behind this nightmare would probably be basing their operations out of Portland, as well.

The drive from Portland to Newport took around three hours, give or take. Carol doubted that someone would want to make that trip immediately before an assassination attempt.

And by the same logic, she figured they weren't likely to travel all the way back to Portland on Saturday, just to turn around and make another two-hour trip back to Grand River the very next day.

She studied the map. It was only about an hour from Newport to Grand River, easy enough for the murderer — or murderers — to have stayed on the coast the night after the Ruiz's boat went down, and then make the short drive east the next day to kill Russell. Or they might have just as easily booked a hotel somewhere in, or near, Grand River.

All well and good, in theory, but how do you search every hotel registry if you don't have a name to work with? Still, Carol knew she should run this by someone. Someone besides Harrison. Heading back to her desk, she opened her lap drawer and fished out the business card Samantha Ledbetter had left behind.

"LOOK, WE KNOW it's a long shot," Sam admitted to Orbison's assistant, Kyle Washington, "but it's still a shot, right? The Grand River PD doesn't have the resources to manage this kind of inquiry and neither do we, but if your office works with the State Police ..."

Washington's end of the line was silent for a moment. "Let me get this straight," he said at last. "You want us to search every hotel register in the immediate area of Newport, Grand River, and Albany, compile a database, and cross-reference for any commonalities? Do you have any idea what you're asking? In the first place, we'll need a search warrant, and you can be sure we're going to have to narrow things down a hell of a lot more than what you've given me so far. Do you at least have a name and a date range we can work with?"

"The Ruizes' boat went down on May 30th. If our hunch is correct, our hitman would have arrived in Newport at least a day or two earlier."

"What about Grand River and Albany?" Washington asked.

"Check in would be some time around May 30th," Sam told him. "As for a name, there's a strong Russian connection to this case."

She heard Kyle sigh at the other end of the line. "That's a little vague, Miss Maxwell. And judges tend to take a dim view of ethnic profiling."

Across the conference table, Paul leaned closer to the speaker phone. "Let's go with Eveginy Polyakov," he said. "He's a known criminal, on the Bureau's watch list for organized crime, and he's connected to both Adam and the Kozlovs. That should be enough to satisfy the judge. But we're going to want to look at all of the names when we get the list."

"All right, I'll see what we can do. This is probably going to take two or three days," Kyle warned them.

"One would be better," Sam said.

Orbison's assistant chuckled. "You guys have been working with Dawes too frickin' long. I'll let you know when I get an answer."

"Thanks, Kyle," Paul said. "There's just one more thing …"

Across the table, Sam eyed her partner with curiosity. Paul was going off script here.

"Oh Jesus, what now?" Washington said, with a half-serious groan.

"Compared to the hotel thing, this should be a piece of cake," Paul assured him. "I was wondering if we could get the security footage from the parking garage where Manny Cespedes was arrested? Lloyd Center, Wednesday, June 24th, from about three PM on."

"That should be easy enough," Washington admitted. "Tomorrow morning soon enough?"

"Tomorrow morning is fine, Kyle, thanks. And let us know when you have anything on our search warrant."

Sam reached over to the Polycom and disconnected the call. She looked at her partner. "Did you find something else in the Cespedes file that you forgot to share with the rest of the class?"

Paul smiled. "More like what I didn't find."

He got up and grabbed the folder on Myers' murder from the far end of the table. Sitting down next to Sam, he opened it up to the section on the Lloyd Center mall, where the car had been found. "I've been rolling Manny's arrest around in my head since this morning. The pieces weren't all fitting together. Then it hit me."

"What?"

"The police staked out the Dodge until Manny and his girlfriend came back, right?" He paused, apparently waiting for her to have some kind of epiphany.

"Still not getting it, *Sensei*," she admitted in irritation. "Enlighten me."

"Manny walked right into the cops' arms because his car was right where he expected it to be, meaning ..."

And then it hit her. "Meaning that the killer put the Dodge back pretty much where he found it."

Paul's nodded with a grin. "So either he got incredibly lucky, and no one had taken the parking spot while he was off shooting Myers," he said, "or he somehow managed to hold the spot while he was gone."

"I thought the security cameras weren't working in the part of the garage Manny parked in," she pointed out.

"True, but what if the guy we're after followed Manny into the parking garage? The cameras at the entrance to the garage should show us which cars came in after his. Then we check for matches leaving the lot after the car was returned."

Sam considered that in silence.

"I mean, I know it's as much a long shot as the hotel thing," he added, "but ..."

"No, I like it. I really do. Besides," she said with a smile, "play enough long shots and one of them is bound to come in, right?"

Chapter 31

Over the last two decades, the city of Portland had become an eclectic blend of old and new, much more so than Seattle to the north, where shadows cast by modern towers of glass and steel fell less and less frequently on the brick-and-mortar vestiges of the past. According to some, this was because the state of Oregon had done a poorer job of encouraging economic growth than its northern neighbor. But the opposing point of view held that the Rose City simply had a better sense of its history. Whatever the reason, the city on the Willamette exuded a unique and quirky charm Jeff loved.

Repurposed structures from the late 1800s and early 1900s dominated the Pearl District in the northwest part of the city. Old warehouses had been converted into high-end boutiques and restaurants. The landmark Armory Building, with its red brick turrets and narrow slotted gun ports, now hosted stage productions.

One of the earliest reclamation projects had been an old fire house at the corner of 15th and Glisan. The beautiful, two-storey brick building had come within a hundred yards of being torn down in the 1950's, when thirty-six aging city blocks were demolished to accommodate the six-lane trench known now as the 405 Freeway. A few years later, some farsighted entrepreneur decided to open a café and jazz bar in the fire station. Jeff couldn't remember what it used to be called — it had been years since he and Annie had eaten there — but it currently operated as Touché, with a bistro on the main floor and a bar upstairs.

Adam Polyakov had been a Wednesday night regular at Touché, playing pool with friends. And one of those friends had been Crystal Samuels, Rob LaSalle's source on the mysterious 'other woman' in Adam's life. Touché seemed as good a place as any to meet with Samuels, who worked as a nurse at nearby Good Shepherd Hospital.

There were no customers seated in the main dining room downstairs, but four o'clock was probably early for the dinner rush. A curving staircase to the right of the entrance led up to the bar.

Ten small tables had been set up near the vintage oak bar in the rear third of the second floor, while a half dozen regulation-sized pool tables dominated the rest of the room. Jeff felt certain that the firefighters of old would have approved heartily.

A slender blonde sat on a tall stool at the bar, talking to a stocky, bald-headed server. Jeff saw that, other than those two, he had the place to himself.

The bartender wore black pants and a matching shirt. His face — which held a slightly amused expression — tended more toward round than oval. The absence of hair on the top of his head was compensated for by a long, well-formed goatee. A mustache framed his friendly smile, and dark, intelligent eyes watched as Jeff stepped up to the polished oak bar.

"How are you doing tonight?" he asked. His tone matched his smile. "What can I get for you?"

Jeff eyed the well-stocked liquor shelves behind the bar. A drink sounded tempting, he had to admit, but technically he was working. Still, with everything he'd been dealing with lately …

"Are you Jefferson Dawes?" The woman perched two barstools to Jeff's left studied him with interest. He nodded. "Well, then you might as well order something," she told him, a mischievous glint in her dark green eyes, "because I'm not talking to you unless you do."

He laughed. "I'm guessing you must be Crystal Samuels?" He extended his hand. She leaned across the stool between them and shook it, her touch exceptionally soft.

"Just Crystal, please."

Jeff realized immediately that she was a very attractive woman. He guessed her to be in her late twenties, although the older he got, the worse he admittedly became at estimating a woman's age. Eyes the color of deep-green jade watched him with a mix of nervousness and amusement. She wore little makeup, if any, and her honey-blonde hair was pulled back in a ponytail, accentuating her angular features. She'd dressed casually for their meeting. Jeans and a simple loose-fitting blouse gave her a definite Girl Next Door look.

Like most beautiful women, she undoubtedly knew Jeff was studying her … and appreciated what he saw. If that bothered her, however, she hid it well.

"You look like a Scotch man," Crystal said. Jeff shook his head. "Bourbon, then," she amended.

"Nailed it in two," he told her. "So, what can I get for you?"

"Me? I'm a cheap date. It's usually just club soda for me, especially when it's hot outside."

"I think my expense report can handle club soda. As for me …" Jeff surveyed the stocked shelves, searching for the bourbons and finally finding one he hadn't indulged in for a while. "I'll have a Basil Hayden's, neat," he told the server with a smile.

"Good choice." The bartender turned to retrieve the bottle.

"Make it a double, Joe," Crystal advised. "He looks like he could stand to loosen up a bit."

Jeff laughed. "Apparently, I'm having a double."

Joe nodded, amusement reflected in his eyes. "Coming right up."

"Do you want to get a table?" Jeff asked as the barman set their drinks in front of them.

"Absolutely," Crystal said. She turned to the bartender. "Joe?"

He walked to a shelf at the far end of the bar and grabbed a tray of pool balls. A moment later, they sat alongside the drinks.

Jeff eyed the tray. "When I suggested getting a table, I meant … a table," he said, gesturing at the empty seats behind them.

Crystal had already slid off of the stool to stand beside him. The young woman was on the shorter side, probably no more than five-three or so, but she'd made no effort to conceal her height by wearing high heels as so many petite women did, even in casual clothes.

"I'd rather play pool," she told him as she picked up the pool balls. "Besides, this part of the bar will start getting busy soon. If you want to talk, grab the drinks and follow me."

With that Crystal headed off to the other end of the room. Jeff watched her in amusement, trying not to enjoy the view too much. "Why do I get the feeling I'm being hustled?" he said, mostly to himself. The question drew a chuckle from behind the counter.

"Nah, that's just Crystal being Crystal," Joe assured Jeff. "She's always been the shy, retiring type. Did you want to start a tab for the drinks and the table?"

Jeff nodded, handing over his company credit card. Then, he picked up the two glasses and headed toward the pool table.

"What's your game?" Crystal asked as she pulled the balls from their tray and set them on the green baize surface of the table. "Nine ball? Eight ball?"

Jeff got the distinct impression that she was in no hurry to start talking about Adam. *What the hell,* he thought, *it's not like I have anything to go home to right now.* "Whatever you prefer," he told her.

"In that case, it's Jack's Rules." She grinned mischievously as she started to fill the triangular rack. "It's like eight ball, with a few slight modifications. One and the fifteen have to go into a side pocket to stay down. If you scratch, you spot a ball … unless you're shooting at the eight. Then you lose."

Jeff nodded. He'd played something similar a long time ago. "Do we have to call the pocket?"

"Only on the eight ball. But once you call the eight, you're stuck with that pocket for the rest of the game," she added.

"Oh, geez. That sounds like it could get ugly fast," he observed with a chuckle.

"It's a great leveler," she admitted. "You up for it?"

"As long as we're not playing for money, why not? You break."

It didn't take long for Jeff to get the measure of Crystal's game. She shot straight shots with confidence, banks and kick shots far less so. Her greatest weakness came in playing the position game; more often than not, she hit the cue ball too hard to leave a solid follow-up shot. But she knew the game they were playing better than Jeff did, and it showed. On her third turn she passed up an easy shot that he would have gone for, in favor of a tricky angle on the fifteen in the side. When it fell, her smug grin told him he might be in some trouble. Fortunately, she missed her follow-up.

"So, why is this called 'Jack's Rules?'" he asked as he tried a bank, six in the corner. The ball nicked the edge of the pocket and caromed to the right.

Crystal eyed the table, looking for her best shot. "I think Jack was the father-in-law of the guy who taught Adam the game … something like that." She dropped the ten in the far corner, but left herself out of position for the twelve. As she lined up her next shot she paused, looking up over her cue. "Adam didn't do it, you know."

It wasn't a question, but a firm statement. Jeff said nothing, keeping his eyes on the game in front of him. Crystal returned to her shot, but her focus was clearly elsewhere.

"How well did you know him?" Jeff asked.

Crystal smiled. "Honestly? Not as well or as long as I would have liked. Look, Mr. Dawes, I know guys. If you're a woman who is even a little attractive, you meet a lot of douche bags. And, if you're smart, you begin to recognize the warning signs pretty quickly." Her expression grew serious as she added, "Adam was no douche bag, and he was no murderer. He could never have done what they said he did to that woman."

"You're not alone in believing that," Jeff assured her, honestly. "So, let's say you're right, and Adam didn't do those things he was convicted of doing. What do you think really happened?"

She paused. Jeff thought she was considering the question, then he saw Joe coming down to check on them.

"You guys need anything?"

Jeff shook his head. His drink was still half full.

"Actually, Joe," Crystal said, "could you bring me a Moscow Mule?"

Joe's surprise was obvious. He gave Crystal a quiet look, as if to ask if everything was okay. She smiled and nodded.

"On my tab," Jeff reminded him, probably unnecessarily.

Crystal waited until the bartender was out of earshot before she answered Jeff's question.

"I met Adam in October of 2011," she told him. Her voice was quiet, almost contemplative. "I'd just moved up from Salem, and my roommate, Tiffany, brought me to Touché for a drink after work. Adam was playing pool by himself ... at this table, in fact." She ran her hand along the edge of the cushion, lost in the memory for a second.

"You okay?" Jeff asked, softly.

She nodded. "Tiffany was the one who saw him first." Crystal grinned. "But I was the one who asked if we could play pool with him."

"I'm shocked," Jeff said with a smile. "You seem so reserved."

She laughed. "I know, right? Anyway, while Adam did his best to teach us 'Jack's Rules,' poor Tiff tried everything she could think of to get his attention. She finally gave up after the second game. I think she went out and picked up some guy at Henry's out of frustration."

"What about you?" Jeff had the feeling Crystal just needed to talk. He was more than happy to give her the opportunity to do just that.

"Me? I'm an optimist, so I stuck around. Besides, Adam was good company. By that time, his usual Wednesday night group had shown up, and they invited me to join them. Good guys ... Frank has actually taught me most of what I know about pool, but they're all great, really. Rick, Fred, Jimmy, Jon ... all of them. Even after what happened to Adam ..." She paused and looked down at the table.

"Let me go check on your drink," Jeff offered, giving her a moment to collect herself.

The bar had started to get busy by this time. The front two pool tables were occupied, and Joe was trying to take drink orders from three people at once. When Jeff stepped up to the bar, Joe shot an apologetic look his way.

"Sorry about that," he said when he'd served the last of the new customers. He set a copper mug, filled to the brim and garnished with a lime slice, in front of Jeff.

"Don't worry about it," Jeff told him. He eyed the cup. "Moscow Mule?" he asked.

Joe nodded. "Is Crystal all right?"

"I think she's fine," Jeff assured him. "It's just a little tough remembering, that's all."

"This is about Adam, right? Yeah, they were close."

"So I gather."

"Just go easy on her, all right?" Joe's expression, and the sudden edge in his voice, made it clear that he didn't mean it as a request.

Jeff nodded and carried the drink back to the pool table. Loyalty was refreshing, whatever form it took, he realized.

"Thanks," Crystal said as he handed her drink over. "Let me guess; did Joe go all protective on your ass?" She smiled, knowingly, as she asked.

"Little bit," Jeff admitted.

Crystal took a long sip from her drink. Then she looked at Jeff. "So, Mister Dawes, ask your questions."

"What about the game?"

She cocked her head in surprise. "Is it still my shot?" He nodded. She lined up on the twelve again but missed badly, her mind undoubtedly still on other things. "Your turn," she told him.

This time he sank the six, corner pocket.

"I know what you're thinking," she said as he surveyed the table for his next shot. He looked at her, waiting. "You're wondering if we ever hooked up, right?"

Instead of answering, Jeff let the question hang for a moment. He lined up on the two and dropped it into the side. The cue ball travelled to the far end of the table on the follow. Jeff moved into position behind it, looking his options over.

"Did you?" he asked, finally, as he lined up his next shot.

"No. I wish we had, though." Jeff glanced over to see her blush, slightly. "We even had a running bet; if I won two out of three games, he had to take me out on a date," she admitted.

"And did you ever get to collect on your bet?"

Crystal shook her head. "He was too good a player. I might manage to win a game once in a while, but usually I'd have to distract him to even manage that much."

"Oh? And how would you do that?" Jeff asked with a smile.

"Why don't you go ahead and shoot, and I'll show you" she told him, a sly look in her eyes. He obediently bent over his cue once more.

Crystal moved into position immediately in front of his target ball and leaned forward. The loose-fitting shirt she wore fell away from her body a little, revealing a disconcerting amount of cleavage. Jeff tried to focus, but the view was pretty damned enticing. He considered standing up and resetting, but male pride kicked in and he took his shot. He missed, badly.

"That must be what they mean by 'Dirty Pool,'" Jeff said with a laugh as Crystal settled in behind the cue ball. "And you never managed to win two out of three, even with a tactic like that? Adam must have had better powers of concentration than I do."

"Actually, he was such a nice guy I felt a little guilty about playing that card very often," she admitted.

The thirteen ball ran the length of the table and into the corner pocket, leaving Crystal set up perfectly for a follow-up on the twelve. She dropped that one, as well. Only the fourteen and the eight stood in the way of her victory. Fortunately for Jeff, she'd left herself completely blocked in behind two of his balls. She tried a kick shot, but missed her target by a good two inches. The cue ball dropped into the side pocket with a *thunk*.

"What happens now?" he asked.

"I have to pull one." Crystal centered the ten on the spot. "You get ball-in-hand, anywhere in the kitchen," she added, sending the cue ball rolling his way. He picked it up and walked to the far end of the table.

"So, was Adam still dating Larissa Kozlov when you met him?" he asked as he lined up on the three and dropped it in the side pocket. He'd left himself set up nicely on the seven in the corner.

"No. He'd quit seeing her before we met, thank God. That bitch was the worst thing that ever happened to him." She saw the look Jeff gave her and shrugged. "His words," she told him, unapologetically, "not mine. Well, except for the *bitch* part. That's mine."

Jeff sank the seven, but managed to tuck himself behind the eight ball in the process. The only clear shot he had was the one ball in the corner.

"I'd take the one if I were you," she advised.

"I thought the one and fifteen had to go in the side pockets."

"To stay down, they do. But if you sink the one in the corner, we just spot it and you keep shooting."

He followed her advice and dropped it in the pocket. Once Crystal spotted it, he was perfectly lined up on the one in the side.

"Nicely done," she said as he made the follow up, evening the game.

"Thanks." He chalked his stick and moved into position behind the cue ball. "So, if Adam wasn't still dating Larissa Kozlov, or anyone else, when you met him, I'm surprised you couldn't get farther with him."

"Maybe he just thought of me as 'one of the guys,'" Crystal offered with a laugh.

"Not a chance," Jeff assured her.

She blushed a little at the obvious compliment. "Actually, I think he was still hung up on his ex," she admitted, after a moment. "The one before Kozlov, I mean. I know he still felt guilty about her."

Jeff had been sighting in on the four, but he straightened and looked over at Crystal. "Guilty, how?" he asked.

"Apparently, she caught him screwing around on her with that Kozlov chick … in the worst possible way," she added with a smile.

"And Adam blamed Larissa?" He threw the suggestion out casually as he settled back in over his cue and took his shot.

The four ball made a satisfying thump as it dropped into the pocket. When he stood again, Crystal was looking at him with an irritated expression on her face.

"You're looking for motive, aren't you?" she asked, accusingly. He nodded. "Well, sorry to disappoint you, but he blamed himself for what happened, not Larissa. That's why he didn't want to date anyone new."

"But Rob's article quoted you as saying that Adam *was* seeing someone," he pointed out.

"That didn't start until we'd known each other for a while ... sometime around the end of February, probably, or the beginning of March."

"Did he tell you anything about this new woman?"

Crystal shook her head. "All I know is that she'd come into town to see him about every other week. I think she might have been in sales or something, maybe someone he met at Connectivity. Unfortunately, her visits always seemed to fall on Wednesdays, so Adam started missing a lot of pool nights."

Wednesdays again ... Jeff let that process as he sank the five in the corner. "He never told you who she was, or where they'd met?"

She shook her head as he moved around the table to get to the eight ball. He had a decent angle on a shot in the side pocket. It would be tight, but it was definitely manageable with a little finesse. "Over there," he called, indicating the target with his cue.

Crystal smirked. "Side pocket? You're sure?"

"I think so," he said, puzzled. "Why wouldn't I be?"

"No reason," she told him. Her tone was less than convincing, however. When his shot nicked off of the corner of the pocket and rolled halfway down to the end of the table, he realized his mistake. Under 'Jack's Rules,' once he called the eight, that pocket was his target for the rest of the game; the odds of his getting a decent angle on the side-pocket again were probably slim to none.

Crystal immediately made him pay by sinking her last two balls in quick succession. "Far corner," she announced.

The eight rolled to a stop just shy of her pocket. In its current position, Jeff would be lucky if he didn't accidentally drop it in for her.

"When was the last time you saw Adam?" he asked, while he considered his situation.

"The night before he was arrested. He played pool with us until about nine, then he got a call and left to meet someone."

"Larissa, or the other woman?"

"He didn't say, but whoever it was, he seemed surprised to hear from them. I tried to visit him at the jail to find out who had called, but he refused to see me. I couldn't bring myself to go to the trial," she added, quietly.

He nodded. Adam had even refused visitation to his own parents at that point.

It might be interesting to see who did get in to see him, he thought as he studied the table, *and who else had tried to.* Orbison's office should be able to pull that kind of information together pretty quickly.

Making a mental note to call the request in, Jeff refocused his attention on the game. He was facing an almost-impossible shot; Crystal had left the eight ball planted near the edge of her pocket, to the right side of the opening. The gap to the left might … *might* … be wide enough to get the cue ball into and, hopefully, force the eight ball away from the corner. The question was whether he could manage that trick without scratching in the process.

He caught Crystal watching him, a look of amused triumph in her eyes.

Jeff settled in low and gave the cue ball a solid poke. It kicked hard off of the cushion and into the eight, with just enough momentum to stay out of the pocket on the carom. The eight bounced off of the opposite rail, coming to rest near the middle of the table.

"You've played pool before, haven't you?" Crystal observed, dryly. He'd left her with a long bank, the kind of shot she'd shown some hesitancy in taking during the game. This time, however, she stepped right up and hit the cue ball with a confident stroke. Jeff knew by the way the eight came off of the far cushion that he'd lost.

"Two out of three?" she asked as the ball dropped into her pocket, a decidedly mischievous cast to her jade-green eyes.

IT WAS HALF-PAST five by the time Jeff made it back to his car. He dialed the DA's office and asked for Kyle Washington. Orbison's assistant answered on the second ring.

"Hey, Jeff, I was just on my way out the door. What's up?"

"I was wondering if you could do a favor for me? I need to see Adam Polyakov's visitation logs while he was locked up."

"City jail or state prison? Or both?"

"Both, if you can manage."

"No problem. Digital okay, or do you need hard copies?" Kyle asked.

"Digital is fine," Jeff assured him.

"Good. Then I should be able to get them to you by the morning. Oh, and tell Paul and Samantha that the judge came through on the warrant; we'll have those hotel registers within twenty-four hours, if not sooner."

"I'll let them know," Jeff assured Kyle, wondering just what his investigators were up to.

Chapter 32

Markus already had the morning edition of *The Oregonian* on Jeff's desk when he arrived at Ferrum's offices a little before seven. "You look tired, boss," his assistant observed as he set a cup of coffee on the blotter in front of him. "Rough night?"

"I've had better," Jeff admitted. Annie had come home unexpectedly around ten the night before. Barely acknowledging his presence, she'd headed up to their room and crawled into bed, leaving him to figure out what to do next. Not up to a late-night confrontation, he'd opted for the couch in the den.

Discretion may be the better of valor, he thought as he sipped the strong black coffee, *but it isn't exactly conducive to a restful night's sleep.*

"I put the Norinda contract on your desk," Markus told him when he'd settled in. "They're hoping to hear back on their counteroffer by noon," he added, an amused expression on his face.

Jeff chuckled as he handed the file back. "Well, since the answer is still going to be no, we could end the suspense right now, couldn't we? But let's wait until eleven-thirty, just to let them know we gave it serious consideration. Paul and Samantha in yet?" he asked.

"You and I are the only ones who come in this early," his assistant reminded him.

"Let me know when they arrive. I'll just do a bit of catching up here."

As it turned out, there wasn't a hell of a lot for Jeff to catch up on; between Markus and Carl Henderson, the office had hummed along nicely in his absence. He spent about an hour going over a couple of contracts Legal had asked him to review, and then sent off a quick email to Ahmad Durrell in the Seattle office, with recommendations for the International Trade Fair detail in September. With that taken care of, he opened up the DA's file on the Kozlov murder.

Every time Jeff had reviewed the casework, he found himself coming to the same inescapable conclusion; the evidence pointed convincingly to Adam's guilt. The right man had gone to prison.

So why would Vasily Kozlov be so concerned about someone investigating his niece's murder again?

Probably because, like everything else in this goddamned case, nothing is as obvious as it seems.

The initial call regarding the murder came from the cleaning woman, Agnes Conrad, reporting a dead woman "chained to the bed" in Adam Polyakov's apartment. The identification in the victim's wallet confirmed that she was Larissa Kozlov.

A warrant was issued for Adam, as a "person of interest." Forty minutes later he was taken into custody, without incident, at the Connectivity corporate offices in Beaverton.

Adam's first mistake had been to waive his right to have an attorney present during questioning. Maybe he felt that he'd look more innocent by doing that, or maybe he actually did want to cooperate and saw no need for representation. Either way, the move had immediately put him at a tremendous disadvantage. The detectives could ask anything they wanted, in any way that they wanted. Everything Adam said would be compared, point-by-point, to the facts gathered at the crime scene. Even the slightest discrepancy could then be a building block in the detectives' case against him. They really didn't need him to admit he was guilty … they just needed him to screw up enough to convince a jury that he was hiding his guilt.

Opportunity was a slam dunk; the body had been discovered in Adam's apartment. He didn't have a roommate. By his own admission, he didn't know of anyone else who had a key other than the maid service. And he'd been home on the night in question.

Motive wasn't a problem, either. Interviews with the management team at Connectivity had quickly turned up Larissa's obsession with having Adam fired.

Apparently, though, no one in the company had been aware that the two had ever dated … no one, that is, except for the company's Chief Counsel, Daniel Radisson. Radisson admitted to having been "intimate" with Larissa since just *before* she'd broken it off with Adam. For the detectives on the case, it probably felt like they'd hit the Daily Double.

Their theory was that Adam must have found out about their relationship and killed his ex in a jealous rage, probably fueled by her determination to destroy his career in the company.

Jeff compared Motive A — Larissa's desire to see Adam out of the company — and Motive B — the jilted lover out for revenge — against what he had gleaned from Andrei Kozlov and Crystal Samuels.

Larissa wanted Adam's head, undoubtedly. But Andrei had made it clear that his daughter didn't have the authority to fire him. What's more, Adam had offered to resign to avoid family conflict, at least according to Andrei's version.

The jealousy angle had its own problems, if Crystal's story was to be believed. She was convinced that Adam not only had no lingering feelings for Larissa, but regretted even having been with her in the first place. Why kill a woman you were glad to be rid of?

Only Andrei's assertions would have been admissible as direct evidence in court, of course. Alex would have had no problem getting Crystal's testimony thrown out as hearsay. But Jeff absolutely believed that she had been telling the truth … or what she believed to be the truth, at least.

Nothing seemed to be lining up the way Jeff had expected. He turned to the transcript from Adam's first interview with the detectives, hoping for something approaching insight.

The detectives who conducted the interrogation, Donovan and Mateo, began by reminding Adam of his rights. He'd waived them once again, assuring them he had nothing to hide.

```
Q: Mr. Polyakov, can you tell us where you were
   last night?
A: I played pool with some friends at Touché until
   around nine. Then I left to meet someone.
Q: Miss Kozlov.
A: Not Larissa, no.
Q: So, you're seeing another woman then.
A: There is no other woman. I'm not seeing anyone.
Q: Then who did you go to meet?
A: It doesn't matter. They never showed up. I went
   home.
```

The detectives hadn't pushed for the name of the mystery person Adam said he'd been going to meet. Then again, why would they if Adam wanted to leave himself without a viable alibi?

But Jeff knew from his meeting with Crystal that Adam *had* received a phone call from someone. A check of his phone records for that night could have proven that. Adam had offered up no defense, however, so the matter never came up in court.

Jeff jotted *2nd woman* on the notepad by his computer. *Wednesdays only ... why? Frequent flier? Sales? Possible Connectivity vendor.* He underscored *Wednesdays.*

Everything in the Polyakov case seemed to revolve around the same day of the week: the maid service that normally came in on Wednesdays; Adam's other woman, who Crystal said only came to town on Wednesdays ... and the murder that occurred late on a Wednesday.

Coincidences like that pissed Jeff off. The more neatly the planets aligned in a homicide case, the closer you had to look at every fact. He stared at the handful of scribbled words, hoping for an epiphany, a bolt from above. *Nada.* With a sigh, Jeff went back to the transcript.

```
Q: Care to explain how your ex-girlfriend's body
   came to be strapped to your guest bed?
A: Strapped?
Q: Restrained. Handcuffed. How did she get that
   way?
A: I don't know. I don't even know how she got
   there.
Q: You think she let herself in and locked herself
   up like that?
A: No, I … I don't think … Handcuffed?
Q: To the bed. Assaulted. Dead. What happened,
   Adam? Did things just get a little too rough?
   Or was killing her your plan all along?
A: What? No. I would never do that.
Q: Because you loved her?
A: No.
Q: You didn't love her?
A: No.
Q: Or maybe she didn't love you anymore. And that
   made you angry, right?
A: No. We never loved each other.
```

Jeff knew Adam may well have been acting, but even in black and white — with his words stripped of their inflection — Adam seemed genuinely surprised to hear that Larissa had been restrained, even more so that handcuffs were used.

After that interview, he'd exercised his right to counsel. From that point on Adam's attorney, Erin Meadows, had been present whenever he'd met with detectives. Not that it really mattered; Adam had stopped talking by then, anyway. Even as the evidence mounted — his fingerprints on the handcuffs, a definitive DNA match on the semen found on the woman's body — he'd offered no confession, and no defense.

The question Jeff had was why? Or rather, why not? A good defense attorney — and by all accounts, Erin Meadows had been a very good defense attorney — would have advised Adam that much of the evidence the prosecution held in the case was circumstantial. Motive was based on jealousy, and yet the people closest to them hadn't even known they'd been seeing each other. Larissa wanted to fire Adam, but Andrei Kozlov could testify that that was never going to happen. As for the DNA evidence, there was surprisingly little semen found on the victim's body, especially given the prosecution's claims of sexual assault pre- and post-mortem.

Then there was the email to the maid service, the one that had seemed so out-of-character to Rob LaSalle. A search of Adam's hard drive had turned up the email asking the cleaning service to reschedule among his deleted files. The date stamp showed that it had been sent from his personal computer exactly one week before Larissa's body was discovered, on Thursday, at 7:32 in the morning.

Forensics found at least three sets of partial prints on the keyboard, in addition to Adam's. No attempt had been made to identify who they belonged to. Meadows would have jumped all over that, too, if she'd been allowed to. But none of that evidence had ever come up during the trial, either.

Adam hadn't forced the Prosecution to introduce it, because he'd just rolled over for them.

The million-dollar question: Why the hell wouldn't Adam get out of his own way?

A quiet knock on his door interrupted Jeff's thoughts. Markus peeked his head around the door. "Mr. Maxwell and Ms. Ledbetter are in the conference room when you're ready."

"Tell them I'll be right there."

Chapter 33

"I heard from Captain Bailey this morning." Paul had Jeff's full attention. "The lab confirmed explosives residue on several of the pieces of debris from the Ruiz boat. There's a joint news conference scheduled for this morning to announce the formation of a multi-departmental task force to investigate. I guess that means they'll take it from here."

Jeff heard the tone in Paul's voice. "So, what's the problem?"

"With the Feds coming onboard, and the local police involved, you know that Orbison is going to pull us from the investigation."

"That's up to the DA's office," Jeff said. He saw the disappointment at the table, especially in Sam's expression. "Listen, there wouldn't even be any federal investigation, or protective surveillance for the remaining jurors, if not for the work you guys have done," he reminded them both. "We've accomplished a hell of a lot in the last five days. Certainly more than Orbison had any right to expect."

That would be small consolation for having the case pulled out from under them and he knew it. He decided to change tack. "Kyle tells me that your search warrant for the hotel registries went through. Care to fill me in?"

Sam mustered up as much enthusiasm as she could and explained Sergeant Banker's theory about the killer staying overnight somewhere in the Grand River area.

"Certainly worth a shot," Jeff agreed. "Let's hope it pays off. Any word on the two guys Vasily sent to pick me up?"

"Not yet," Paul said. "Yance is still looking into it, but it isn't exactly going to be top priority for the Bureau."

Jeff couldn't argue that. "Any other angles you guys are working?" he asked.

"Paul asked Orbison's office for a copy of the mall's security cams from the day they arrested Cespedes." Sam explained what they were hoping to find.

"So we're in wait-and-see mode," Jeff said. "Until the registers and the security footage come through, there's not much either of you can do. I think you've both earned a break."

Sam looked about to object.

"At least take the morning," Jeff told her firmly. "Get away from the office for a while. I'll let you know if something comes up in the meantime."

"So, what are you going to do with your new-found freedom?" Sam asked as she and Paul waited for the elevator. "Go home and see Lucy?"

Her partner flashed a crooked smile. "I would if I could, but she won't be home from work until at least three. So I guess I have no idea what I'm going to do right now. You?"

"Not a clue," she admitted. "Even if I go home, my mind is still going to be on the case. Do you really think we're going to be pulled off of the investigation?"

"Today or tomorrow," he guessed. "By Friday, at the latest."

"That really sucks."

The elevator doors slid back and they boarded together, both reaching simultaneously for the Lobby button. Sam got there first and grinned triumphantly, eliciting a chuckle from her friend. As they rode down she chewed absently on her bottom lip, lost in thought.

"Is it awful that I don't want this to end yet?" she asked at last.

Paul shook his head. "It's easy to get a little obsessive," he assured her. "I think that's why Jeff wants us to find something to take our minds off of the investigation for a while."

Sam nodded unhappily as the elevator doors opened onto the lobby. Then she looked over at him with a smile. "Well, since we're both at loose ends, how about I buy you a cup of coffee? Maybe we can find a way to distract each other for a few hours."

If that offer had come from any woman but Sam, Paul might have been tempted to read something more into it.

PAUL'S PHONE BUZZED halfway through their coffee and pastries at Lovejoy Bakers. He checked the caller ID to find the DA's assistant was calling.

"Let's hope this is good news," he said to Sam as he answered. "Good morning, Kyle. What's the word?"

"Well, you certainly sound chipper today."

"The boss gave us the morning off," Paul explained, grinning at his partner, "so we're enjoying a relaxing cup of coffee in the sunshine. You should join us."

"I'd love to, but I'm too busy running errands for you guys," Kyle told him. "That's what I'm calling about."

"Where are we at with the hotel registers?"

"Good news, bad news. No obviously Russian names on the hotel registers around Newport on the dates you gave me, and no common names between the hotels in Newport and the Grand River area." the DA's assistant told him. "I've forwarded digital copies to both of your emails, so you can look them over for yourself."

"I hope that's the 'bad' news," Paul said dryly.

"I always start with the bad news. Now for the good. Remember that name you came up with for the search warrant, Eveginy Polyakov? Well, guess who checked out of the Albany Inn and Suites the day after Allen Russell died?"

Paul leaned forward in his seat. Sam, who had been polishing off her Danish, stopped mid-bite to watch him.

"Polyakov?" Paul repeated in surprise. "In Albany? You're kidding."

"Checked in two days before."

He looked over to see Sam grinning. "That's better than 'good' news, Kyle. Thanks. Where are we at with the mall security videos?"

"I couriered them over to your office about twenty minutes ago."

"Eveginy?" Sam asked when Paul ended the call.

He nodded. "Checked into an Albany hotel on the 29th of May, and left the morning after Russell was killed. I think we have our first real break."

"Do we have enough to bring him in?"

"No. Look in the dictionary under 'circumstantial,' and this is pretty much the definition. But for the first time we have a stake in the ground. Now that we know Eveginy is involved, we have a much better chance of tying him in to the other murders."

He finished off the last bite of his strawberry Danish and stood. "Coffee break is over, partner. Time to get back to work."

Chapter 34

Nick Averill studied the old circuit box. It was made to order. By the time he was finished, there would be nothing out of the ordinary to create suspicion, no sign that he'd done a little rewiring. Satisfied, he brushed the sweat beading on his brow away with a gloved hand and looked around the rickety wood-framed garage.

These were the jobs he most enjoyed, the ones that offered a chance at creativity, at artistry. Guns and knives were for the unimaginative. Even poisons, like the one he'd used on Porter up in the woods, seemed almost a cheat. But an old house like this, built in the thirties … He'd finally settled on the circuit box out in the stand-alone garage, but in truth there'd been almost endless opportunities to choose from.

The juror, Joel Williams, lived north of downtown Portland in the quiet neighborhood of St. Johns. According to Eveginy's man, Williams was a lonely old *otshel'nik* — a hermit — leaving his overgrown property only to buy groceries and go to work. No family, no friends, no company to speak of but the faces flashing across his big screen television every night.

Tonight, when Williams came home from work, the power to that television and the rest of the living room would be off. A blown circuit no doubt, and when the old man came out to reset the circuit, the electrical charge that coursed through him when he touched the box should be enough to kill him outright. If it didn't … well, the fire that followed would take care of the rest and destroy any evidence of Nick's presence. It wouldn't require much accelerant to ensure that, not in this tinderbox of a garage.

Satisfied with the plan, Nick was about to get started when he heard voices outside. He risked a glance through the dust-covered window to his left just as two men emerged from around the corner of the old man's house. One wore a patrolman's uniform. For an anxious moment, Nick imagined that some neighbor had seen him entering the yard and alerted the police. But he quickly dismissed the thought; Williams' landscaping was too unkempt and overgrown to allow for prying eyes.

Both men carried sidearms, which meant both were police. At least the weapons were still holstered, so they obviously weren't anticipating trouble.

Across the yard, the uniformed officer climbed the three steps up to the back porch of the house and tested the door, clearly making sure that it was locked. Then the two started toward the garage.

Nick calmly drew his 9mm Beretta and crouched low in a gap between two shelving units at the far end of the room. He was running on instinct now. No over-thinking. No hesitation. The Beretta didn't have the stopping power to take on body armor, but in close quarters it should be all he needed. He eyed the distance to the door. *Three and a half meters, give or take.* The uniform would have to go first. He'd probably be wearing Kevlar, so it would take a head shot. Once the patrolman went down, the element of surprise should give Nick enough time to take out the second man. There was no immediate cover at that end of the garage. Simple enough, if they came in together, he decided. If they didn't …

If they didn't, Nick would simply improvise.

The door swung back half way, kicking up dust motes that floated in the early afternoon light. Nick waited patiently, pistol raised to firing position, as the patrolman stepped part-way into the garage. The second man waited outside. The uniformed cop gave the darkened garage a perfunctory once-over before pulling the door closed once more.

Nick exhaled slowly but stayed put. Sweat trickled down his neck and back as he forced himself to be patient. He could hear the two men talking through the garage's thin siding, but he couldn't quite make out what they were saying. Then their voices faded completely.

He waited almost twenty minutes before emerging cautiously from the garage. There was no sign of the cops. Nick considered taking the time to rig the circuit panel anyway, the idea of killing the old man right under the watchful eyes of the police almost too tantalizing to pass up. In the end, however, discretion won out over ego.

To hell with the hit, he thought as he made his way to the edge of the yard.

He'd already discarded the original plan to leave the way he'd come in, through a gap in the thick shrubbery and trees at the front of the property. Instead, he took a more circuitous route back to his car, through the neighbor's yard to the east. Fortunately, no one appeared to take any notice of him ... the only thing that seemed to be going right, all of a sudden.

Nick opened the driver's door, stepping back to let the summer heat inside the Audi dissipate a little before climbing in. *They've put Williams under surveillance. That's the only thing that makes sense,* he decided.

And if Williams was under surveillance, then so were the others.

To confirm his suspicions, he pulled away from the curb and cruised slowly past the juror's house. A dark green Chevy sedan was parked in front. The plainclothes officer behind the wheel barely glanced in Nick's direction as he drove by.

Eveginy or no Eveginy, this useless exercise in retribution was over.

It now came down to survival ... Nick's survival. All he needed was a few hours more to put his contingency arrangements into motion. As he drove west onto the St. Johns Bridge, Nick called the number his cousin had given him. Eveginy's man answered on the third ring.

"Did you find the girl?" Nick asked, without preamble.

"Of course I did." The man sounded almost offended by the question. Nick smiled at the professional pride.

"And Mrs. Dawes?"

"I forwarded her information on to you. Does this mean it's time to move?"

"Soon. Keep an eye on the girl and I'll be in touch."

Chapter 35

Jeff began combing through the jail and prison visitation logs Kyle Washington had sent from the DA's office as soon as they hit his inbox. Someone had thoughtfully compiled the list of people who had actually made it in to see Adam into a spreadsheet. The file contained times, dates, and the visitors' relationship to the prisoner. Aside from the usual list of people associated with the investigation, only Adam's attorney, Erin Meadows, and his parents — Fyodor and Anya — had been granted access to him while he awaited trial.

As it turned out, the list of visitors after his conviction proved even shorter; only Eveginy Polyakov had been allowed to see him in Salem … once, in August of 2012, shortly after Adam's transfer to the State penitentiary.

The full list of visitation requests — coming in the form of scanned log pages — was much, much longer. Half of the journalists in the city, along with dozens from the national press outlets, had asked for — and been denied — access to the accused. Amazing what murdering an heiress will do for your media profile, Jeff thought, sourly.

Even Eveginy had been declined visitation on four occasions before Adam's sentencing. There were other names Jeff recognized, like Rob LaSalle and Crystal Samuels, but only one caught him by surprise: *Kozlov, S.* The same delicate handwriting appeared seven times over the first year of Adam's confinement, starting with the day after his arrest in Portland.

When he'd gleaned what he could from the register, Jeff dialed the number he had for Fyodor Polyakov. The call went straight to voice mail. He left a brief message, along with his cell number. Then he placed a second call, this one to the University of Washington's registrar's office. After explaining who he was, and what he was looking for, he was assured that they could get the information he wanted within a couple of hours, if not sooner, provided Jeff could obtain a warrant.

The next call went to Kyle Washington, at Orbison's office. Washington said he'd get right on the warrant request. Jeff thanked him just as Paul ducked his head through the doorway.

"I think you better see this," he said. Not waiting for an answer, he disappeared back into the outer hall. By the time Jeff caught up with him, they were halfway to the conference room.

"I was reviewing the security footage from the day Manny Cespedes was arrested, and I almost missed it," Paul said over his shoulder.

"Missed what?"

Paul didn't answer, striding into their war room instead. Sam sat at the conference table with pages of hotel registers spread out in front of her. She grinned when they entered. "We did it, boss," she said. "We fucking did it!"

Paul sat down in front of his laptop. The fifty-inch monitor behind him had been linked wirelessly to the computer. When he clicked on a video file that had already been queued up, the black-and-white image of one of the Lloyd Center mall's parking entrances filled the center of the screen.

"Here is Cespedes and his girlfriend, pulling into the parking garage across the street from the theater," Paul said, hitting the pause icon as Manny's distinctive 1970 Dodge Coronet pulled into the frame. The time stamp in the lower right showed *3:52 PM*.

"I assumed that anyone following Manny would be right behind him," he continued, pressing the play icon, "but what I didn't take into consideration was just how damned unique the Coronet is. It would take a blind man to not be able to spot that car in the garage."

Over the next two minutes, two more cars entered the garage, then nothing for almost another minute. At the 3:56 mark of the footage, Paul hit pause once more. A light-colored, late model Audi — an A4, from what Jeff could see — had taken center-frame. Without explaining its significance, Paul fast-forwarded through the footage.

"Manny's car — with our shooter inside, presumably — leaves the garage again at 4:10. Then, at 5:15, it pulls back in. Now, here's where it gets interesting. That Audi that we saw earlier? Here it is at 5:21; six minutes after Manny's Coronet was returned."

"And two minutes after someone anonymously tipped off police as to where they could find the car," Sam added.

From the angle of the camera, Jeff could see that there were two men in the front seat. Their faces were impossible to make out, however. "It could just be a coincidence," he pointed out.

Paul smiled and shook his head. "I was pretty sure I recognized that car, and a quick check of the license plate confirmed that it's registered to one Leonid Konigsberg, but currently being driven by … Nicholas Averill."

Jeff looked over. "Nicholas Averill, as in the travel writer whose rental car was used in the Meadows' hit-and-run?"

"And guess who checked into the Water Street Inn in Newport two days before the Ruizes' boat blew up?" Sam asked with a satisfied smirk.

"I'll be a sonofabitch," Jeff said, matching their smiles with a grin of his own. "Who else have you told?"

"Just you so far," Paul said.

"All right, I want the Feds all over this. Call your friend at the FBI … what was his name? Yance?" Paul nodded. "Let Yance know, so they can put out a warrant for Eveginy and Averill. I'll let Orbison know what you've found."

Neither Sam nor Paul seemed overjoyed about his plan.

"Look, I know you want to finish this," Jeff said, "but there are too many lives at stake, and we need everyone on this we can get. You guys have done a fantastic job, but let's let the police do their job."

MARKUS WAS ON the phone with Fyodor Polyakov when Jeff entered the outer office. Jeff waited until his office door closed before picking up line one. "Mr. Polyakov?" he said, settling into his chair.

"Fyodor, please," his caller reminded him, gently. "I just got home and saw that you had called. What can I do for you, Jeffery? More questions?"

"Just one. Do you know who Adam was dating before he started up with Larissa Kozlov?"

The Russian chuckled. "Could you be more specific? My son was a very popular young man."

"Probably someone special," Jeff told him. "Someone he might have been seeing right before he met Larissa Kozlov."

"Adam never allowed himself to get serious about any girl in school, and after ..." Polyakov's voice trailed off for a moment. "He did tell his mother about someone, though, after he went to work for the security company."

"Did he mention her name?" Jeff asked.

"No. I'm sorry, but for some reason he didn't want to go into details. Even his mother couldn't get him to say much, not even where they'd met. I'm afraid I haven't been much help," Fyodor added, apologetically.

"Actually, Fyodor, I think you may have been of great help," Jeff assured him. "I'll be in touch."

"Well, that's that," Paul told Sam as he hung up the phone. "With that information about Averill and Eveginy Polyakov, Yance is going to be a rock star at the Bureau for the next few days."

"So, the Feds are going to pick them up?"

Paul nodded. "I gave Averill's last known address to Yance, the one at the yacht club. Presumably they should have some idea where to find Eveginy, since they've been looking into his activities for a while."

"In the meantime, we're on the outside looking in," Sam said. Resignation was etched into her expression.

"Where Averill and the Ruiz case is concerned, yeah," he admitted. "Yance did promise to keep us posted. The other murders don't fall into the Bureau's jurisdiction, although I'm sure they'll cooperate with the DA's office in any way they can."

"And how long do you think Orbison is going to let us keep looking into the other deaths?" Sam asked.

Paul shrugged. He guessed that they both knew the answer to that.

Chapter 36

Jeff's call caught the DA in her office between meetings. He filled her in on what Paul and Sam had uncovered.

"I'll ask the Chief's office to coordinate with the FBI on the arrests," Orbison assured him, relief clear in her voice. "And we'll reopen those cases, too. Looks like you guys have aced yourselves out of a job. Tell Niko that the department will still pay for the full month of your services," she added.

"I'm sure he'll be relieved to hear that. What about Manny Cespedes?"

He heard Orbison sigh. "We'll have to cut him loose. It's been nice having him off the streets for a while, but ..."

Jeff thought about Paul's theory on why Cespedes had been framed for Myer's murder. "Hold off on that for another day or two," he urged. "At least until you have Averill and Polyakov in custody. I'm working on an angle that might ... *might* ..." he emphasized, "help you nail Manny on those Eastside shootings."

"An angle?" Orbison sounded confused, and a little concerned. "Jeff, I appreciate what you and your team have done, but it's out of your hands now. I can't back you anymore."

"This isn't about the trial murders," he assured her. "Not directly, anyway. Just do what you can about Manny. I'll let you know what I find out."

"Whatever you have in mind, keep this office out of it."

"Of course." He disconnected with Orbison, then he buzzed Markus. "See if you can get in touch with Andrei Kozlov. He's probably at his house on Orcas Island."

"What should I tell him it's regarding?" his assistant asked.

"Tell Mr. Kozlov that I need to come back to see him. Tomorrow, if possible. Tell him ..." Jeff paused a moment. *At least Markus has plausible deniability in all of this,* he realized. *He doesn't know that Orbison just dropped us from the case. No sense in taking anyone else down with me.*

"Tell him that the DA's office has just a few more questions about his daughter's murder," he said at last. "And Markus? Get me on the first flight to Seattle in the morning, with a connection to Orcas Island."

Chapter 37

Nick had picked up on the surveillance teams before they were even in place. Federal agents, he guessed. So far he'd only spotted the two sitting in a dark SUV at the far end of the yacht club's parking lot. *But Feds are like ants,* he thought with irritation. *If you see two, there's bound to be a nest of them nearby.* It hadn't escaped his notice that the Sheriff's patrol boat had idled by twice in the last hour, either. The wolves were most definitely at the door.

He picked up his mobile and dialed Eveginy's man. "Pick the girl up," he said, simply. He disconnected before the man at the other end could answer. Then he punched a new number into his phone.

"Mrs. Dawes?" he said quietly. "I'd like to speak to you about your husband … and your daughter."

Chapter 38

Markus stepped into Jeff's office. "There's someone named Vasily holding on line one," he said, quietly. "He wouldn't give me a last name. I tried to explain that you were unavailable."

"That's okay, Markus," Jeff told him with a smile. "I've been expecting his call."

He waited until the door had closed behind his assistant, then he picked up the receiver. "Mr. Kozlov," he said cheerfully. "I was wondering when you were going to call."

"I thought we'd agreed that you were through looking into my niece's case." The Russian's accent seemed more pronounced with his anger.

"That's funny. I don't recall agreeing to that."

Jeff's mobile phone started to vibrate on his desktop. He glanced down and saw that Annie was trying to reach him. He sent the call to voice mail.

"Why are you seeing my brother tomorrow?" Kozlov's voice rumbled through the phone.

"I'm guessing we both know the answer to that," Jeff told him. "So let's talk about Eveginy Polyakov, instead."

There was a moment's silence at the other end of the line. "What about Eveginy?"

"He's managed to put your organization under the FBI's magnifying glass." Jeff paused to let that resonate. "I might be able to minimize the damage," he added, "but this is a limited-time offer."

While Vasily mulled that over, Jeff's phone started buzzing on the desk again. *Jesus, Annie,* he thought with irritation. *Give it a rest.*

"I'll be arriving at SeaTac tomorrow morning," he told the Russian. "Meet me in the lobby of the Airport Marriott around eight, and we can discuss this before I catch my flight to Orcas Island."

Jeff hung up before Kozlov could answer.

He leaned back in his desk chair, trying not to think about all of the ways this plan could blow up in his face. Then he picked up his mobile and called his wife back.

"Sorry about that, Annie," he said when she answered. "I was in the middle of an important call ..."

"What the hell are you in to?" Her voice was so shrill he instinctively yanked the phone away from his ear.

"Annie, calm down! Tell me what's going on."

"Don't tell me to calm down. Don't you dare fucking tell me to calm down." She sounded as though she was teetering on the edge of hysteria. "He said he was going to kill Mikaela ... and me ... if you didn't call them off."

Oh, sweet Jesus, no.

"Call who off, Annie?" he asked, struggling to keep his own voice calm. "Who did he say he wanted me to call off?"

"The federal agents, or police, or whoever the fuck is watching him," she screamed before she dissolved into racking sobs.

"Annie, listen to me ... Honey? Please, just listen to me. I'll take care of this. I promise I will."

"Just call them off, Jeff," she pleaded, her voice now little more than a whimper. "Just call them off ..."

"Where are you, Annie? Are you at home?"

"Yes," she managed.

"Stay there. Lock the doors and don't let anyone in until the police arrive. Where is Mikaela?" he asked. Annie didn't answer; he could hear her crying softly in the background.

Frustrated, he hung up and shouted for Markus as he dialed his daughter's number. His assistant popped his head through the doorway immediately, a look of concern on his face.

"Call Orbison's office. Tell them one of their suspects just called in a threat to my wife and daughter. Have them send a unit to my house immediately ... Mikaela? Baby, are you all right?"

"Of course I'm all right," his daughter said in an exasperated tone.

"Where are you?"

"What do you mean, where am I? What the hell …"

"Mikaela, I don't have time for this right now," he snapped. "Just tell me where you are."

The other end went quiet for a second, then, "I'm at Palatine Coffee, just off campus," she whispered, all traces of irritation replaced by anxiety.

"Stay right where you are. The police will be there in a few minutes." He lowered the phone and turned back to Markus. "Mikaela is at Palatine Coffee, by the Lewis and Clark campus."

Markus hurried back to his desk.

"Dad? You're scaring me. What's going on? Is Mom all right?"

"I'm sorry, Baby," he said, managing a little calm in his tone. "Mom is fine, and everything is going to be all right. It is." *Please, God, let everything be all right.* "Just go with the police when they arrive, and I'll explain it all later. I promise."

Markus hurried back in. "ETA of four minutes for both Annie and Mikaela," he said. "Cynthia Orbison is holding on line two."

Jeff nodded. "Baby," he said softly to his daughter, "I have to go now, but you call me if you need me."

"Be careful, Dad."

He smiled, emotion almost getting the best of him. "I will," he promised. "I love you, Kiddo."

Markus watched him anxiously. Jeff managed a tense smile. "I'm fine. Do me a favor; call Paul and Samantha and let them know what's going on."

Markus headed back to his desk once more. Jeff took a long breath and exhaled slowly. Then he picked up his office line. "Cynthia, either Averill or Polyakov — or both — know they're being watched."

"I know, Jeff. Markus filled me in. Patrol units should be with your family any minute, and I've been in touch with the FBI. They're pulling back from Averill's place for the time being."

"What about Eveginy Polyakov?"

"They don't know where he is, yet. Apparently, he hasn't been under active surveillance for some time. How are you holding up?"

He laughed softly. "Twenty years wearing a badge and nothing like this ever happened. One week working for you ..."

"Yeah, yeah. Are Maxwell and Ledbetter okay?"

"I sent them home after you let us go," he told her. "Markus is touching base with them now."

Chapter 39

Paul pulled into his driveway behind Lucy's Honda Civic. Seeing her battered old car brought a smile. This would be the first time in a week he'd made it home before nine. His body creaked as he climbed out of the Blazer. Tired didn't begin to describe how he felt, now that the pressure had been lifted off of the team. What he really wanted to do was lay down and sleep for two days. Somehow he doubted that would go over well with Lucy. She had been incredibly understanding, but this wasn't what she'd signed up for.

Maybe dinner at Andina tonight, he thought as he unlocked the front door and stepped into the dark house. Like most homes in Portland, his didn't have air conditioning. With the notable exception of this year's heat wave, temperatures in the Rose City usually reached the 90's a handful of times all year. With the forecast calling for another scorcher, Paul had left the ceiling fans running all morning and the curtains drawn to block the afternoon sun. As a result, the house felt at least a few of degrees cooler inside than out.

He set his cell phone and keys in the little porcelain dish on the table near the door. "Lucy, I'm home," he called out in his best Ricky Ricardo accent, a joke his girlfriend never failed to roll her eyes at.

The only response he got was Barenaked Ladies' *Who Needs Sleep*, thumping away on the stereo at a notch louder than Paul would have preferred. It was one of the differences between the two of them; the first thing Lucy always did when she got home was turn Pandora on, while he was much more of an ESPN kind of guy.

That's what man caves are for, I guess. Of course he hadn't gotten much traction on his plan to convert the spare bedroom into a 'guy space' since Lucy had moved in. He smiled at the thought. It was a small enough price to have her in his life.

Wandering into the kitchen, Paul snagged a Black Butte Porter from the fridge and looked around for the bottle opener that used to be on the side of the refrigerator. *Used to be,* he remembered with a sigh. Now it resided in the drawer by the sink, neatly arranged with all of the utensils he'd never given much thought to before.

Somehow, Lucy had managed to nudge him gently towards her ideas on domesticity and housekeeping over the last six months.

Frankly, he liked it, even if it did mean no more drinking from the milk carton.

He heard a tinny version of Michael Jackson's *Beat It* start up. Her smart phone was propped up against the napkin holder on the small kitchen table, ringing merrily away. If there was one thing he would change about Lucy, it was her choice of ring tones. *Michael Jackson? Seriously?*

Paul ignored it and continued savoring his beer. He prided himself on not being one of those insecure assholes who had to check the caller ID to see what his girlfriend was up to. *You either trust the person you're with or you don't. End of story,* he thought as the phone stopped ringing.

A moment later, it started up again. After four rings it stopped … and then began ringing once more.

Accepting that there was a limit to even his lack of curiosity, Paul set his beer down on the counter and wandered over to Lucy's phone. *Unknown,* he saw on the caller ID before the caller hung up a third time.

"Goddamned telemarketers," he muttered, even as an unsettling feeling began to creep over him. Why the hell didn't she come and answer her phone?

"Lucy?" he called out, again. Still no response.

"Beat it, Beat it …" rang out once more, echoing in the otherwise quiet kitchen.

This time Paul reached out and picked up the phone, swiping his finger across the screen to answer. "Hello?" he said, irritated by the tension in his own voice.

"I was beginning to think you would never pick up, Paul."

He recognized the voice at once. Averill. Cold fear spread through him.

"What have you done with her?" he asked, battling to sound more calm than he felt.

"Oh, good," said the man at the other end of the line. "I was afraid I'd have to spell out the obvious. Lucy is fine … she will continue to be fine as long as you prove helpful."

"Barking up the wrong tree, Nick. You have me confused with someone who has pull."

Averill laughed. "It wouldn't be the first mistake I've made, obviously."

The line went quiet for a moment before he added, quietly, "If I am wrong, however, Lucy will suffer needlessly. I'm very sorry for that."

"Let her go right now, and I'll do whatever you ask me to."

Another laugh. "Oh, please. I acknowledge the gesture, but we both know life is about leverage, and right now I have leverage."

Paul slowly sank down onto the straight-backed chair beside him. "What do you want?" he asked.

"For now, very little. No more FBI or police at my doorstep, or I kill Lucy. No more patrol boats that just happen to drift by, or I kill Lucy. The wrong helicopter circles overhead and …" Averill paused a moment, an obviously dramatic pause. "Well, there's really no need to be redundant, is there?"

"I'll do what I can," Paul said.

"Please do. And I will do what I can to keep your girlfriend safe." Then the line went dead.

Paul held Lucy's phone tight against the side of his face for several moments. *Control … control,* he vowed. *I can't help her if I lose control. I can't help her if …* He took a deep breath. *I can't help her … I can't …*

He realized that his own phone was buzzing in the other room. How long had it been ringing? He hurried in, checked the caller ID. It was Sam.

"Paul?" She sounded frantic. "Jesus! Markus and I have both been trying to reach you! Did you hear what happened?"

"He's got Lucy, Sam," Paul managed. Everything was crashing down around him. "Averill's got Lucy."

Chapter 40

Lucy faded in and out of awareness. Fragments of thoughts and memories drifted in her head. The air around her felt … heavy. The floor shifted and rolled beneath her. She tried to focus in the darkness, tried to …

Her eyelids — as heavy as the air around her — closed slowly. *So tired …*

A sudden lurch jolted her back into semi-consciousness. Lucy willed herself to open her eyes again, to stay awake, but the absence of light was very nearly complete. There was only motion and a low, rhythmic hum. Some part of her brain registered the sound as tires on pavement. She must have been put into a car after … *after what? What happened?* As hard as she tried, Lucy couldn't remember, couldn't concentrate. Couldn't clear the fog that had settled around her thoughts.

The motion and the road noise lulled her quickly back into unconsciousness.

SHE WOKE FROM a dreamless sleep, only to find herself in an even deeper darkness. The motion and road noise were gone. It took Lucy a moment to realize that someone had placed a mask securely over her eyes. She could feel the coarse cloth pulled tight against her face. They'd also gagged her, possibly with the same material. Her jaw ached from being held open for too long.

How long have I been here? she wondered.

Her head rested on a firm pillow. That was the only part of her situation that had improved. They — whoever they were — had laid her on the floor, on her side, against a wall. She could feel cool air along the floorboard. Her arms were secured awkwardly behind her back, her legs bound at the ankles. Struggling against her restraints only caused them to dig painfully into her skin. Lucy forced herself to relax, to try to recall how she'd gotten there.

She remembered turning on the stereo when she'd gotten home from work. Then she'd gone into the bedroom to change.

As she'd started unbuttoning her blouse ... Lucy vaguely remembered a hand over her mouth ... Panic as an arm wrapped around hers to keep her from struggling.

Whatever they'd used on her had put Lucy out for quite a while. It had also left her with a hell of a headache, and a mouth as dry as dust. But why had they taken her ... and what were they going to do? She felt the panic start to build anew. Lucy fought against her restraints as tears welled up, quickly soaking through the heavy material over her eyes.

"Please, you'll hurt yourself." The words came from somewhere above her ... like the Voice of God. The man's voice was gentle and deep, his words tinged with an accent.

Lucy stopped struggling. Then she screamed into her gag in frustration, the sound comically muffled in her ears. When at last she ran out of breath, Lucy heard a creaking noise nearby, like the ancient springs of an old bed.

"Do you feel better?" the man asked softly. There was a trace of humor in his tone and, somehow, empathy. "I'm sorry about putting you on the floor, but I was afraid you'd roll off the bed and injure yourself."

Eastern European, she thought. The tumblers fell into place. *This is one of the people Paul is after.*

"I'm going to help you up now," he told her, "and set you on the bed. Do you understand?"

She nodded, too frightened and too tired to manage anything else.

"Good ... I don't want to hurt you, and I won't if you follow my instructions. I would imagine you are thirsty, yes?"

Again she nodded.

"That usually happens," he said, reassuringly. "I will remove your gag and give you water. No one can hear you here, but if you scream too much, it will go right back on."

Lucy heard the bed groan under his weight. Large, strong hands grasped her upper arms with surprising gentleness and lifted her easily onto the mattress.

"Move back," he urged, guiding her until the backs of her legs were up against the side of the bed. Then she felt him fumbling with the gag in her mouth.

At last it came free. Lucy worked her jaw back and forth, trying to ease the dull, aching pain. A plastic bottle was pressed to her lips and she gulped the water greedily. The man's hand supported the back of her head as she drank.

"Thank you," she whispered when at last he pulled the bottle away.

"You're welcome. Would you like some more?" Even as he asked, he returned the bottle to her mouth.

Lucy drank again. After a few moments she gently nudged the container away from her lips as water trickled down her chin and onto her chest.

"I'm glad that you are all right," her captor said, his voice maddeningly pleasant.

"Why are you doing this to me?" Her own voice sounded raspy and harsh by comparison.

Instead of answering, he gently laid her back onto the bed, a pillow once more beneath her head. "In a few minutes you will be asleep again," he told her.

She shook her head, then realized what he must mean; "The water?" she asked.

"It's better this way." The bed shifted beneath her as he pulled himself away. "Rest. This will all be over soon enough."

"Why?" It was more plea than question. The door clicked closed in response, his footsteps fading into the other room.

"WHY?" Lucy screamed into the darkness, her anger and frustration seeking release. Her cry went unanswered.

Chapter 41

If the conference room at Ferrum Security hadn't felt like an actual War Room before, Sam thought, it sure as hell did now. Jeff paced anxiously in the back of the room, talking to someone at the DA's office about Annie and Mikaela. On the other side of the conference table, Paul stared silently at the victim board as though he expected to see Lucy's picture appear suddenly.

For the first time, Sam found herself thankful that Jen had moved on with her life. The thought of Averill threatening someone she loved … she shivered despite the warmth of the room, and whispered a prayer for Lucy.

The FBI had taken Averill's threats very seriously. The yacht club had been closed off to the public, and everyone in the surrounding houseboats had been contacted and evacuated. Surveillance teams had been pulled back to a more discreet distance, and the Sheriff's patrol boats had been ordered to position themselves at least three hundred yards — upriver and down — from the houseboat. From there, they could prevent any river traffic from approaching from either direction and still keep an eye on the yacht club. Averill wasn't going anywhere.

Jeff put his phone down on the table and settled heavily into the chair beside Sam.

"How are Annie and Mikaela doing?" she asked.

He shrugged. "They're safe. And Annie sounds very, very pissed. Orbison put them both up in a suite at the Hilton, so at least they have room service," he added with a half-hearted smile.

Sam nodded. "Why don't you go be with them?" she asked.

Jeff glanced over to where Paul was sitting. "There's still work to be done," he said, simply.

Paul looked up at that. He turned from the board to face them. "There are plenty of people on this," he said, his voice quiet. "Go to your family."

Sam saw the conflict in Jeff's eyes. "Are you sure?"

"I'm sure."

Jeff stood, reluctantly. "You need me, you call me."

"Damn right we will," Paul assured him. "Now go."

Jeff nodded unhappily and moved to the door. As he started to open it, he turned back to look at them. "I am so sorry that I got you involved."

"And if you hadn't, these bastards would still be out there killing people," Paul pointed out, his voice uncharacteristically tight with emotion. "Never apologize for doing what's right. No one could have anticipated this."

Jeff took that in, then stepped out into the hall. The door closed behind him with a soft click. Sam said nothing, waiting patiently for her partner to break the silence. Paul was once again staring at the whiteboard, deep in thought.

"Tell me what the damned point is," he asked at last. His anger had a strange, almost molten quality to it. "Averill is no closer to getting away now than he was before. Less so, in fact. This paints a huge target on his ass. So why take Lucy? Why add kidnapping to his laundry list?"

Sam said nothing. This was new territory for them both, probably, but certainly for her. Paul scowled from the other side of the table.

"Come on, Sam," he urged, "I can't do this by myself. Averill isn't a fucking idiot. He knows the FBI will move in eventually, whether he has a hostage or not. What the fuck are we missing?"

"All right," she said, tentatively, stepping over to the board. She might not have a background in law enforcement, but the Marine Corps must have taught her something about strategy and planning. She studied the pictures and their captions. Finally, she turned to her partner.

"Averill's a professional, right?" she asked. Paul nodded in agreement. "Well, a professional would undoubtedly have prepared a Plan B, an escape if something went wrong," she reasoned. "If so, then grabbing Lucy probably wasn't spontaneous, or an act of desperation."

"You think this was his exit strategy all along, if things went south. That makes sense," Paul admitted.

"So, let's start with what we know about Averill." She looked over the list of victims so far, trying hard not to imagine Lucy's picture alongside the others. "We can't be sure if Polyakov was directly involved in any of these, so let's focus on the ones that Averill almost certainly handled … like Porter Richardson's death out in the woods," Sam said, pointing to the juror's profile on the board.

"And Alex Burwell," Paul said. "A high-profile 'suicide' in a locked car can't be that easy to pull off cleanly."

He studied the other victims' profiles for a moment. "Gatimo could have been either Polyakov or Averill," he reasoned. "Pushing someone down a flight of stairs isn't exactly elegant. Neither was Erin Meadows' hit-and-run."

"Agreed," Sam said. "Same goes for Alan Russell taking a header off a bridge. Besides, we know Eveginy was checked into a hotel near Grand River the night before. What about Vonetta Myers?" she asked.

"Two shots, pretty much center-mass, from a moving car? That has 'professional' written all over it. And the Ruiz murders were obviously Averill. Between methodically sabotaging their boat and …" Paul's thought trailed off.

Sam could see something simmering behind his eyes. "What?"

He got up and walked over to stand in front of the Ruiz photos. "You have got to be fucking kidding me," he muttered to himself. He was so focused on the board, Sam might not even be in the room.

"Hey, you want to share with the rest of the class?" she asked, frustrated at suddenly being left out of the process.

"You were right, Sam," he said. "This *was* the plan, all along. The son of a bitch has been preparing his escape from the beginning. And I think I know how he's going to do it."

Chapter 42

Sam guided her Subaru south along Macadam. The Willamette River was on her left, flowing back the way she'd just come … back toward the city. The water looked ink-black now that the sun had set behind the West Hills.

Paul sat beside her, trying to get through to his friend, Yance, at the Bureau's Portland office.

"Shit," he muttered. "Goddamned voice mail." He paused, waiting for the greeting to finish, then, "Yance, this is Paul … I think I know what Averill is up to. Call me as soon as you can."

He terminated the call and slumped back in his seat. "If Yance is at the yacht club, it might be a while before he checks his messages," he said, clearly frustrated. He raised the phone again and punched another number in.

"Plan B?" Sam asked. Paul nodded.

"I need to reach Agent Yance Cooper as soon as possible," he told the person who answered. "I know that he's out of the office. That's why I need to reach him." Paul sounded like he was struggling to stay patient, and losing the fight. "Look, just get word to him that Paul Maxwell is trying to get in touch. Tell him that I think I know what Averill is up to, but we have to act fast."

Sam focused on her driving. For once she was staying a little below the posted speed limit. They'd cleared the dense commercial district traffic south of the city and now traveled through a mix of strip malls and aging office complexes to their right, more upscale buildings to their left. Sam stayed as close to the river as possible, turning left whenever a side road opened to the east.

"Well,' Paul said as he hung up, "let's hope that idiot takes me seriously and gets the message to Yance before they're too late. How far from the yacht club are we?"

"I'm guessing about a mile, give or take."

"Should be something soon, then." He studied the properties bordering the river as they passed by.

"It would help if we knew what we were looking for," she pointed out.

Paul didn't respond, his focus on the passing scenery. Headlights filled the rearview mirror for a moment, then an old Jeep Wrangler roared past on their left with a blare of the horn. Sam glared as the vehicle's tail lights faded into the distance.

"They drive like you do, don't they?" Paul said, with a chuckle.

Sam ignored the jab. "How sure are you about this?" she asked. "I mean, if you're right about Averill's plan, we can't even be certain that he'll head for this side of the river."

"The risks go up if he tries to cross to the east bank," Paul pointed out. "If there's one thing I'm sure of with this bastard, it's that any risk he takes is going to be calculated, and minimized as much as possible. What we're looking for is somewhere along here."

Sam still had her doubts. Paul's theory hinged upon they're being right about how Averill had managed the Ruiz boat sabotage in Newport. But this still beat sitting at a conference table waiting for something to happen, so she kept her pessimism to herself.

They were about a half-mile out from the yacht club now, passing an old manufacturing or warehouse facility along the waterfront. It was all peeling paint and rusted metal. The asphalt pad beyond the chain-link fence was cracked and uneven. Tall weeds pushed up through the pavement. As the Subaru drew even with the gated entrance, Sam slowed and rolled the window down to get a better look.

"See something?" Paul asked, leaning forward to look past her as she braked the car to a gentle stop along the narrow shoulder of the road, opposite the gate.

She didn't answer immediately as she studied the apparently deserted property. Most of the area beyond the fence lay in darkness. There were two large structures at the far side of the property, long and narrow, built parallel to the river and to each other. The ground-floor windows Sam could see from the road were boarded up and barred. The upper windows, and the skylights running the length of the buildings, were dark.

"I think I saw an SUV or a pickup parked between those two buildings," she told Paul. She backed the Subaru up slowly to give them a better sightline. Sam could just make out the grill and headlights of a large, dark-colored vehicle. "Doesn't mean anything, necessarily," she admitted, "but it just seemed out of place."

"God, I love your instincts," Paul told her, quietly. He gave her a nudge, pointing over to a sign attached to the fence.

This property monitored by WHITEMAN SECURITY

"Come on," he said. "Let's get in there and take a look."

Sam saw the determination in his eyes. "All right, but we're calling the boss first."

JEFF SHOWED HIS ID to the uniformed officer standing guard outside of the hotel room. The officer — Sanchez, according to his nametag — waved off Jeff's driver's license. "I know who you are, Mr. Dawes. I started at Metro during your last year there."

Jeff managed a tired smile. "So, how are they doing?" he asked, nodding toward the door.

Sanchez shrugged. "Your wife was pretty shook up when they arrived, I guess. The DA's office arranged for a doctor to come check on her. That was about an hour ago. It's been pretty quiet in there since then."

"How about Mikaela?"

"Your daughter?" Sanchez shook his head, the beginnings of a grin on his face. "That girl is something else. I pity anyone who tries to come after her."

Jeff couldn't help but laugh. "Try raising her," he said. "Can I go in?"

Mikaela threw the door back before Sanchez could even knock. "I thought I heard you out here. Where have you *been*?" The irritation in her voice didn't quite sync up with the relief Jeff saw in his daughter's eyes. Then her arms were around him and they hugged, fiercely.

Sanchez smiled as he nudged the door to the room open a little wider, a gentle reminder that they were still exposed in the hallway.

Jeff nodded his thanks and guided his daughter back through the doorway. Sanchez closed the door behind them.

The county had arranged for a suite; two bedrooms, separated by a living room. There was no sign of Annie. "The doctor gave mom a sedative," Mikaela explained as they settled on the sofa. "That — along with a couple of vodka tonics from room service — and she was out like a light."

He thought he detected an undercurrent of disapproval in her tone. "How are you holding up?" he asked.

"Me?" She wrapped her arms around herself, leaning back into the far corner of the couch. "Okay, I guess, now that you're here. What's this all about, Dad? Who's threatening us?"

Jeff gave her the *CliffsNotes* version of the investigation, starting with Alex's theory and ending with Averill's call to Annie. He decided to leave his theory about Adam out of the narrative, however, and Lucy's disappearance. Mikaela had enough to deal with.

"So, what happens next?" she asked.

"As far as I'm concerned, there is no next. I didn't want any part of this to begin with. Now that I've involved you and your mom ..."

"I don't see how you involved us," his daughter pointed out. She studied him in silence. When he didn't answer with anything but a shrug of his shoulders, Mikaela got up and walked over to the mini-bar. Jeff watched her pick up what looked suspiciously like a bottle of Knob Creek bourbon. "Amazing what you can order through room service," she said over her shoulder as she dropped ice into two tumblers. "I figured we could both use a drink tonight."

She returned to the sofa, handing one of the glasses to her father as she sat back down. He could tell something was weighing on her, so he sipped his drink and waited in silence.

"I haven't been the best daughter for a while," she said at last. Her voice was so soft, she might have been speaking to herself.

He couldn't help but chuckle. "What the hell are you talking about?"

Mikaela looked at him, tilting her head in that way she had of saying, *I'll talk, you listen.*

He sat back and took another sip of bourbon. Apparently satisfied that her father had gotten the message, she continued. "Before Mom's second vodka tonic kicked in, she filled me in on a few things."

Jeff decided to let this one play out. He took a deep drink and nodded for her to continue.

"You weren't the one having an affair, were you?" she asked. It was clear from her tone that she already knew the answer.

His stomach twisted as he looked down at the glass in his hand. "It's not that simple, Kiddo," he said at last. "If I hadn't been so focused on work, if I'd been more available ..."

She reached out and gave his hand a squeeze to silence him. "Don't you dare make excuses for her. There is no way to justify what she did to you."

"Maybe not," he allowed. "But nothing happens in a vacuum."

"She cheated on you with Alex Burwell! With your best friend! And then accused you of having an affair with his wife. I don't get how you can be so goddamned calm about this." She paused, obviously trying to get her anger under control. Then, in a steadier voice, she asked, "Is their affair why you bailed on the job at the DA's office?"

Jeff sat back, taking another long pull from his drink. Then he shook his head. "I wish I could say that it was," he said. "but I'd already put my notice in before I found out."

Mikaela looked surprised. "So, if the affair wasn't the reason, why *did* you leave your job?"

He managed a tired smile. "Honestly, I don't think that I'm ready to talk to you about that," he told her. The look in her eyes told him that she wasn't going to settle for that, however. "I crossed a line I shouldn't have."

"With one of your cases?"

He didn't answer, and watched his daughter's surprise transition into curiosity. "Wow! Nothing ominous about that," she said. Before she could push for more, his phone picked that moment to ring.

Jeff glanced at the caller ID. *Samantha Ledbetter*. He resisted the urge to answer.

"You should get that, Dad," Mikaela told him. "I'm guessing it's probably important." There was no sarcasm, not even resignation in her voice.

She is clearly not her mother's child, he thought as he answered the phone. "What's going on, Sam?" he asked, his eyes still on his daughter. "Any news on Lucy?"

"Not yet, but Paul thinks he knows what Averill's escape plan is." She quickly laid Paul's theory out for him. "We think we may have found something, too. There's a newer SUV parked in what looks to be an abandoned warehouse complex, about a half-mile downriver from the yacht club. Oh, and there's a Whiteman Security sign posted out front," she added. "We're going in to take look around."

Jeff leaned forward. "The hell you are, Sam. Leave it to the police."

"How long have you known Paul?" Sam asked.

"Listen, I'm serious," he said, adamantly. "Do not put yourself in danger, do you understand? Tell me where you're at."

Jeff had her repeat the address twice. "I'm calling this in," he told her. "Then I'm on my way to you. Both of you stay put."

The other end of the line was quiet for a moment, then, "I'll do what I can," Sam promised unenthusiastically. "We'll let you know if anything breaks."

Jeff disconnected, then speed-dialed Cynthia Orbison's mobile number. Mikaela was watching him closely.

"This is Jeff," he said when the DA answered. "Paul and Samantha think they may have a lead on Averill … 4211 Riverside Road. It's an old warehouse facility or something. Get someone there as soon as possible, okay? And have them go in quietly, Cynthia. For all we know, that could be where they're holding Lucy. I'll be there in twenty minutes."

"Who is Lucy?" Mikaela asked when he'd disconnected.

Jeff held up his hand. He hit redial for Sam, but the call went straight to voicemail. He left a brief message to let her know that the police were on their way, and reminded them to sit tight. Then he tried Paul's number with the same result. Frustrated, he disconnected.

"Dad, tell me who Lucy is," Mikaela insisted, impatiently.

"Lucy is Paul's girlfriend." He hesitated, then ... "She's been taken."

"By the people who threatened Mom?" Jeff nodded. "Dad, you have to finish this. Now."

Chapter 43

Nick had practiced this so many times, he could practically do it with his eyes closed. Just let the current do its job. Five minutes in, a hundred yards or so. He decided to risk a quick glance.

The nearest patrol boat was at least a click away, much too far to see him bobbing in the dark waters of the Willamette. He glanced at the Hammerhead watch strapped to his wrist. *9:58 … two minutes to go. Then we'll see how well this plan works.*

Someone on the patrol boat cast a perfunctory searchlight across the water, probably more from boredom than from a genuine hope of spotting anything. Nick slid quietly beneath the surface and relaxed, letting the river current slowly close the distance between himself and the police.

Chapter 44

Lucy's eyes fluttered open and closed a few times before she realized that the mask — or whatever they'd used to keep her blind — had been removed while she'd slept. The room around her was dark, the only light a soft glow coming from under the closed door a few feet away.

She was still on the bed, in pretty much the same position she remembered herself in before whatever they'd put in the water had knocked her out again. But the restraints at her wrists and ankles were gone. Lucy sat up slowly, cringing at the squawking bedsprings beneath her. Her head felt fuzzy. She took deep breaths, exhaling slowly while she tried to attach a little bit of rational thought to what was going on.

She swung her legs slowly over the side of the mattress and stood. Her legs felt shaky, but they held. A few awkward steps and she was at the closed door. It may have been only three feet from the bed, but it felt like the longest three feet of her life. She prayed for the room to stop revolving and her head to clear.

There was no sound from outside the room, she realized. No TV, no radio … nothing. *And if I go out there, what? A bullet between the eyes?*

Lucy took a slow breath. If they'd wanted her dead, she reasoned, she'd be dead. If they'd wanted her to stay put, they wouldn't have removed her restraints. She pushed the door open cautiously, her eyes squinting against the light coming from the overhead fixture in the hallway beyond. The only things that greeted her were a battered, threadbare old couch and a fragile-looking coffee table. No pictures on the walls, no drapes covering the grimy windows. Overgrown shrubs blocked any view of the world outside.

A door to Lucy's right led to a tiny bathroom. An opening at the other end of what passed for a living room led to a small kitchenette. Both rooms were empty. Lucy was alone. On the counter, by the ancient refrigerator, she found an old flip-phone. She snatched at it, praying that it still worked, that it wasn't some cruel trick.

As the phone powered up, Lucy noticed a piece of paper folded neatly beneath it. She opened it with shaking hands to find an address, typed, and beneath that, a simple instruction: *Call the police.*

Lucy held herself together long enough to make the call to 911. Then, slumping against the wall and trembling uncontrollably, she broke down and wept.

Chapter 45

The padlock at the entrance had been cut so neatly that it would have been easy to miss at first glance. "We're definitely in the right place," Paul said, pushing the gates apart.

Sam hesitated. "Jeff said we're supposed to be waiting for the police," she reminded him once more.

"Look, if Lucy is in there, two of us will attract a hell of a lot less attention than a tactical team will," he pointed out as he stepped through.

"But you don't think that she is in there, do you?" Sam was already pulling her Glock G30S as they moved quickly for the cover of the two buildings. It felt strange to hold the sidearm outside of the firing range, but her training was quickly reasserting itself as she scanned her surroundings.

"No," her partner admitted. He had also pulled his sidearm, a HK45. "This is a solo escape route, so either she'll still be at the yacht club, or she's been taken somewhere else."

They covered the open ground between the gate and the nearest building. The lower windows were all boarded up inside, and barred outside. Thick cobwebs could be seen behind the grimy glass panes. There were traces of rust on the metal bars, and padlocks on the doors. The same held true of the second warehouse, as well.

While Sam checked the buildings, Paul made his way over to the SUV. The dark green, late model Chevy Equinox had rental plates. The doors were locked, and the alarm had been set. Paul pulled a small flashlight from his pocket and scanned the interior. "Definitely Averill," he confirmed, quietly. "Take a look."

Sam stepped up to the Chevy. A pair of pants and a shirt lay folded on the front passenger seat. There was only the one outfit. But what caught Sam's attention was the large beach towel spread across the back seat. The long lump beneath it looked ominously shotgun-shaped.

Their hit man clearly had no intention of going down without a fight.

Chapter 46

Cynthia Orbison's caller ID popped up on Jeff's dashboard display. He answered as he drove.

"Where are you?" she asked.

He checked the GPS; "I'm about two minutes out from the address I gave you. What about the police?"

"There are a couple of units waiting for you. They found Miss Ledbetter's car parked across the street, but there's no sign of her or Paul. And the lock on the gate has been cut," she added.

Shit! "That means they're inside already," he said, flatly, hopefully masking his frustration and anxiety.

Cynthia didn't even try. "You told me they were going to wait for backup. What the hell are they thinking?" The line went quiet for a moment, then, "Are they armed?"

"They'd better be, if this does turn out to be Averill's escape route," he told her. "Don't worry, they were cleared to carry by your office."

"Which is fine, except for the fact that, strictly speaking, they're not with my office anymore," the DA pointed out, her voice low. "I suppose I'll have to rectify that, temporarily."

He managed a weak laugh. "Probably not a bad idea."

Orbison hesitated, then asked, "Can I at least count on them not to fuck things up and get themselves killed?"

Jeff spotted Sam's Subaru and pulled in behind it, across from the gate leading to the abandoned warehouse complex. The entrance had been blocked by a patrol car and an unmarked unit, a dark gray Dodge Charger, both with their lights off. Two uniformed officers stood near the hood of the Dodge, watching as Jeff brought the Audi to a stop. The guy closest to the Dodge — a sergeant — looked familiar to Jeff, but he couldn't immediately place the face.

He gave the sergeant a quick wave. *Danielson*, he remembered. *Scott Danielson.* He'd been a patrolman at Central, when Jeff had been with Homicide.

"Well?" Orbison asked again. "Can I count on them?"

"I wouldn't have brought them in on this if I didn't trust them," Jeff told her.

"Except when it comes to following orders, apparently," she pointed out. "Well, there's nothing we can do to help them at this point without a warrant to go inside."

"What about 'probable cause?'" Jeff suggested as he pulled his cell phone from its cradle and climbed out of the car. "After all, you said that the lock on the gate had been cut."

"I'm not sure that will hold up, given that it was probably your people who cut it."

Jeff couldn't help but smile. "You mean *your* people, don't you?"

MIKAELA SAT IN the quiet darkness of the hotel room, suddenly aware of just how quiet 'quiet' could be. Her dad was already on his way to meet up with his team, and her mother would probably be dead to the world for hours. Mikaela felt incredibly alone. She wanted to at least let Jim know that she was all right but, aside from one quick call to him when the police had taken her into protective custody, she'd been told — in no uncertain terms — not to contact anyone.

She sipped at her second bourbon in frustration, her mind wandering off in a dozen different directions at once. The threat from that man, her mother's affair ... it felt like the ground had broken loose beneath her feet.

She drained the last of her drink and flipped the television on, hoping for some distraction. What she got was the exact opposite. One of the local news stations was covering a breaking story along the Willamette River. Multiple law enforcement agencies had responded to a hostage situation at the Lattimer Yacht Club in southwest Portland.

Lucy.

Suddenly the room seemed ten degrees colder. *That could have been Mom ... or me.* Her father had been in law enforcement for most of her life, but she'd never experienced this kind of immediacy before. Hell, Mikaela hadn't even met Lucy, but what she saw unfolding across the screen felt intensely personal.

A wave of guilt passed over her. Lucy's life was in danger and here Mikaela sat — safe and secure in her hotel suite — watching the aerial footage of flashing lights and police barricades …

And then the world exploded.

Chapter 47

Even from half a click away, the sound of the detonation rippling through the water vibrated in Nick's chest.

I never really get to see them go off. All that work, and I have to settle once more for the video replay on the news.

He waited patiently until the reverberation died off. Then he heard what he'd been waiting for. The engines of the Sheriff's boat — now probably less than a half-click away — roared into life as it sped toward the yacht club.

PAUL AND SAM both looked up at the distant sound of the explosion. "Lucy's not there," he said firmly, but Sam saw the desperation in his eyes.

"Paul ..."

"She is not ... fucking ... there." He glared at Sam. "Averill doesn't gain anything by killing her. This is just a distraction. He's on his way, and we'd better be ready for him when he gets here."

Sam nodded. Whatever Paul had going on inside, she was determined to ride with it. She owed him that much.

He glanced around, then focused on a small shed about twenty-five yards away, on the southern edge of the property. The corrugated metal building sat half-hidden behind overgrown shrubs and Vine maples. "I need you to go over there and take up a position," he said. "Keep those oil drums to your back."

"Fuck that," she told him, her voice almost a growl. "I'm staying with you."

Paul gave her a hard look. "Didn't the Marines teach you anything about field of fire? Besides, there's barely enough cover here for one of us. Together, we're too easy a target. Separated, we have the advantage."

"Then you go," she said, firmly.

"This isn't a debate, Sam." Paul put his hand on her shoulder. "If it helps any, think of this as my pulling rank, but I need you over there. Find good cover, and keep low," he added.

Chapter 48

Nick pulled himself from the water as quietly as possible. He stood slowly, staying behind a small rock outcropping as he looked around. The grounds appeared to be deserted. The warehouse facility was dark.

He peeled the wetsuit from his body. After tucking the suit behind the rocks he paused, listening for any sound of company. All he heard were distant sirens responding to the marina fire.

The warm night air felt welcome on his skin after so much time in the cool water. Reluctantly, Nick pulled a thin, long-sleeved black t-shirt from the small waterproof bag he'd kept strapped to his side during the swim. He put it on, then extracted the Beretta 92 Compact from the bag, and the custom noise suppressor that had lain underneath. With a practiced hand, he threaded the suppressor onto the barrel of the Beretta while he surveyed the property, alert for any sign of movement, any indication that his plan had been compromised.

Reassured, he pulled the two spare magazines from the bag. Then he made his way along the edge of the grounds toward the small equipment shed, near the southwest corner of the property. He would have decent cover from there, and a clear view of the main structures where he'd hidden the rental car. He approached the outbuilding quietly, staying low to the ground and utilizing what little cover the untamed shrubs and spindly trees on the lot provided. As he moved around to the back side of the building, Nick froze in place …

Someone was crouched by the shed, waiting.

Nick couldn't make out much detail from where he stood. Between Nick and the watcher was a stack of empty oil barrels, barrels Nick had stacked as cover himself. Now, they were working against him, preventing a clean shot.

He forced himself to take a deep breath. *Focus … patience.* Where there was one watcher, he knew, there would be others. His instincts told him this would be a small team; two only, perhaps. Three, at the outside. Committing more people until they were certain of what they had stumbled upon would make no sense.

Nick was confident that no one was behind him. That left the main buildings. He pictured the best places for cover and surveillance in his mind. The shed, some old packing crates stacked at the nearest end of the western warehouse, the pile of rotting lumber north of the buildings.

The last would be too far away to be of immediate danger, and anywhere else on the property would be too exposed.

So, the systematic approach … first take out the one by the shed, then we see who else raises their head.

With the Beretta in his left hand, his shooting hand, he cautiously left the security of the shadows.

Chapter 49

Paul had tucked himself in behind the only real cover available to him, a couple of old, empty shipping crates stacked at an angle near the outer wall of the building closest the road. The wooden barricade probably wouldn't stop a bullet, but the position gave him a good view of the approach from the river. He glanced through an opening between the crates to where Sam had settled in by the shed. She had positioned herself well, keeping the rusting oil drums at her back. From there, she should have a clear view of the area between the buildings, including the SUV. That would do until reinforcements arrived.

If they arrive.

Even as that grim thought crossed his mind, he caught a flicker of movement in the darkness. At first Paul thought it had been his imagination, or shadows cast by headlights from the street, but then he saw it again, moving low, slowly and methodically toward the shed … toward Sam.

There was no time to warn her. And no chance at a clean shot through the crates.

Paul stood and broke quickly to his right, his pistol in firing position. Sam's head snapped his direction at the movement.

"Sam, behind you!" Paul shouted as he squeezed the trigger twice.

The shadow vanished behind the oil drums.

Paul saw Sam lunge forward, past the corner of the shed. She twisted and rolled up against the tangle of tall weeds growing along the outer wall. Her pistol was already trained back the way she'd come.

Three flashes, three dull pops came from the direction of the barrels. Three bullets thwacked into the weathered wood of the warehouse to Paul's left. He abandoned the crates and ran for the southwest corner of the building. *Close … too fucking close,* he realized. But Averill had missed, the distance probably too great for an accurate shot.

As he passed the far end of the old warehouse, Paul planted his left leg and cut back to his right.

Something gave inside. Sharp pain ripped through his knee as he threw himself past the corner and out of sight.

Another bullet from Averill gashed the edge of the warehouse. Bits of weathered wood and paint fluttered down harmlessly as Paul writhed on the ground below.

NICK RISKED A quick glance around the rusted barrels. The area between the two warehouses — and the SUV — was clear. *And no one is shooting at me ... good. Then it is only the two of them, after all.*

He cursed himself for losing patience. Maxwell — Nick had recognized him even in the dim light — had broken for the far end of the building before Nick could set himself properly for the shot. Even so, the third round had missed the investigator by no more than a centimeter or two. But the last ... that had been pointless. Wasting rounds out of frustration solved nothing.

He ejected the half-empty mag from the Beretta and inserted a new one.

The fact that Maxwell had not reappeared to return fire was a very good sign. The way the investigator had cried out as he went down behind the warehouse, he'd almost certainly torn a ligament, probably an ACL or MCL. That would keep him out of the equation for the moment.

Nick stilled his breathing, listening in vain for any sound of movement from Maxwell's partner. Then he stood slowly, his back to the tall stack of empty oil drums, Beretta at the ready. He took a slow breath, then exhaled as he pushed back, toppling the upper barrels.

They dropped to the pavement with a deafening metallic clang. Nick spun as they fell, ready to fire, but there was no one there.

Without hesitation, Nick hurried to the corner of the shed. With his left hand, he reached out around the edge of the hut and snapped off two blind shots— one low and one high — hoping to catch Maxwell's partner unprepared.

THE EXPLOSION OF pain in Paul's knee had been enough to make him drop the HK45 when he'd fallen. But Sam was still out there.

Paul spotted his pistol, lying just a few, agonizing feet away. Grimacing from the effort, he dragged himself over to retrieve it just as two more muffled shots echoed across the deserted property.

Sam.

Chapter 50

"Tactical is four minutes out," Officer Rizzo informed Jeff and Sergeant Danielson, who had hunkered down behind the patrol car. "We've been ordered to stay put until they arrive."

Before Jeff could say anything, two more angry pops sounded in the muggy night air.

"I've got people in there," he argued. "What the hell are they supposed to do while we sit on our asses?"

"I'm sorry, Dawes," Danielson said, "but we don't even know what we're facing. And there's no way that three of us can cover that much ground without leaving ourselves vulnerable. We wait."

Jeff fought his anger. He knew it was the right move, the smart move, but that left Paul and Sam to deal with Averill alone. For the first time in a long time, he regretted not carrying a sidearm.

"All right," he agreed at last. "But if we aren't going in, let's at least let them know we're here."

Officer Rizzo looked at the sergeant, who nodded. "Sounds like a plan to me," he said. "Sirens and lights, Rizzo."

SAM HEARD THE two muffled shots from Averill's pistol. Too close to be directed at Paul, she guessed he'd probably made the corner of the shed and fired blindly, trying to catch her off-guard. Staying close to the little building, Sam moved quickly, quietly. She wanted to circle around on the bastard. At the very least, she might be able to put herself in a better position to take Averill out if he made a break for the SUV.

She peeked cautiously around the back corner of the shed. The toppled oil drums were in front of her now, but there was no sign of Averill. She stood still and listened. All she could hear was distant traffic from the freeway to the west, and the faint keening of sirens at the marina.

Then, from somewhere in the direction of the gate, another siren whooped. Blue lights danced across the back of the property.

Hallelujah, Sam thought. *The fucking cavalry has finally arrived. Let's just hope I live long enough to see them.*

Chapter 51

At the sound of the siren, Nick knew he'd run out of both time and options. It would be suicide trying to make it to the Chevrolet now. Maxwell's partner was still out there somewhere, taking up a new position, waiting for him to move. *And if I do make it to the car, what then? The police are outside the gate, and more will be on their way.*

His only chance now was to head for the southwest corner of the property. If he could get over the fence he might be able to escape the area on foot and steal a car.

First, though, he had to get past Maxwell.

SAM EMERGED FROM behind the shed just as Averill broke for the far corner of the warehouse. Even from a distance, she could see the long-barreled automatic in his left hand. She settled into firing position and calmly squeezed the trigger. At the last moment, Averill changed direction, cutting back away from the building at an angle. The bullet splintered the wall just to the right of target.

Shit! Sam adjusted her aim, leading her target. Averill had almost made it to the corner of the warehouse. Sam saw him bring his pistol up across his body. She couldn't be sure who he was aiming at, but she had a good idea. *Paul.*

She squeezed off two more rounds.

Averill staggered as at least one of the bullets struck home. Yet, even as he fell, he somehow managed to twist back, bringing the barrel of his gun around to Sam.

Paul looked up at the sound of two shots, echoing loudly off the buildings. Averill stumbled into view, his features ghostly and contorted in the flashing blue lights coming from the gate. The assassin rolled as he fell, the pistol with its silencer swinging back toward the source of the gunfire like an accusing finger.

Paul snapped off three quick rounds. Averill fell heavily to the ground, flopped over onto his stomach, and slid to a stop.

Chapter 52

Sam kicked the Beretta away from Averill's outstretched left hand, her Glock steady on target. *There have been enough surprises,* she thought. But Averill had no more surprises left in him. He was bleeding heavily from three wounds, wounds she could see even in the dim light. One, at least, she knew had been from the shots she had fired.

His breathing came in slow, rattling gasps. Sam knelt and checked for a pulse ... weak and thready ... and saw that his pupils were unresponsive.

A steady wail of sirens grew louder by the minute. She caught sight of flashing lights at the gated entrance. *If they don't get in here soon they're not going to be able to do you much good,* she thought, looking down at the man on the ground. *Please God, let him hang in there long enough to tell us where Lucy is.*

Sam picked up Averill's Beretta and hurried over to where Paul lay. "You doing okay?" he asked as she approached.

"Better than he is," she said, glancing back in Averill's direction. "How about you?"

"Fan-fucking-tastic," he managed with a grimace, then nodded toward the emergency vehicles gathering at the gates. "Better let them know it's safe to come in," he added, looking over to where Nick Averill lay. "With any luck, the son of a bitch can hold on long enough to tell us something."

Sam called 911 and explained the situation to the dispatcher. Then she helped Paul into a more comfortable position, sitting with his back against the wall of the warehouse.

"You know what this means, don't you?" he asked, teeth clenched against the pain as he settled in. "You owe me. I saved your life."

"Nice try," she said with a tight smile, "but I slowed him down for you."

"Fine. We'll call it a draw then," he allowed, eyeing the body lying on the concrete.

Chapter 53

Mikaela watched nervously as the scene played out across the big screen. The initial explosion had sent a fireball nearly a hundred feet up above the marina, destroying the floating home the FBI had reportedly been watching. The dock and three neighboring homes were ablaze, and threatening others nearby. Sheriff's patrol boats had arrived on the scene almost immediately, and fire boats had been dispatched.

There'd been no mention of a hostage, no word of the other murders or the men her father had been hunting. As she watched the events unfolding, unable to look away, a Breaking News scrawl appeared along the bottom off the television screen.

... Police are responding to shots fired along Riverside Road in SW Portland. Preliminary reports indicate that at least one person has been badly wounded and is being transported to a nearby hospital.

Nothing tied this latest event to the fire at the yacht club, but Mikaela knew. She looked over at the door to her mother's room. *How many times have you watched the news, not knowing if Dad would ever make it home?* The anger she'd felt earlier toward her mother had ebbed over the last hour. Vestiges of the betrayal still simmered — probably always would — but none of that mattered at that moment. Apparently, kidnapping and murder had a way of putting things in perspective.

Mikaela jumped when someone knocked at the door to the suite. She practically ran to answer.

Her father stood in the doorway, a reassuring smile on his face. For the second time that evening Mikaela wrapped her arms around him tightly, but this time her emotions got the better of her. She felt her father pull her close as she wept.

"It's okay, Kiddo," he whispered. His hand came up to stroke her hair, the way he'd comforted her a thousand times before. "Everything is going to be okay, now."

Mikaela nodded, but the tears still flowed, and she still held tight. He bent slightly and lifted, carrying her back into the room. The door closed quietly behind them as he set her down gently. That seemed to break the spell. She reluctantly stepped away, using the back of her hand to swipe at the tears, and looked up at her father.

"It's been a while since you've picked me up like that," she said, managing an embarrassed laugh.

He grinned down at her. "It's been a while since I've seen you cry."

"Yeah, well, it's been that kind of night."

His smile faded at that. "I know, Kiddo. I'm so sorry." He glanced over to the closed bedroom door. "Is your mom still out?"

"Slept through the entire thing," Mikaela assured him. They walked over to the long couch. Her father used the remote to turn off the television, then glanced down at the two bourbon glasses. Both were now empty.

"I don't remember finishing that," he said with amusement.

Mikaela shrugged. "Like I said, it's been that kind of night. I'll pour another." She gathered both glasses and carried them to the bar. When she reached for the bottle, however, her hands were shaking. She felt her control slipping away once more.

Her father stepped up behind her, his hands on her shoulders, and kissed the top of her head, softly. She squeezed her eyes shut for a moment, not quite ready to let herself cry again. "What about that girl, Lucy?" she whispered. "I saw the explosion ..."

"Lucy is fine. They let her go. She called the police from a cabin out in Sandy, just before the explosion at the marina."

Relief washed over her. For the first time in hours, she felt like everything just might be okay. She took a deep breath, then reached once more for the bottle of bourbon. Her hand was more steady this time.

"Sandy? That's almost to Mt. Hood," she said as she managed to pour drinks for them both. "I don't understand. Why take her there just to let her go?"

"To keep the police busy long enough to get clear ... or try to." He took his glass from her, then explained about Averill's escape plan.

By the time he was finished, the drinks in their hands had been largely forgotten

"The news said that someone had been shot tonight," Mikaela told her father.

He nodded. "Averill. It doesn't look like he's going to make it."

"Good." He shot a surprised look at her. "I'm sorry," she told him without conviction, "but he killed all of those people ... and those are just the ones you know of. He deserves whatever happens to him."

They sipped at their drinks in silence for a few moments. Then she asked, "What about the other one?"

"Eveginy Polyakov? The FBI are looking for him in connection to the Ruiz murders, but no luck so far. I'm guessing you're probably going to be enjoying the county's hospitality for a couple more days, at least."

"Well, at least the hotel has air conditioning," she told him with a smile. "Beats the hell out of my apartment right now." She turned serious once more. "If Averill dies, how solid is your case against Polyakov?"

Her father frowned. "Frankly, the only evidence we have tying him to any of the deaths is completely circumstantial."

"Are you telling me he's going to get away with this?"

Her dad leaned back against the cushions. "Quite possibly," he admitted, "unless ..." He let the rest fade out and took a drink of his bourbon. "Anyway, the FBI and police have things under control as far as this case is concerned," he said after a moment.

His daughter must have picked up on some subtle, unintended inflection in his voice. "What do you mean, 'this case?' Are you working on another one, too?"

Jeff hesitated. "No," he said. "Well ... not really another case, but ..."

Mikaela held him in a piercing, uncomfortable stare. *God, even at five-foot tall she's going to make the most intimidating attorney in the city,* he decided.

"What else are you working on, Dad?" she asked firmly.

He smiled. "Did anyone ever tell you you're a pushy kid?"

"All the time," she admitted, a touch of a smile showing at the edges of her mouth. "And you know I'm not going to let you off the hook until you talk, so ..."

"All right. This all started when Adam Polyakov went to prison for killing his ex-girlfriend. The problem is, I don't think he was guilty."

Curiosity and surprise showed in his daughter's expression. "Are you sure?" she asked.

He nodded. "Pretty sure. I should have the last piece of evidence any time, now."

"And then you're going after the person who killed her, right?" She said it so matter-of-factly, as if it was a foregone conclusion, as inevitable as the sun coming up the next day.

"That was the plan," he admitted. "But ... well, it's complicated, Kiddo, and with everything that's going on with you and your mom ..."

Mikaela turned her attention back to the glass in her hand. She took a long drink, rocked the tumbler back and forth, and watched the amber liquid swirl for a moment.

"Growing up, I loved that my dad was a cop," she said, her voice contemplative. "Coolest thing in the world, although you did intimidate more than a few of my friends," she added with a laugh. "God, Courtney was completely paranoid around you back in high school."

Jeff grinned. Courtney was Mikaela's 'Wild Child' friend; beautiful and bright, but as impulsive as they came.

"You're the reason I'm going to law school," Mikaela continued. "You are the voice in my head that tells me right from wrong. And when you left the DA's office, when you went corporate on me ... that was the first time you ever really disappointed me. I blamed Mom, mostly, with all of her 'money and status' crap ..."

"Mikaela, that's not fair," he objected, but she held her hand up. He stopped talking.

"Oh, believe me," she said, "I was just as pissed at you for caving in to her. The work you did was so damned important ... I loved the sense of justice I saw in you, Dad. I needed to see that. I still do," she added.

"Your own personal St. George, fighting the dragon?" Jeff asked with a self-conscious grin.

Mikaela smiled indulgently. "Something like that, I guess." She studied him for moment. "You have something planned, don't you?" she asked.

He nodded. "It's a long shot but, yes, I have a plan. In fact, I'm booked on a flight to Seattle in the morning." Jeff smiled at his daughter. "I just don't know how I'm going to explain why I'm going to your mother."

"Leave Mom to me. We have a few things to talk about anyway." She saw the worried expression on his face. "If you're worried about Mom and me, we'll be fine. I don't think I'm ready to forgive what she did to you but, after tonight, I might understand her a little better. Besides, the last thing I need right now is to be trapped in a hotel room while you guys try to deal with your personal issues," she added with a sly smile.

"How did you get so smart?" he asked.

"Obviously not genetics," she teased. "Now, you need to go home and get some sleep. You look like crap."

He laughed. "Harsh, but I'll let it slide this time. I love you, Kiddo."

"Love you, too, Pops," Mikaela whispered as she leaned in for a long hug. Then she nudged him away gently. "Call us as soon as this is over," she told him. "And be careful."

"Always," he promised. "Are you sure there isn't anything else I can do for you?"

"Well …" she said, a familiar, mischievous light beginning to show in her eyes, "if I *am* going to be stuck here for a couple more days, it would be nice if I had a little company besides Mom."

"James?" he asked. Mikaela nodded, smiling. "You know, there are some things a father should never be asked to arrange for his unmarried daughter," he told her, "but I'm sure the DA can be persuaded to extend protective custody to your fiancé," he added with a wink.

Chapter 54

The lobby of the SeaTac Marriott had settled into a steady flow of traffic by eight in the morning. Guests catching early flights from Seattle had already checked out and caught shuttles to their terminals. That left the hotel to the more leisurely travelers, who wandered, bleary eyed, down to the restaurant for breakfast. Many wore outfits just shy of pajamas, and sported serious bed head.

By contrast, Jeff had dressed to the nines for this trip. After all, he was representing the Multnomah County District Attorney's office … at least as far as the Kozlovs knew. With the trial murders solved, any legitimate reasons Jeff had for making this trip had come to an end. Nick Averill had gone down, and Eveginy Polyakov had made it onto the FBI's ten-most-wanted list.

That left just this one last loose end for Jeff to tie up. A loose end Cynthia Orbison knew nothing about.

The events of the last twenty-four hours ran through his head. So many things had gone wrong, but they could have gone far worse. Paul and Sam had been lucky, but only because they were good. Even so, Averill had had his chances. If Paul hadn't seen him moving up behind Sam's position … If she hadn't gotten off a good shot when Averill made a break toward Paul …

Don't worry about 'ifs' that didn't happen, Jeff thought, remembering the old policeman's adage; 'Any day you make it to the end of your shift is a successful day.'

Paul had spent the night at Good Shepherd, where an MRI had confirmed that he'd torn his anterior cruciate ligament when he'd gone down behind the warehouse. It would probably be three or four weeks before the swelling subsided enough to undergo reconstruction, and six to nine months more for rehab and healing. Niko would burst a blood vessel when the workers' comp claim went through, but it was a hell of a lot better than paying out death benefits.

Besides, Niko would just find some way to roll everything into his bill to the DA's office, anyway.

Out of the corner of his eye, Jeff spotted the arrival of the Russians at the hotel entrance. Kozlov had sent the same two men who had picked him up on Orcas Island.

The younger one — Victor, Jeff remembered — glowered menacingly from across the lobby as soon as he walked in. The bigger of the two merely smirked at Jeff, nodding his head back toward the hotel entrance.

Here we go. Let's hope to God I'm as smart as I think I am.

Jeff walked past the two men without a word, and stepped outside. Two black Mercedes limousines were waiting. An enormous, uniformed chauffer held the door of the lead car open. Jeff climbed in, nodding at Vasily Kozlov as he settled into one of the rear facing seats. To his surprise, the door closed behind him immediately, leaving him alone with the *Bratva* boss.

"Marat and Victor will follow in the other car," Kozlov told him. "This way we can speak without interruption."

The limo pulled away from the hotel, followed closely by its twin. When they had merged with the traffic flowing toward the airport, Vasily slid a small hidden door back, revealing a compartment filled with liquor.

"Drink?" he asked as he half-filled a small crystal tumbler with something that looked like whiskey from a matching crystal decanter.

"It's eight in the morning," Jeff pointed out with a smile. "I'll take a coffee, if you have it."

His host shook his head in disappointment, then looked past Jeff to the driver. "*Misha, my dolzhny kofe,*" he said. Kozlov turned back to his guest. "I presume you have no objections if I have something besides coffee, even at eight in the morning?"

Jeff laughed. "None whatsoever."

Misha managed to maneuver the long car into a Starbucks parking lot. The second limo pulled up alongside, remaining just back of the doors. Victor got out and stepped over just as Kozlov rolled the window down.

"Tell Victor what you want," Kozlov said. "He will go inside."

"Tall Americano," Jeff told him. Seeing the irritation on the bodyguard's face, he added, "Get some of those little vanilla scones, too."

The young Russian scowled, then turned and headed into the coffee shop. Kozlov laughed. "I don't think Victor cares for you very much," he said as he rolled the window up once more.

"I have that effect on people sometimes."

"I imagine you do." Vasily grew more serious. "Tell me about Eveginy."

"He and a man named Nick Averill have been systematically killing anyone connected with Adam Polyakov's murder trial." At the mention of Averill, Jeff thought he'd caught a strange light in the Russian's eyes, there briefly but quickly extinguished.

Kozlov sipped at his whiskey and looked out the window. He said nothing more until after Victor had returned with the coffee and scones. Only when the two limos had pulled back out into traffic did the Russian speak again.

"Say this is true, that they have been eliminating these people ... this has nothing to do with me or my family."

Jeff nodded. "You and I both know that. I doubt the Justice Department will be as easy to convince."

Vasily leaned forward. "What interest would the Justice Department have in this?"

"In addition to the judge and jury, Eveginy and Averill assassinated the judge's husband, a Federal Prosecutor named Antonio Ruiz. Turns out, he specialized in organized crime."

"*Sukin syn*," Kozlov muttered. Judging by the anger on the big man's florid face, Jeff didn't need a translation to get the gist.

"They also framed a drug-dealing rival of yours for one of the murders," Jeff added, "and used one of your business fronts — Whiteman Security — in an attempt to escape last night." The part about Whiteman was still a guess, but an educated one. When he saw irritation flare in the Russian's expression, he knew he'd hit target.

"Which drug dealer?" Kozlov asked after a moment.

"Manny Cespedes," Jeff told him. "Or perhaps you know him as *Lagarto*."

Kozlov dismissed the importance of the Mexican thug with a wave of his hand. "Cespedes is little more than an animal," the Russian growled. "Barely worth my time."

Jeff said nothing. Outside, the streets around SeaTac were heavy with traffic. The limo seemed to be headed for no particular destination; they drove so far in one direction, then a turn or two would take them in another. He had the feeling that Kozlov's driver was keeping them in a holding pattern around the airport.

"I will take care of Eveginy myself," Vasily said at last.

Jeff shook his head and smiled.

"I'd give that some serious thought if I were you," he said. "If Eveginy disappears, or turns up dead, the DOJ is going to assume that you had him killed to silence him. As it stands, they're going to do everything in their power to connect you to Ruizes' assassination. And no matter what they're trying to prove against you and your organization, think of what the Feds will uncover along the way. The spotlight Eveginy has put you under is going to get very, very hot."

Vasily frowned, but offered no argument. "I take it you have another suggestion."

"Let's call it a compromise, one that will give us both what we want … more or less. Part of my price involves Manny Cespedes."

"And this visit to my brother? That is also part of your price?"

"Non-negotiable," Jeff assured him. He looked at his wristwatch. "And you'll need to decide soon, because my flight to Orcas Island leaves in an hour."

The Russian studied him for a few moments, then, "Misha, *prinyat' nas. Mwe gotovy.*" The limo made a u-turn at the next light, taking them back toward the airport. "I have made alternate arrangements for our trip to the island," Kozlov told him. "We will discuss your compromise in greater detail along the way. But understand," he said as he leaned forward, a very dark look in his eyes, "I've agreed to nothing, yet. And if I am to gamble with my family, then you are most assuredly gambling with yours."

Chapter 55

A light breeze blew through the open windows of Andrei Kozlov's gate house. It brought some relief from the afternoon heat, but it did nothing to sooth Eveginy's nerves. The explosion at the houseboat in Portland — Nikki's escape plan — had made the news, even in Seattle. There had also been a report of a shooting near the marina. Someone had been taken to the hospital in the aftermath, but there'd been no indication that the two events were related in any way. The police in Portland seemed unable — or unwilling — to provide any further information.

And still there was no word from his cousin.

I should be there, Eveginy thought, frustration getting the better of him. *I should be looking for Nikki instead of babysitting Andrei Kozlov's fucking security detail.* Why Vasily had chosen him to review security at the compound, today of all days, was beyond baffling. Every man on Andrei's protection team had been hand-chosen for their jobs. Most were former Russian Army or *Spetsnaz* … Special Purposes Forces who had learned their craft in the civil war in Tajikistan, or in Chechnya, before discovering that there were far more rewarding opportunities to be had with Vasily's organization. They knew their business far better than Eveginy did.

His dark mood had not infected the men in the gate house, who largely ignored him while they joked and played cards. Convinced the walls would close in on him if he remained another moment, Eveginy announced that he was going down to check on things at the house.

The security team's leader, Russak, looked up from his poker hand. "Better stay put," he advised. "Vasily is on his way."

"Vasily is coming here?" Eveginy asked. "I've heard nothing of this."

Russak pushed a small stack of chips into the middle of the table. "He called from the helicopter while you were checking the fences. Something about an urgent matter with his brother. Sit," he urged with a grin. "Watch television. The car should be here in a few minutes."

Irritated, Eveginy took a seat on the sofa and checked his phone. No messages from either Nikki or Vasily, he noted with frustration. *And here I sit with my thumb up my ass.*

Fifteen minutes later, Vasily's silver Escalade pulled up to the gate. Russak and Eveginy went out to greet the boss, followed by a couple of the more curious bodyguards.

"Is everything all right?" the team leader asked as Vasily rolled the window down. Eveginy could see someone else sitting in the shadows across from Kozlov, but he couldn't make out any detail.

"Everything is fine," Vasily assured them. He smiled when he saw his number two man standing nearby. "I just need to speak with my brother. Eveginy, get in. This should interest you."

Russak opened the front passenger door and Eveginy climbed in, noting with surprise that the privacy screen separating the front and rear compartments had been raised almost to the roof of the SUV.

"*Govorit' ostorozhno. Mwe ne odni,*" Vasily advised. 'Speak carefully. We are not alone.' Nothing in Vasily's tone indicated tension, however. Eveginy glanced at the driver, Misha, who merely shrugged in response as he pulled the car forward.

"How did your review of my brother's security go?" Vasily asked, in English.

Eveginy hesitated a moment, confused by the mixed signals the boss had been sending. "Everything is well," he said at last.

"Good, good." Then, presumably to the person sitting in the back with him, Vasily said, "Eveginy has done an outstanding job seeing to my brother's protection. I couldn't ask for more." Misha smiled at that, and Eveginy felt himself relax a little as the SUV pulled up in front of the house.

Andrei Kozlov's estate had been developed as a vacation retreat, an escape from the rigors of running a company. As far as Eveginy was concerned, the posh house on Orcas Island now amounted to little more than a well-appointed prison. Since his eldest daughter's death, Andrei rarely left the grounds, and only when business on the mainland absolutely required him to. For the last several months, even his youngest daughter, Stefanya, had joined him in his self-imposed exile.

All because that bitch, Larissa, had gotten herself killed. Eveginy had met Larissa twice only, but the spoiled little rich girl had left a lingering, unpleasant impression. Arrogant, demanding … the mystery, as far as he was concerned, wasn't why Adam had murdered her, but how he had allowed himself to become involved with her in the first place.

The Escalade pulled up in front of the main house. Eveginy let himself out, then waited patiently for Misha to come around from the driver's side to open the door for Vasily.

The man who climbed out first was unfamiliar to Eveginy; clean shaven, with short, dark hair that was just beginning to show a touch of gray at the temples, he moved as though he had taken care of himself. Broad shoulders were obvious beneath the expensive suit he wore. He nodded to Misha, who held the door for him, before his eyes came to rest on Eveginy. The look was cold and appraising.

Eveginy might have taken him for a cop but for the expensive clothes he wore. Of course, if the man was in Vasily's pocket, a badge and an Armani suit wouldn't be mutually exclusive.

The boss got out next. The two of them, Vasily and the stranger, chatted like old friends about some visit to Charleston the new man had taken recently. They moved toward the house, walking almost past Eveginy before Vasily thought to acknowledge him.

"Come," he said with a smile. "You and Misha should be here for this,"

Without waiting for an answer, Vasily opened the front door and walked inside. Eveginy cast a questioning glance at Misha as they followed.

Chapter 56

Jeff followed Vasily as he guided them all through the living room and out onto the back deck. Andrei and a young woman — Stefanya Kozlov, presumably — were enjoying the morning sun at the large table. Andrei jumped up from his seat when he realized he had guests.

"Brother, why didn't you tell me you were coming?" He looked over at Jeff, surprise evident in his expression. "And Mr. Dawes! Did I have the wrong time for our meeting?"

Vasily smiled. "I ran into Mr. Dawes at the airport, and we flew in together," he explained. "I asked if I could be here for this."

Andrei seemed confused and anxious. He looked back and forth between his brother and Jeff. "You know each other? But I thought you were with the District Attorney's office."

"I think that's why your brother wanted to be here," Jeff told him with an encouraging smile. "To protect your family's interests. And this, I presume, must be your daughter?"

"Yes, I'm sorry ..." Andrei said, regaining his composure a bit. "Stefanya, this is Jefferson Dawes, an investigator with the Multnomah County District Attorney's office."

Stefanya rose from her chair, a troubled look in her olive-green eyes. Jeff studied her as he stepped forward. The youngest Kozlov had inherited her father's slender physique, if not his height. But the twenty-four-year old seemed more gaunt than lean. Her wispy blue and yellow sundress hung almost shapeless from her shoulders, and despite the long, hot summer the Northwest had been enduring, her complexion looked almost pallid.

Stefanya's eyes flicked nervously to her uncle, then to her father and back to Jeff. The depth of the sadness he saw in her gaze was striking, especially is someone so young.

"Sweetheart, I'm afraid we have matters to discuss," Andrei said gently. "Why don't you leave us for a few minutes?"

"Actually," Jeff said, "I'd prefer that she join us for the time being."

"Yes, brother, let her stay," Vasily agreed. Andrei cast a surprised and worried look at his brother, then motioned for Stefanya to sit beside him.

EVEGINY STOOD NEXT to Misha, his mind racing. *Jefferson Dawes … the man Nikki said had visited Uncle Fedya … here, with Vasily? How could this be?*

Vasily and Dawes had taken seats across the table from Andrei and his daughter. Eveginy edged a little closer so that he might better hear their conversation. Misha seemed content to remain near the door to the house, arms folded across his massive chest.

"THIS IS ABOUT your case, then, the deaths of those jurors?" Andrei asked.

Jeff shook his head. "Actually, we closed that case last night. The person who committed all the murders was a man named Averill. We think he may have been a contract killer, possibly tied to organized crime."

The businessman glanced quickly at his brother. "I had nothing to do with this," Vasily assured him with a grim smile.

Andrei looked unconvinced, but turned back to Jeff. "I don't understand. If you have closed your case, why then are you here?" he asked. "What more can I tell you?"

"Well, for starters, you can tell me when you first learned that Stefanya was responsible for her sister's death." Jeff's voice was level, matter-of-fact. Although he had addressed the question to Andrei, he was watching the daughter's reaction.

Stefanya bit her lower lip and looked down at her lap. Her father sagged back in his chair, his expression anxious. "This is … absurd," he managed at last. "How could you think that she might be involved?"

Jeff smiled, not unkindly. "It really wasn't that difficult. In fact, Adam figured it out almost immediately, didn't he, Stefanya?"

She looked up at her name but didn't respond, remaining quiet and watchful as Jeff continued.

"As soon as Adam saw the evidence the police had, he stopped protesting his innocence. In fact, he wouldn't even let his attorney mount a defense. That didn't make any sense to me, unless he was protecting someone." Jeff held the girl's gaze. "Adam was protecting you, wasn't he, Stefanya?"

Still, she said nothing. But the emotional dam she'd been hiding behind showed signs of cracking. Tears welled up in her eyes. Her breathing grew shallow.

"I will not have you accuse my daughter like this," Andrei roared. He began to stand, but Stefanya reached out and took his hand.

"Enough, Papa. No more … no more," she said again, more softly as he sat back down in defeat. Then, while she tenderly stroked her father's hand, Stefanya turned to Jeff. She wiped away her tears with her free hand. "I didn't tell my father until after Adam died. But how did you find out?"

"An educated guess," Jeff admitted. "You tried to visit Adam several times, beginning right after his arrest and then later in prison. I couldn't help but wonder why you would want to see the man who killed your sister, or why you'd be so persistent about it. And then I saw that your visits always fell on Wednesdays … the same day of the week Larissa died. The same day Adam's mystery woman came to Portland in the weeks before — and on the night of — the murder."

Andrei had turned away, staring out at the water beyond the rails of his deck as Jeff continued.

"I decided to check with the Registrar's Office at the university. It took some doing, but I finally got access to your school records. You carried a full schedule that Spring, but you didn't have any classes on Wednesdays. Nothing until late Thursday afternoon, in fact. Plenty of time to get down to Portland and back. What I don't understand is why you started seeing Adam again. Were you just trying to find some way to hurt him for the way he betrayed you with Larissa?"

Stefanya nodded. "They humiliated me. No," she corrected herself, "Larissa humiliated me. She tricked Adam, seduced him. The night I killed her, my sister bragged about how she'd gotten him drunk, how she'd planned everything so that I would find them together in bed."

"Larissa hated you that much?" Jeff asked.

The tears rolled freely down Stefanya's cheeks now. She wiped at them again with the back of her left hand. Andrei looked over at her with deep sadness. He took Stefanya's other hand and gave it a quick, reassuring squeeze.

"You must understand," he said. "My daughter ... my Larissa ... was sick. Her mother's death poisoned her soul, I think. I was simply too blind to see."

"It wasn't your fault, Poppa," Stefanya protested. "None of this was your fault."

"She's right, Andrei," Vasily agreed. "Larissa was far too careful to let you see behind the mask."

EVEGINY'S HAND MOVED to the Glock in his shoulder harness almost of its own accord.

Adam is dead, Aunt Anya is dead, and God knows where Nikki is, all because this stupid girl had to have her pathetic revenge?

In the back of Eveginy's mind, he knew that Nikki would have urged patience. He would have reminded his cousin that retribution requires caution and planning. But Nikki wasn't here. Nikki was probably sitting in a jail cell, three hundred miles away, because of this worthless little bitch and her vanity.

JEFF HEARD A strangled cry behind him. Stefanya's eyes grew wide as she looked past his shoulder. He turned to see Vasily's driver squeezing Eveginy's neck in the crook of his massive right arm. In his left hand, Misha held the smaller man's right wrist, the fingers of Polyakov's hand inches from the butt of his pistol. Eveginy struggled to break free, his feet dangling comically an inch or two above the deck.

A second man — the one who had met them at the gate house, Jeff realized — stood just behind the driver. He watched the one-sided battle between Misha and Eveginy play out with obvious amusement. Vasily stood and walked to where his second-in-command now wriggled more and more feebly, and plucked the handgun from its holster.

"Take him to the kitchen and wait for me," Vasily said to Misha, as Eveginy slipped into unconsciousness. "I'll be with you soon." The driver nodded. The other guard stepped up. Working together, they carried Eveginy Polyakov into the house.

"Vasily!" Andrei's confusion was obvious. "What is happening? What are your men doing?"

"Mr. Dawes will explain," he told his brother. Then looking at Jeff; "We have an understanding, yes?"

"We do," Jeff assured him.

The elder Kozlov followed his men back into the house. When the sliding door had been drawn closed behind them, Jeff turned to Andrei and Stefanya.

"Eveginy and Nick Averill were behind the murders of the people connected to Adam's trial," he explained. "Adam was Eveginy's cousin."

"So, he killed all of those people because of what happened to Adam?" Stefanya whispered. "Because of what I did?"

"Indirectly, yes," Jeff admitted. "But the thought that Adam might have been innocent in Larissa's death probably never even occurred to him."

"I don't understand," Andrei said, his voice quiet, pained. "If he thought his cousin had been guilty of the crime, why go through with his revenge?"

"I'm not sure," Jeff said. "Family loyalty, most likely. After all, the murders didn't begin when Adam was convicted, but after his death … and his mother's suicide."

Stefanya fell back in her chair as though she'd been struck. "Adam's mother?" she whispered. "Dead?"

He nodded, and she broke down completely. Her father pulled her close. She nestled her head in against his neck and sobbed uncontrollably.

Chapter 57

Eveginy's head throbbed. His arms were pulled back, wrists secured through the back of the heavy wooden kitchen chair by what felt like zip ties. Misha stood near him to the right, Russak to the left. Arms crossed, they watched Eveginy impassively. Neither managed to convey as much menace as Vasily. He had straddled a chair in front of Eveginy, leaning forward until his face was inches away from his lieutenant's.

"*Sukyn syn*" … Son of a bitch ... "You put my organization … you put all of us in jeopardy." Vasily's tone was somehow all the more intimidating for its calmness. "How could you be such a fucking idiot?"

"My family …" Eveginy whispered. His throat was still tender from the chokehold Misha had put him in.

Vasily cocked his head at that, his expression thoughtful. "All right," he said with a nod. "Family I understand, but what of the Federal Prosecutor, Ruiz? He had nothing to do with your cousin's trial."

Eveginy shrugged as best he could with his arms pinned behind him. "The Columbians had a bounty out … two hundred fifty thousand."

"So, you and Nikki saw an opportunity." Vasily shook his head sadly as he stood. Misha stepped up and pulled the empty chair to the side. "Well now I have an opportunity, and I'm going to take it."

Eveginy looked up into his boss's face. "What opportunity?" he asked, tensely.

"I've made arrangements for you to go back with Mr. Dawes and answer for what you've done."

"But they have nothing on me," Eveginy protested. "Nothing that they could make stand up in court."

The answering smile chilled him. "Perhaps not yet," Vasily admitted, cradling Eveginy's chin firmly in his calloused hand, "but they will. They will, because you are going to give them everything they need."

Eveginy jerked his head away. "No. I will not help them put together a case against my cousin," he growled.

"Eveginy, why would they need to build a case against a dead man?" his boss asked quietly.

"A dead man?" He blinked in disbelief. "Nikki? It's not possible."

Vasily nodded, a grim smile on his face. "Nick Krupin died last night because of your pathetic, meaningless attempt at revenge."

"You're lying!" Eveginy's words came out in a raspy, angry cry. Kozlov backhanded him across the face. Eveginy's head snapped painfully over into his right shoulder.

"The next time you raise your voice at me, Eveginy Sergeiovitch, I will cut your tongue out and shove it firmly up your ass. Do you understand?"

The beaten man managed a sullen nod as he sagged back into his chair.

"Good," Kozlov said. "Now, let's discuss what you will tell the District Attorney."

Misha shifted awkwardly. "Vasily, are you sure about this? What if he decides to give them something on you?"

Kozlov smiled at that. "You won't do that, will you, Eveginy?" he asked, gripping Polyakov's chin again to look into his eyes. "Because you know me ... you know what I would do. You see, Misha, family is Eveginy's weakness, the reason he's here in the first place. He will do anything to protect what little family he still has, here and back home. Won't you, Eveginy?"

The man in the chair closed his eyes and nodded in defeat.

Chapter 58

Jeff watched in silence as Andrei wrapped Stefanya in his arms, whispering softly in her ear as she cried. Father and daughter, riding out the storm together. Jeff wanted to let their mutual grief play out in privacy, but there were questions he still needed answers to.

"Stefanya," Jeff said when, at last, the young woman's wracking sobs had slowed. "There's something I still don't understand. You said that Larissa admitted Adam had been tricked into betraying you. If that's true, then why did you still frame him for her death?"

She managed to look at him through red, puffy eyes.

"Don't you think I've asked myself that a thousand times?" she whispered. "I don't know ... I don't think I even processed what she'd told me. Not really. I just knew that I wanted her dead more than ever. But the way she'd manipulated Adam ... I think I only accepted that afterwards. And by then he'd worked out what had happened ..."

"The handcuffs," Jeff guessed, remembering Adam's reaction when the detectives had told him that Larissa had been chained to the bed.

Stefanya nodded. "I'd brought them with me the last time I'd stayed with him. I told him it would add some excitement to our love-making. He wanted nothing to do with them. I had to insist."

Jeff nodded. "And the DNA evidence?" he asked.

The young woman bit her lower lip and blushed, glancing quickly over at her father. Jeff didn't push. He didn't need to. As carefully as Stefanya had obviously thought her plan through, Jeff could fill in enough of the probabilities by working backward. Getting Adam's prints on the cuffs, collecting the semen she'd need to plant on Larissa's body, the email to the maid service ...

"You wanted Adam to know what you'd done, didn't you?" Stefanya didn't answer. "The handcuffs, the DNA samples you introduced ... That's why you didn't try very hard to cover your tracks ... because you were counting on him to piece things together. You wanted him to know what he'd turned you into."

Jeff had never seen as much pain in anyone's gaze as he saw in Stefanya's as she nodded.

"Why do you think he protected you after everything you'd done?"

"Because he still loved me," she whispered. "Because he blamed himself … for letting Larissa betray us." Tears rolled freely down her cheeks. "It wasn't his fault, but still he blamed himself."

She dropped her head and broke down once more. Her shoulders shook with sobs. Her father reached over, putting his arm around her. "That's enough for now," Andrei said quietly to Jeff as he stood and helped Stefanya to her feet. "There will be time for more questions later."

As if by some signal, the housekeeper, Marie, appeared and hurried over to help Stefanya. The two men watched in silence as Marie guided her back inside to rest.

"What happens now?" Andrei asked when the door had closed behind them.

Jeff managed something close to a smile. "To your daughter? Nothing," he said. Kozlov looked at him in surprise. "I made an agreement with your brother; in exchange for my silence about what really happened to Larissa, he hands Eveginy over to me."

Andrei considered that for a moment. Then he walked over to the outdoor bar. Without asking, he poured three fingers of what looked like bourbon into two tumblers.

"Forgive me," he said as he handed one of the heavy crystal glasses to Jeff, "but you don't strike me as a man who would make such a deal."

"I'm a complicated guy, I guess," Jeff said as he swirled the amber liquid in his glass.

Andrei smiled. It was warm and genuine, if a little sad. "Maybe not so complicated," he said. "Everything you have on Stefanya is circumstantial. None of it would hold up in court without her confession." He paused, but Jeff didn't offer any argument.

"No," the Russian continued, "I think you played a bluff. My daughter for Eveginy. And my dear, overly-protective brother couldn't risk calling you on it."

Jeff merely shrugged at the suggestion and took another drink.

"But if this was all about getting Eveginy, why insist on coming here to confront Stefanya at all?" Andrei asked.

"Someone needed to know what really happened," Jeff told him. "I felt as though Adam deserved at least that much."

Kozlov's smile turned even more sad at that. "No, that is where you are wrong," he said. "Adam deserved much, much more."

Chapter 59

Cynthia Orbison slid the file she'd been reading across the desk toward Jeff Dawes. He didn't even bother to open it up.

"The DOJ hasn't released Eveginy Polyakov to us yet," she told him, "but they have thoughtfully provided us with a transcript of his statement. So far, he's admitted to being an accessory in the murders of Judge Ruiz and her husband. And Alex. And the jurors ... he's even copped to being behind the wheel when Erin Meadows was killed."

She watched Jeff, searching for some reaction. "You don't seem very surprised," Cynthia said at last.

"Should I be?"

"Given the fact that we had no real evidence on him when he turned himself in, I would say that his full confession could be considered ... surprising, yes."

He smiled at that. "I guess some people are just burdened with a guilty conscience."

Cynthia laughed. "Yeah, I'm sure that applies here."

"I guess this means Manny Cespedes walks in the Myers shooting, then." Jeff didn't seem too troubled by the thought.

"I guess so." She looked at the clock on her desk. "They should be breaking the good news to him any time now."

"I wish I could be there when they tell him," Jeff said as he stood. "Unfortunately, I have an office to run. It's been nice working with you, Ms. Orbison."

"It's certainly been ... interesting," she admitted with a smile. They shook hands. "Are you sure you wouldn't like to come back to the department?" she asked.

Jeff chuckled. "You couldn't afford me," he pointed out.

Just as he reached the door to the outer office she said, "You know, Alex was right about you."

Jeff paused, his hand resting on the door knob, and looked back. "How so?" he asked.

"You are a pain in the ass," Cynthia told him with a smile. "And you're damned good at what you do."

DETECTIVES MILLARD AND Dunlop led Manny Cespedes, dressed in his county-issued neon orange jumpsuit, into the interrogation room. He shuffled to a chair where they removed the restraint from his left wrist. Detective Millard attached it to the thick steel ring set in the middle of the heavy metal table.

"You look good in orange, Manny." Dunlap said, a cheerful grin on his round face. He had the build of an aging prize fighter; stocky, a little heavy in the jowls, but still muscular and vaguely intimidating.

"Fuck you," Manny growled, his accent thick.

"Watch your goddamned mouth, Cespedes," Detective Millard said quietly. Taller, and more lean than his partner, Millard carried himself with a dangerous energy, like a switchblade about to open.

"Easy, Kevin," Dunlap soothed. "Under the circumstances, you can't blame Mr. Cespedes for being irritated. After all, we've been holding him for almost three weeks now." He turned to Manny. "I have good news, buddy. We're dropping all the charges against you in the Myers murder. Turns out we had the wrong guy after all."

"No fucking shit. What about the drug charges?"

"The DA is dropping those, too," Millard muttered unhappily.

"Good." Manny tugged impatiently at his restraints. "Then get these fucking things off me so I can get out of here."

Dunlap looked over and smiled. "In due time," he said, picking up a file folder that had been sitting in front of him. He opened it and studied the contents for a moment, then looked up at his prisoner. "Had an interesting conversation with a couple of friends of yours the other morning … the Rojas brothers."

Manny stopped pulling at his chains. "What the fuck you talking about?" he asked. His voice was low, his tone suddenly less … arrogant.

Dunlap ignored the question. He returned his attention to the contents of the file. "They brought us a little present," he continued.

He pulled an 8x10 photograph from the file and set it on the table for Manny to see. "FN 57," he said, tapping a finger on the photo of a handgun.

"Only one set of fingerprints on it, too," Millard added. The scowl on his face had been replaced with a Cheshire Cat grin. "Yours. And guess what? Ballistics matched your gun with the one used in the murder of three kids on the east side last June."

Dunlap pulled another photograph from the file. This one showed the trio of teenagers sprawled across the grass, what was left of their faces unrecognizable under masks of blood.

Manny looked at the picture in silence.

"You should try being nicer to the hired help, Cespedes," Millard told him. "The Rojas brothers decided to hang on to the gun you asked them to get rid of, in case they ever needed a little leverage against you. Seems it came in handy, after all."

"This is bullshit! Bullshit! You got nothing," Manny shouted. He yanked at his cuffs again in frustration. "Nothing! They won't ever testify against me."

Dunlap smiled as he put the photos back into the folder. "Oh, I'm pretty sure they will. Turns out, there are people out there even scarier than you. Manuel Cespedes, you're under arrest for the murders of Michael Bebniv, Anthony Yeltsin, and Anton Dubrovsky. Oh, and a little advice for the future ... the next time you go after rival drug dealers, I'd try to avoid the Russian ones."

Chapter 60

Paul maneuvered through the crowded bar at Portland City Grill with difficulty. Crutches were a pain in the ass, at best, but during Happy Hour they were an accident waiting to happen. Somehow, he managed to get to the seats by the window, where Jeff and Sam were waiting, without mishap.

Leaning the crutches against the wall, Paul settled himself onto the low couch beside Sam. Jeff grinned at him as he got comfortable. "How goes it, Hop-a-long?" he asked.

Paul gave his boss a half-hearted scowl. "I'm sure I'll find that amusing after I've had a drink ... or two."

"Or three," Sam offered.

"Now you're talking," Paul said, signaling for the waiter. A selection of appetizers was arrayed on the low table between them: plates of cheeses and crackers, crab cakes, and spring rolls that looked almost untouched.

"What, you guys waited for me?" Paul asked as he grabbed a small plate and helped himself to the food.

"Clearly, you've forgotten who you're dealing with," Sam laughed. "The waiter just dropped them off."

Paul grinned. It felt good to be back with the team. Both Sam and Jeff had been around frequently to visit him while he recuperated from his injuries, but this marked the first time they'd gotten together socially since the night Averill had died.

There had been a lot to process for everyone.

The waiter arrived to take their drink order — Paul's first round, their second — and headed back to the bar. While they waited for him to return, the three of them talked shop — upcoming projects and staffing issues, mostly — while working their way through the excellent food. Somehow though, after what they'd been through together, business as usual seemed less than enthralling.

"How is Lucy doing?" Jeff asked at last.

Paul frowned. "I don't really know. She went back to Pittsburgh to spend some time with her family. We haven't spoken in about a week."

"Lucy's been through a lot," Sam reminded him, "but she'll come around."

He nodded, clearly unconvinced, as the waiter returned with their drinks.

"To Lucy coming around," Jeff said, raising his glass, "and to successful conclusions." The others joined in the toast, their enthusiasm tempered by memories of what it had taken to get to this celebration.

"Speaking of successful conclusions," Jeff added, "I heard from Cynthia Orbison just before I left the office to come here. Stefanya Kozlov turned herself in for her sister's murder this afternoon."

"You're kidding," Paul said. "She was free and clear."

Sam looked over at her boss and smiled. "You knew she would do this, didn't you?"

"Let's say that I had a hunch," Jeff admitted. "Honestly, I think Stefanya would have turned herself in three years ago, if Adam had asked her to. All I needed to do was give her a nudge in the right direction."

"What do you think is going to happen to her?" Paul asked.

"I'm guessing the DA's office will be as lenient as possible, under the circumstances."

"Because you asked Orbison to go easy," Sam guessed.

"I might have put in a word on her behalf," Jeff admitted with a hint of a smile. "But regardless of what they decide to do with Stefanya, Adam's conviction will be vacated. That will go a long way toward helping her heal from all of this."

"And Adam's father," Sam added.

"Him, too," Jeff agreed, thoughtfully. "Him, too … and on that note," he added, tossing back the rest of his drink, "I should get going."

"But it's early yet," Sam protested. "At least stick around for one more."

He shook his head. "Someone has to be the responsible one in this group," he said with a smile, "and God knows it isn't going to be either of you. Besides, there are a couple of contracts on my desk that I need to wrap up before I head home." Jeff stood, looking down at his friends. "Have a great weekend, guys. And try to stay out of trouble."

Sam watched as their boss made his way over to their waiter.

"Do you think he's all right?" she asked Paul. "Markus tells me he's been staying late at work a lot, lately."

"He's fine," Paul assured her as he watched Jeff hand the waiter some cash, gesturing back toward their table.

"And something tells me that we have another round or two coming our way," he added. "Of course, since you're the responsible driver, I'll be willing to pick up your slack."

Sam laughed. "That won't be necessary, tonight. I took a cab, just in case."

"Really? Miss 'Prim-and-Proper?'" Paul managed a look of shock. "You've been holding out on me."

She grinned "Oh, there's a lot about me you still don't know."

"Is that right? Name three things," he challenged.

"All right." Sam held up three fingers. "For starters, I'm half-Irish, which means I can drink your ass under the table. Anytime. Anywhere …" she said, lowering the first digit. "Second, I've been known to tear it up like Lady Gaga on karaoke night at the neighborhood bar."

"Lady Gaga? Funny, I would have pegged you as more of a Taylor Swift kind of girl," he chuckled. "All right, that's two. So, what's number three?"

"Oh, yeah, number three." Sam glanced back over toward the entrance of the bar for a moment. Then she leaned in close, her mouth only an inch away. "The third thing," she whispered, her breath warm on his ear, "is that I don't *always* bat for the other team."

With that, she stood and smiled down at him.

"I'll be right back," she said. "If the waiter comes by while I'm gone, I'll take a double Jameson, neat." Then she wandered off in the direction of the restrooms, leaving a very confused Paul in her wake.

Notes and Acknowledgements

A Matter of Justice is my second novel, and the first in the Jefferson Dawes series. I suspect all Jeff's adventures will be set largely in the Pacific Northwest. Fortunately, the diversity of landscapes and people in the region should be sufficient to fill my "canvases" for many books to come.

Those of you who have read my first novel, *Drawn Back*, were probably surprised to see Patrick and Rachel O'Connell make an appearance in this book. This wasn't simply because readers kept asking me what happened to them after *Drawn Back* ended (and a gratifying number of people did care enough to ask); after living with Patrick and Rachel for so long, I am more than happy to revisit them from time to time.

SO MANY PEOPLE are involved in the writing process that it isn't possible for me to acknowledge them all in a paragraph or two. Here, then, are but a few to whom I owe much:

Thank you to D.J. Bershaw, Tim Burgess, and Chris Trujillo—writers of talent and generosity—who volunteered to read early versions of this story and provide their invaluable feedback. Thanks also to Jane Rossiter, a dear friend (and my first paying reader). Jane saw this story in its rawest form, and provided encouragement chapter-by-chapter, as they were written. And special appreciation to my sister, Karalee German, for her proofreading efforts; I hope I got them all, Sis.

Special thanks, also, to my niece, Katelynn Burns, and my good friend, Rick Meikle, who created the original cover for this book. Even though commercial realities forced me to go a different direction, I was blown away by the talent, time, and effort they put into their work.

Finally, my eternal thanks—and my deepest love—to my wife and family, who are always in my corner. Living with a writer can't be easy but, somehow, they've managed it admirably.

Keith Tittle

About the Author

Keith Tittle is a software trainer by vocation, and a writer by compulsion. He was the winner of the 2016 Chanticleer Clue Award for Suspense/Thrillers — for A Matter of Justice *— and twice was a finalist in the PNWA contest for Mainstream Short Fiction.*

Keith self-published his first novel, Drawn Back, *in 2014.*

A native and lifelong resident of the Pacific Northwest, Keith lives with his oh-so-patient wife — and assorted felines — in Southwest Washington.